Genevieve, the Fix

Mack Lines

ISBN: 979-8-218-62335-7

Before they started multiplying,

there was only one.

Its name was Venn.

Before humans united to stop them,

there was only one.

Her name was Genevieve.

THE STORY

1

THE TROUBLE WITH PANCAKES

I used to think a lot about dying, but never about getting killed. Even if I did, I would never have imagined anything like this.

The neighbors were fascinated when the airplanes first arrived—standing on their lawns squinting to see the jets lap the sky. Everybody enjoyed the odd air show. But all I saw were vultures. If my regular Rochester Hills subdivision were the World Trade Center, people would have deciphered the threats scrolled in their vapor trails.

Fighter jets cut the show short though, flying low, crisscrossing the sky. BOOM! BOOM! BOOM! The shockwaves extinguished the happy oohs and aahs, replacing them with shrieks for God. I was able to ignore my windows rattling in their sockets, but I couldn't ignore the crash of my mom's China against the floor.

When I didn't surrender, it sent the drones. Most were the size of frisbees, others were tiny. They swarmed my house like dirty clouds of chaos—bloodthirsty metal mosquitos. A lot of them died trying to use their propellers to saw into the attic, but the roof was too strong. Their dead bodies stuffed the gutters until they overflowed like storm water.

Others slammed into the house—making loud threats as they pecked at the brick.

I could have given in—made them all go away with a few of clicks on my phone. Everybody would have been safe—at least for a little while. But being safe forever is way better, so I stuck to the plan.

Keep it together Genevieve, you've got this.

• • • •

Two weeks earlier …

It all started on the anniversary of Moo-Ha! McNuggets Meltdown. Yeah, that was me. It's a long story but it accidentally made me sort of famous—extremely famous by Rochester, Michigan standards. It wasn't my idea—and I wish I could undo it—but I'm kind of a YouTube star.

When I first saw the video, I laughed like everybody else. It's *really* funny—a squirrel-cheeked girl hammered on fentanyl, mooing, laughing and demanding McNuggets and Ranch. Speed it up and loop it and it's priceless. Good thing my "friends" were there to catch it all on video—and to post it online—right? Take it from me, keep your friends away when you're waking up from anesthesia. Last time I checked it had forty-one *million* views and counting … translated into eighteen languages. Yep, now everybody thinks they know me. You probably do too. No offense, but you don't. Maybe nobody does anymore.

Anyhow, just as my life was getting back to normal, the video went viral again. On the video's first birthday, my face showed up online with Sammy Griner, Maggie Goldenberger, Kyle Craven, and a bunch of other memes in a "Where are they now?" clickbait story. And of course, everybody clicked. I don't know, I guess people got sentimental about it—like it was some happy childhood memory or something. Anyhow, my phone started blowing up again. Calls—how do people get my number? DMs, tweets, texts … a thousand irritating alarm clocks vibrated, chirped, beeped, and squawked me awake.

I buried my phone under a pile of dirty laundry, blankets, pillows, and books, until I couldn't hear it anymore. It was an impressive pile. It was surprising some superfan didn't somehow snap a picture and send a hilarious "MOO-HA SHUT-UP PHONE!'" meme into the world.

Sorry … I know it's what everybody wants—to get famous. I guess I was just tired. I was tired of it all. Everything was complicated now. I used to have a couple of good friends—which was enough. Now I had hundreds of people saying they were my "best friend." It was getting hard to pick out the real ones from the imposters.

Good thing it was a Saturday. I lucked into the smell of "dad breakfast" halfway down the steps. No offense to my mom's cooking, but dad breakfast always made me feel better—especially the times I dragged him out of bed to make it.

Tired eyes looked me in the face.

I forced a smile back at him.

"What's up, kid?"

"I'm okay."

Knowing that "I'm okay" meant "I'm not okay," he forced a smile of his own and snuck a deep breath mixed with a soft "Help me, Jesus." Then he asked the only question I really wanted to answer—"Want some breakfast?"

"Yeah."

"Good! Pancakes for one is no fun." He always said that.

But the truth is, my dad never makes pancakes for one. He makes as many as it takes for the smell to drag someone into the kitchen to join him. Dad takes great satisfaction in building enormous stacks. The stacks can get pretty tall if nobody comes down—so high the plastic wrap sticks to ceiling of the fridge.

I love my dad, but sometimes I don't come down when I smell them. I know it's a bummer for him, but most of the time, I don't want to talk about it—whatever "it" is. Plus, I prefer pancakes cold and with no syrup or butter—"cold and dry" he calls it. There's nothing better than peeling a few cold pancakes off the stack and eating them from under a blanket on the couch. I know, right?

But that day … I got warm pancakes, with blueberries. If you've gotta have warm pancakes, blueberry pancakes are the way to go. I still skipped the syrup though. I like picking them up and eating them like a squirrel—another meme, ready to go viral. Sorry, I worry about weird stuff. I'm tired.

"Yawwwwwnnnn! Uh … Sorry, kid. My phone started ringing at three—three a.m., really? How'd they even get my number? I chucked it out the bathroom window. I'll get it when I take the dog out. The battery should be good and dead by then—just the way I like it." He laughed for real.

"Sorry, Dad."

He whipped up another smile. "Well, at least I know the ringer works." He laughed again. That's his way of complaining that nobody calls him anymore. It wasn't funny, but I laughed too. It felt good to laugh.

As always, the laughter dragged my mom into the kitchen. Pancakes have no effect on her—she prefers "just coffee." I usually escape her hugs pretty fast, but that day I just surrendered and let her do it. Between the pancakes, my mom's death grip and her kisses on the top of my head, I started to feel better. We knew the drill … we were all going to get way too much attention for a couple of months, but after that, people would start forgetting. That was the hope, at least.

But unfortunately, that wasn't everybody's hope.

With two quick knocks, our front door burst open, bouncing the handle off the recently repaired hole in the wall. "Trouble" rambled in.

My parents used to call them by their names, but after posting the original video, "Trouble" seemed more fitting. Issy backed in through the doorway first, making sure she was perfectly framed on her "boyfriend" Josiah's phone. Jo gave me a helpless shrug and a familiar

"I'm sorry" look when he saw my face. He knew it was a cruel thing to do but fell in line with Issy's instructions anyway.

She shouted in a stern voice, "Okay. Roll it!" then switched to the more likeable, completely fake version of herself she'd been trying to make famous. "Good morning, friends! Can you believe it? It's been a year since I introduced you to my personal friend, Moo-Ha! McNuggets and Ranch Girl, and made her famous. I know, right? Well, I figured it'd be fun to pop in to say hello and celebrate the anniversary of the day I made her *a star!*"

She rushed me, swung her arm around me and planted a loud, overly lip-glossed kiss on my cheek, before I could pull the pancake out of my mouth—"Mwah!"

The smell of her lip gloss mingling with my morning breath and blueberries was gross. Worse, the smell wasn't nearly as repulsive as the look of my "freshly woken from a nightmare" stylings, set against Issy's "on point" outfit and perfect eyebrows. Sorry, I never say "on point." That's her phrase. I prefer "fake." I know that sounds mean, and not super creative, but it was fitting, and it was early.

I stared into his phone as the camera recorded. I must have looked desperate, because my dad sprang into action. "Jo!" he thundered.

Josiah panned his phone to my dad barging into the kitchen. His giant hand eclipsed the lens and snatched the phone. Josiah backed up. He's terrified of my dad. Ever since he caught us kissing in the driveway, Josiah's never been the same. That was a long time ago … a mistake … and I'm not sure why I even brought it up.

Anyhow, my dad kept his cool on the outside. But I could tell by the way he was holding the phone, if I didn't do something quick he was going to bend it in half. I should have let him do it, but … it wasn't Josiah's fault. I know he saved up a long time for that phone, and I could never resist his sad eyes.

So … I scooted over and placed my hands gently on my dad's hairy knuckles and whispered, "I'm okay. I got this." That helped loosen his grip enough so I could pry it from his fingers.

I hoped the phone would still be unlocked so I could delete the video, but nope. An old picture of the three of us looked back at me from his locked screen. Lucky for him, that softened my rage a bit (I miss those people). Sensing that I had the situation under control, my parents excused themselves, moved to the other room and pretended to be busy while listening closely.

With my parents out of the room, *Issy Show* Issy returned as if the camera was still shooting. "Oh, thank you, you're a lifesaver, Gena." She reached for the phone.

I glared back and shot the phone high over my head. It would have felt amazing to smash it. "Hold on! What makes you think you're getting it back? I didn't invite you over. Nobody let you in. And I certainly didn't agree to participate in another of your get-famous-fast schemes. Best of luck and everything, but leave me out of it!"

Real Issy shot back, "Yeah, sorry. That's not going to happen. You're in it."

Then the much sweeter *Issy Show* Issy tagged in to try and help. "Eh-hem." She cleared the meanness out of her throat. "I'm sorry, I know the last year has been tough on our friendship. I'm sorry we don't hang out the way we used to. With my career and all, everything's gotten really busy. You understand, right?"

"You're crazy! I don't even know who you are anymore." I turned from Issy to Jo. "What's your password? *Now!* I'll delete the video, and the phone's all yours, safe and sound. Piece of cake."

Jo broke eye contact and looked down at the countertop. "Okay. But I'm not giving you my password. I'll key it in."

"Nope! Ain't happening! You're not laying a finger on your phone until the video's gone. Or"—I gripped the phone hard and jerked it toward the concrete countertops—"I'll take care of it my way!"

"Stop!" Jo squeaked out a shout. "Okay! ... Okay," he continued nervously. "It's 71 ... 10 ... 1."

I tried to ignore that his password was my birthday—July, 10th 2001. Hearing the lock spring, Issy rushed me again. I hip checked her hard as I turned away. With my back toward them and the phone held out of their reach, I selected the video and deleted it from his library. "This morning never happened!" I announced, then turned around and chucked the phone hard and fast, hitting Jo in his boney chest. Don't worry, he caught it before it could crash against the tile.

Issy was furious, but Josiah was grateful. "Thanks, Gena. And don't worry, I'll pull the video off the cloud too."

Ugh. It was on the cloud too? Perfect.

Issy cut back in, "Oh no you're not! You're not deleting anything. That content is gold! We're posting it." She turned back at me over her shoulder. "Sorry, sweetie, there's nothing you can do about it."

Issy was right. My life had been reduced to "content." Greasy haired me with no makeup, wearing sweats that look like they survived a zombie apocalypse and a T-shirt from seventh grade basketball camp would soon be seen by millions of people, curious what happened to Moo-ha! McNuggets Ranch Girl. Perfect.

But then the Josiah I used to know stood up tall from his slump, cleared his throat and put on his deep, manly voice. "Eh-hem! Uh. Sorry, babe. I said I was going to delete it, and I'm going to. I promised, and it's the right thing to do."

Issy slit his throat with dagger eyes. He was dead meat. I didn't know how she was going to make him suffer, but I knew there would be weeping and gnashing of teeth to come.

I know … I should have just left it at that and let them sort it out. I mean, I won, and I never win at things. But before I could stop myself, my big mouth threw Jo a life raft instead. If we were in a *Terminator* movie, someone in the future would travel back in time to stop me from opening my mouth. But unfortunately, nobody launched a rocket through the window. "Thanks, Josiah, but maybe it is time for an update from the McNuggets Girl. Issy, do you want the exclusive?"

She dropped her daggers and leaned in. "I'm listening …"

"Well … everybody knows you work really hard on The *Issy Show*. You're always perfectly lit and framed—Jo makes it look like you have a professional crew. So … do you really think you'd be happy with what you shot today? I mean, look around, the lighting in here is horrible. Don't take this the wrong way, but when I first saw you, I thought you might be sick."

She winced.

"Don't worry, it's not you. The lighting in here does that to everybody. I mean look at Josiah."

Issy glanced at Jo and shook her head in agreement. "Yeah, you don't look so good, babe."

I continued. "So, how about this … come back after dinner, and we can stage the whole thing in my room—with a good camera and perfect lighting. I'll even make my bed—it'll be a real shoot. You can bust in, I'll act surprised, we'll hug and kiss, I'll say that you look amazing and thank you for being my best friend. Gold, right?"

She was hooked. "Okay. We'll go remote and shoot in your room. It'll be priceless" She grabbed Jo by the hoodie and dragged him down the hall. "Don't worry. I'll plan it all out. Jo will be here at three sharp to set up." *Slam!*

My parents popped back into the kitchen. I brushed by them, escaping down the hall and up the stairs to my room. I didn't have time to stop and talk. My room was trashed.

2

AMAZING (I DIDN'T BARF)

Jo arrived at 2:55. He was dependable that way. My mom greeted him at the door with a smile and a hug—like the old days. Jo used to come over a lot—we were buds … and we thought we were in love. Okay, I said it. But I was a kid then, and it isn't that way anymore. It's been almost a year since we even really talked—and that was more of a yell than a talk. Now we're more businesslike than anything. Ha! *Business*—that's a good word for it. Before they removed my wisdom teeth, I was just a regular senior girl at Rochester High. I got Bs, had a boyfriend, went to church … I was a good but forgettable girl. I flew under every radar. Now I'm a "business" with millions of customers devoted to my "product"—millions of people who love me but don't know me.

I listened to Jo thump his stuff up the stairs and get up his nerve before he knocked. "Gen?" A gentle *tap, tap, tap* muffled through. "Uh … can I come in?"

"Yeah, I guess." I opened the door, and he banged through my doorway with his first load of gear—big black plastic cases stickered with "The *Issy Show*" and layered with not so sticky pink lip-print stickers that left a trail of glitter across my floor.

I hope to never get used to seeing Jo this way. I prefer seeing him the old way—when I admired him and didn't pity him. He dropped his last load in the only empty spot left on my floor and he started setting up. At first, I sat up tall in my bed and watched. He snapped open the first case, releasing Issy stink—I mean, her "iconic fragrance." Though Issy wasn't famous—at all—she was prepared for fame with a full catalogue of *Issy Show* branded trinkets and taglines to share with her public.

"New cologne, Jo? What do you call it?" I teased.

Jo ignored me and continued working in silence. For the last year, our conversations had pretty much been me joking and him ignoring. We were good at it. It wasn't that we didn't have real stuff to talk about, but neither of us wanted to uncork that bottle. It was better that way. I wouldn't get hurt, and he wouldn't get killed.

No matter, I had a lot to think about while he worked. I plopped back into a pile of pillows and clicked some notes into my phone. What am I going to say? I had no obvious answer. I'd been hiding out since the video went viral. Yes, what mean girls said about me was true— "Gena couldn't handle it" … "it wrecked her" … "she went dark" … "just disappeared."

With some convincing, my mom agreed to homeschool me the rest of my senior year, and I dropped out of everything else—my friends, my church … my dreams. For a while I even thought about completely dropping out. Nobody officially knows, but if I'd gone through with it, nobody would have been surprised. I was glad that was over. Maybe it was just a fantasy, but I was hoping that if I came out of the shadow and said something, maybe I could put all of this behind me and start living again. I had no control over getting famous, but maybe if I tell my story, I could get back to being regular again. Unlike the first video, I was in control this time. But … Issy had different plans.

Jo's phone buzzed with a text, signaling her arrival. He shot down the steps with his camera and slipped out the front door. One minute later he stuck his head back in and announced: *"Quiet on the set!"* It was showtime.

I slid my window open to listen in on the action outside.

With artificially perky whispers, *Issy Show* Issy began her act, "Shhhhhh! Hi, everybody. It's me, Issy, from the *Issy Show*, here with an *Issy Show* exclusive that's going to break the internet. Sorry internet!" She squeaked out an *Issy Show* snort. "It's been a year since I introduced you to my very best friend—The Moo-Ha mamma, McNuggets and Ranch Girl. Super funny, right? I know. Well, it's been a year, and it's about time for an *Issy Show* pop-in—don't you think?"

My front door creaked open, and Issy overacted her way in and up the stairs with Jo following behind, carefully ensuring her overly exercised, yoga-pants-wrapped rear end was in frame. She whispered a countdown outside my door, and I took a deep breath. Then, with a quick turn of the knob, Issy threw herself into my room. "Surprise! It's Issy!"

Even though I knew it was coming, I jumped anyhow. I can be a bit jumpy. Jo zoomed in to catch my surprise.

"No way! You really got me, Issy!" I waved to the camera. "Hi, everybo—"

"Cut!" Real Issy shouted. "Sorry, that was sweet and all, but first things first." Jo repositioned the camera facing the door as Issy stepped out and closed it behind her. "Action!" My door flung wide open again, nearly hitting Jo's camera. He jumped back as *Issy Show* Issy jumped in. "Surprise! It's Issy!" She cha-cha'd across my room and threw herself on top of me on the bed—bouncing my body against my mattress as she buried my face in overly lip-glossed kisses. Jo followed her in for a close-up. Having completed the *Issy Show* barrage of slobber, she lifted her mouth and yelled in my face, "Cut!"

I pushed her off me, accidentally sending her to the floor with a loud bang. My floor isn't very soft. I scooted off to help her up, but Jo was already there. He swung his camera around to his back and gave her his hand. It would have been really sweet, except it was fear that sprung him into action. She looked back at me for a second before pulling Jo in for a long kiss. It was an impressive kiss. They must practice a lot. It was much better than the oddly dry, severely misaligned kiss Jo debuted on me. With her point made, Issy wiped the gloss from his lips with a tissue. "Thanks, babe."

"So …" I interrupted, "Thanks for coming over! Always good to see you guys. Let me help you pack up." I lifted one of the black plastic cases and moved toward my door, but Issy ripped it out of my hand.

"Oh, we're not done! We're just getting started. Next, I'm giving you a makeover. People live for my makeup tips, and sweetie … you could use some help. I'll ask you questions, we'll talk, and Jo will cut out the boring stuff."

Jo rolled. Knowing that kicking them out of my house on camera wouldn't help my cause, I sat back down while Jo reset the lighting and Issy set up the *Issy Show* makeup kit on a stand in front of me.

"Roll already!" My eyes squinted in the bright lights as Issy addressed the camera. "I'm here with my friend and creation, Moo-ha! McNuggets and Ranch Girl. Say hi to everybody in Issy land."

I rolled my eyes and answered sarcastically, "Uh … hi, everybody … in … 'Issy land'."

Jo zoomed back in on Issy, just as they rehearsed.

"Well, friends, it looks like I got here in the nick of time. Someone needs an *Issy Show* pick-me-up and I've got just the thing!"

The camera swung back and Jo signaled me to smile. There was no way I was smiling. I responded sarcastically, "Uh … yeah, Issy, I could really use a pick-me-up. Do you have any makeup tips for me? I'm sure that's all I need to fix my life. Please help me, Issy. That would be amazing."

Real Issy shot back, "So, that's how you want to play?"

Jo started to put down his camera.

"No! Don't you dare stop rolling!"

He kept rolling.

"Maybe you'd rather talk about something else—like how you ditched your friends and became a complete loser after we made you famous. I'm sure everybody would like to hear about how little miss Moo-Ha lives her life now. Wanna tell us about it, McNuggets Ranch Girl?"

I thought about it for a second. Maybe it would be better if people knew the truth. But who knows what she'd do with the footage—send it to TMZ probably. So, I gave in and did it her way. Maybe if everybody thought I was okay, I wouldn't be a story, and this could all go away. I took a deep breath and relaxed my face before forcing it into a toothy smile. Issy smiled back with approval. "That's more like the Gena I remember!"

"Take two! … Hi, friends. A year ago, I introduced you to my very best friend, Gena Mucha—you may know her as Moo-Ha! McNuggets and Ranch Girl."

"Hi, everybody!" I smiled and waved like a beauty queen on a float. "Thanks for coming over, Issy—you look amazing!" I said "amazing" a lot over the next hour as my face got Issy'd up. It was "amazing"— "amazing" that Issy picked me and made me a star. This last year was "amazing" too. "Amazing … amazing … amazing—amazing" The fact that I didn't throw up in my mouth saying it, that's what was really amazing. When she was done, we debated who looked more "amazing." "You look amazing." "No, *you* look amazing!" Then we blew kisses to Jo's camera. There was not much more to it. Once I gave her what she wanted, "Trouble" packed up and left.

3

BLOOD IN THE WATER

I sat quietly in the aftermath. Somehow, the smell of pancakes broke through the lingering Issy odor, but I didn't go down this time. Instead, I buried myself under my pillows again to feel horrible … fake … dirty … used … etcetera … again. It was hard to pray.

Yeah … I pray. But don't worry, I'm not going to preach to you about it. The truth is, I don't know how to explain it, but ever since I yelled at my ceiling on that dark day, God's felt close. Yeah, I know, "God's everywhere, of course he's close!" but it was different. It just felt different. Ha-ha—and before that day, I felt like praying was helping—like maybe God was fixing stuff. I was starting to like myself again, starting to trust again. Even my parents noticed. Now, I felt craptastic all over again.

I worked myself up out of bed to my mirror. It used to be a lot harder to get out of bed—so, that's something. I was surprised by the pretty girl looking back in my reflection. She wasn't real, but I thanked her for lying for me on the video. I couldn't have said the stuff she did. She made me a non-story, and pacified Issy, so I was grateful. I took

14

one last look before sending her away. "No offense, chick, but it's time for you to go."

I went through a lot of wipes before I could see my real skin again. "Hello, freckles!" It took lots of scrubbing, but eventually the me popped through the not-me.

It'd been a while since I looked long at myself in a mirror. It was just my normal face, but I was fascinated with it. I looked for a creepy long time. My eyes looked different than I remembered. They looked stronger—not ashamed, insecure, or alone. I don't know, it's hard to explain. I looked deeper again, and I started to tingle inside. That—the tingling—happened a lot those days. I'm pretty sure that's how God tells me I'm not alone.

I still don't know what I'm supposed to do when the tingling happens. Sometimes I say stuff. Sometimes I sit and enjoy it and listen. Maybe you know what I'm talking about. If not … sorry, I told you it's hard to explain. Anyhow, when the tingling was over, I knew what I had to do. It was time to tell my real story.

I slid the pile of wipes into the trash and moved fast, before I could lose my nerve. It was time for the world to hear my real story—just me this time, live, with no makeup and full freckles.

I gave myself a pep talk as I opened YouTube and chose live streaming. "'Go live any time for any reason.' I guess this qualifies. You want the truth about McNuggets Girl? Well, all right. 'Get Started.'" With a couple more clicks, the recording light was glowing red, and my face was full screen. I propped my phone up against the mirror.

"Uh … hi, everybody! I'm Gena, but you probably know me from the video of me asking for Chicken McNuggets and Ranch. If you were wondering … the Moo-Ha part is what my last name sounds like if you care enough to say it right. Or, if you're saying it over and over again with gauze packed into your cheeks. Actually, my last name is pronounced Mucha. It's Polish. So, yeah, that was me. I thought it was funny when I saw it too. Uh …" I took another deep breath and forced myself to keep going.

"So, earlier today I made a video with Issy, talking about how amazing the last year has been. Well, that's not exactly true. The truth is … being the McNuggets and Ranch Girl has been the opposite. I don't want you to feel bad for laughing. And if you were one of the thousands of people who sent chicken nuggets and bottles of ranch to my house … well … I'm sure you were just trying to … be nice, I guess.

"So… the truth is, that video wrecked me. Or maybe I let it wreck me, I don't know. Long story, but … I was terrified about getting my wisdom teeth pulled. My boyfriend and best friend surprised me in the waiting room. They were exactly what I needed. 'Don't worry, Gen. You're going to be great. When you wake up, we'll be here waiting for you.' Jo—my almost boyfriend—was convincing.

"My friend Issy reassured me. 'Yep. I had mine pulled last year. One second you're counting down from ten, and the next second you're waking up and it's over. All the bloody gauze packed in the holes is gross, but that's normal. Once the swelling and bruising goes away, you'll start looking human again. Just don't get dry sockets. I know a girl who got dry sockets, and she said it was the most painful thing she—'

"Seeing that I was getting nervous again, Jo jumped back in. '—but that's not going to happen to you, Gen. You're going to be great.' See, he used to be sweet.

"Issy prodded Jo to kiss me for good luck—warning him to 'Do it now. You won't want to kiss her afterwards.' It was our second and last kiss—but not because of my gross mouth. Afterwards he was the one too repulsive to kiss.

"I don't remember them shooting the video. When I came out of it, I just remember that everyone was happy, smiling and laughing around my bed. I got my fat cheeks to sort of smile back. Surgery was over, and I was surrounded by my favorite people.

"Yeah … so … it wasn't until the next morning that I found out about the video. I felt beat up from the surgery. My face bruised bad.

The thought of changing out the bloody gauze still makes me sick to my stomach. But seeing the video hurt more. It was a punch to the stomach.

Issy rationalized it, saying, 'I don't know what you're so upset about. It's funny—and you're famous!' They were right, it was so funny that millions of people laughed—at me. I was famous for something I don't even remember doing. I wish my parents were in the room, then there wouldn't be a video, but they weren't. I didn't talk to them for a long time for letting it happen.

"My dad blamed himself. It's his job to protect me—those were his words. I remember yelling them back at him, 'You're right, it was your job to protect me! Where were you?' I hurt him bad, and it wasn't fair. He didn't know he had to protect me from my friends … neither did I. I would have skipped having friends if I knew the danger.

"So, it's been a year, and I've survived just fine without them. Yep, I'm a survivor, but I'd much rather just be normal—like before. Surviving's hard. Three months after it happened, I almost wasn't a survivor. I didn't see much of a point in it all …"

I did a good job holding it together up until then, but now my head throbbed from holding back the emotion. I reached to stop recording, but just then the tingling came back. I pointed the camera at the ceiling while I tried to compose myself, resting in the warm tingle.

In the Bible—yeah, I read the Bible now too. I hope that doesn't weird you out. I'm still getting used to the idea that I'm a "Bible reader" myself. Anyhow, somewhere in there, I remember Jesus saying that he wanted to pull the people close to him, like a hen pulls her chicks under her wings. I don't know much about chickens, but that's how the tingle feels. It's warm in there.

Well … when my courage came back, I set my phone back in place. I was still streaming. My screen had a weird flicker, but I didn't think much of it—I always got the hand-me-down phones. It's old and it can be glitchy, but it works most of the time, so I don't complain.

"So, three months ago, I almost killed myself. It was the worst and best day of my life. Yeah, I know. I felt really alone. I sat over there, in the dark, every day. I lost track of the time. I didn't know if it was day or night and didn't care. Before, I would have watched videos on my phone to pass the time, but none of them were funny anymore. I just kept imagining the person the day after they got famous … feeling betrayed, used. So, I just slept, and when I wasn't sleeping, I pretended to sleep.

"A lot of bad stuff ran through my mind until it got stuck on the idea of God. I mean, when you get down to it, it's God's job to protect people—right? I was tired of blaming my friends and parents, so I turned the blame on him. I gave it to him. 'And where were you? What? Were you too busy? Too tired? I know I'm not that important, but … Jesus!'

"Those aren't all the words, but you get the point. I've never been good at swearing, but I launched all of them, violently, in his direction. I figured if God was around, he'd be gone for sure now. But … nope. That's when I felt God for the first time. It's hard to explain, but I cried for a long time.

"I was hoping God would yell back, so I could fight him, but he didn't. He was just there, making me tingle deep in my heart. Maybe that's what he does to remind people he's with them, and it's going to be okay." I smiled and whispered, "Thank you, God," under my breath. That was when my phone died.

At first, I thought it just ran out of battery—my battery was old and didn't hold a charge very long. But the bright flash out the speaker holes, the crackle and the smell told me it was dead. They only last so long, you know.

Even though I knew nobody was watching anymore, I finished up. "Thanks for being my friend through all of this. I always wanted to believe. But I didn't really know … that you're real. Or maybe I did know you were real, but I didn't know you cared about me. But I know now. I love you."

I took a deep breath and sat with God for a while before following the tingle to a warm shower and a change of clothes. I felt good—really good—ready to face the world. As I walked down the stairs, I got ready for the questions. I'm pretty sure my parents store up questions for me when I'm not around. Luckily, this time I was saved by the internet.

The internet was out, and when the internet goes out at my house, it's a big deal. Last year Bill, our neighbor, chopped our cable in half. He said it was an accident, but we knew different. He doesn't like us much—so, that was where my dad went to check first.

Dad came back in, proud of the "civil conversation" he had with the neighbor at the cable box hidden in the bushes between our houses. "Sounds like we're not the only ones. The whole neighborhood's out. Our box is completely fried. I mean, the thing is black—sizzling even. Bill thinks there was some kind of power surge."

That kind of made sense. I don't know much about how electricity works, but everything in our house that was connected to the cable was fried—the modem, the wireless router, the TV … everything.

But that didn't explain everything. How could a power surge through the cable fry the wireless stuff too? Our phones, laptops, the wireless in the car, even the wireless thing I use to find my keys burned up. Good thing we had insurance, I guess.

After three days of "quality time" doing puzzles and playing board games with my family, the workers fixed everything. The internet was back on and things started to get back to normal—until everything became the very opposite of normal.

4

NO STRINGS ATTACHED

I was home alone when the doorbell rang. That was a good sign—the doorbell got fried during "the surge" too. Nobody else was home, so I signed for the box. It was addressed to me, but the box was too small to be a jug of Ranch, and it didn't sound like nuggets when I shook it—"Interesting." I took it up to my room and jammed my thumbnail through the tape to open it. A shiny black, perfectly shrink-wrapped box fell out. A phone.

I know, lots of people get new phones all the time, but not me. I only got "new to me" phones—hand-me-downs. So, I figured it was a mistake—it was probably for one of my parents. But the idea of having my very first unboxing experience was irresistible. So, I carefully sliced through the plastic in the gap between the lid and the bottom and worked the lid up.

When I saw it, I knew for sure it was a mistake. It couldn't be a replacement for my fried iPhone 6, this was the newest generation iPhone. It was heavy and had three massive cameras sticking out the back. And it wasn't just the normal-size one, it was huge. I held the glass against my lips and gave it a farewell kiss. If it were for my parents, I knew it would come back to me someday—and I'd remember this moment.

I tucked the phone back into its bed, slid the top back on, then scotch-taped it into the shipper.

That was when it started ringing—yes, ringing. I figured I must have woke it or broke it—I don't know how new phones work—so I ran the box downstairs, added a couple strips of packing tape, and hid it under the welcome mat on the front porch—like nothing happened.

My heart was pumping hard. I didn't get much exercise the last six months, lying in bed. The doorbell rang again, stopping my heart midbeat.

I sat quietly on the step, hoping that whoever it was would think I wasn't home and would just go away. But they kept ringing. I peeked through the curtains. It was the guy who delivered the phone. That made sense—it was all a mistake, and he was just coming back to get it.

"It's there, under the mat! You can stop ringing the doorbell!" I yelled through the door. I knew he heard me. I'm loud. But he kept ringing anyway.

I only opened it a couple of inches at first. "Uh … hi again. Sorry, I figured you'd be coming back for it, so I put the box under the mat. I opened it. You can still take it back, right?"

"Nope. No mistake," he answered with a smile. "It's for you." He folded back the mat, picked up the box and brushed it off before handing it back. "I forgot the envelope that goes with it. Sorry about that." He set the envelope on top of the box, and I opened the door big enough to take it. "Have a great day, Genevieve." Then he left.

Later my parents asked me about the guy. "What did he look like? Was it the Amazon guy? UPS?" I had bad answers. I didn't remember much of anything. He was just a normal guy. The box was no help. It didn't have a shipping label—just my name and address. I need to pay better attention to stuff when it happens.

I opened the letter and read it bunch of times. Seemed friendly enough.

"Hi Gena, I hope you like your new phone. It's yours, no strings attached. It's a limited edition and we set it up especially for you. It comes with unlimited data, and we can switch it to your mobile number in a few seconds, if you'd like. Someone will call you to help.

In addition to a completely free phone, I'd like to run an idea by you: We're getting ready to launch a new world-building game for girls, and we'd like you to help us test it. What do you think?"

If got this letter before I became McNuggets and Ranch Girl, I'd be like you, I would have thought it was some sort of scam. But I got a lot of offers like that after the video—even from McDonald's. They wanted to use the video in a commercial. Their lawyers said it would "make our relationship official." I said 'No!'—eighty times.

I got all kinds of gifts from people who wanted to promote their stuff—"no strings attached." There were always strings. I'd either send their stuff back or give it to Issy. She loved pimpin' products on the *Issy Show*. But they didn't want Issy, so after a while the "gifts" stopped coming. This one was the first one in a long time.

The next line in the letter was the only reason I didn't chuck it and the phone into the trash—*"Because the game is still in development, we'd need you to agree to keep the game and your gameplay confidential."*

Later, my dad explained that. "Confidentiality agreements are just a part of doing business today. They just want to protect their idea until it's ready." That made sense to me.

My mom thought it sounded like a great opportunity. "They want to hire you for your brain, not for the video. Honey, it's time to start living again. It'll feel good to work." That made sense too.

So I reopened the box. And the moment I touched it, the phone started ringing again.

"Uh, hello? This is Gena …"

"Hello, Genevieve. Welcome to the beta team. Over the next year, we'll be working together to test *A Better World*, our latest world-building game. Please join us at nine a.m. tomorrow, May 17th, 2020, at the Beta World headquarters. I will send you an SMS with a map momentarily…"

I was waiting for the guy to take a breath so I could ask some questions, but there were no pauses and none of his sentences ended in a question mark. I figured it was a recording, so I tapped zero to get an operator. There was *no way* I was following a creepy recorded message anywhere. I'm not stupid, I saw *Taken*.

"Beep, beep, beep, beep, beep …" I pushed zero over and over again until the recording stopped.

The voice came back. "Yes, Genevieve. Is there something I can help you with?"

"Yeah, NO. Thanks for the phone and all, but I'm not meeting you at the 'A Better World Headquarters'—for all I know, the address is to a van parked down an alley somewhere. I mean, no offense, but you gotta understand how creepy this sounds, right?"

"I'm sorry, I don't understand, Genevieve. Is there something I can help you with?"

Yeah, I know what I should have done. I should have hung up and called the cops. But I didn't. I kept talking. "First off, I'm not agreeing to anything. I don't even know what a 'world building game' is. I don't know why you'd pick me. None of this makes any sense. And you're a weirdo! I'm done—"

He cut me off before I could hang up. "Hold please."

A different guy jumped on the line and called out frantically, "Gena! Gena! Don't hang up! Sorry! Sorry … dang it."

My thumb hovered over the end-call button.

"Gena, that was our A. I.—Artificial Intelligence. It was a test. We wanted to see how you'd react to it." He pulled himself together, "I know you're there. C'mon, this is important. We need you to help make it better. You're the right person for this … I know it …"

I heard about A.I. but nobody I knew ever talked to one. What was creepy was now curiously creepy—which everybody knows is my favorite kind of creepy. Plus, to be honest, it had been a long time since I did anything "important." So I put the phone back to my face.

Confident me took over. "Ok—I mean maybe. Ugh. Look! I'm not saying I'm going to do it. I'm not promising anything." Until less confident me barged back in—"What am I saying? This is just too weird. I change my mind. Consider me a 'NO.' Sorry for wasting your time. I'm hanging up now. Don't call me again."

That's when I should have hung up and chucked the phone. But I didn't. Instead, I listened quietly to see what he'd say next.

He signed. "I understand. I'm sorry. We could have asked you a hundred better ways. It's my fault and I don't blame you. We'll look for someone else—"

Feeling equally parts sorry for the guy and super creeped out curious about the A.I., I barged back in. "Wait …are you still there."

"Yes. I'm here."

"*if*—you heard the '*if*' part, right? *if* I happen to go temporarily insane and I change my mind, I'll let you know!"

"I'm glad you —"

I killed the call before he could say anything else.

That night, I wrote a long list of reasons why I was wrong for the job. Sure, I was famous, but really, I was a nobody. And I was famous for something dumb, not because I was a super gamer, world-builder. I was only smart-ish. Really, I'm not just saying that, ask my teachers. I didn't get into any of the colleges I really wanted to go to, so I decided to take a gap year. Unfortunately, it was a year of sitting in bed, staring at the ceiling.

I didn't know much about computers, I wasn't a programmer, I didn't even like video games. "Video games." I wasn't even 100% sure people called them that anymore. So, it didn't make sense … right?

I read the list to my parents. No offense, but they were no help. They flipped it on me, changing it from a list of "why me?" into a persuasive list of "of course you!" They'd always believed in me more than I believed in myself. Part of me wanted to explain why they were wrong, but ripping on myself only makes them mad. The truth … I liked their version of me better than the real thing.

Anyhow, after lots of back and forth, they cornered me. "Genevieve, what's the harm in talking to them about it? You're rejecting a really interesting offer that you know nothing about." They were right. And to be completely honest, I wanted to say yes from the beginning. I guess I just needed help getting to "of course you."

Knowing that my dad didn't have the "particular set of skills" necessary to extract me from human traffickers, he dictated a new plan, and I punched it into a text. "New plan. Meet me at the Cuppa Joe on the corner of University and Main at 10 am, this Saturday. This is not a yes. I have lots of questions."

Their response was instantaneous. "Great! See you then!

5

$25K SUCKERS!

Cuppa's is down the hill in our little downtown. It's a busy place—especially on Saturday mornings. People stop there coming and going from the farmer's market.

I got there when the doors opened at seven a.m. to make sure I got the table in the corner, by the window, far away from the door. I sat with my back to the wall, so I could easily see the entire café.

Dad took a seat in one of those gross old leather chairs that they let the crazy people sleep in. He didn't care though, it put him in earshot.

We probably could have waited until nine and been okay, the place didn't start to get busy until then. By the time the game people arrived, my butt was sore, my notebook was filled with doodles, and with three hours of coffee pumping through my brain. I was wired.

At ten sharp, the bell on the door rang and two men and a girl walked in. It was them.

I cleared my throat to signal my dad, but his eyes were already locked on. I figured the short, messy-haired guy was probably the person I talked to on the phone. The other man was my dad's age. And the girl looked about my age. No alarms went off, everybody looked normal and nice enough. They waved and smiled. "Can we get you anything?"

I waved back and shook my head. "No, I'm good! Thanks!" I brushed the muffin crumbs off the table and pitched my empties while they got their drinks.

I stood up politely and reached out with a confident hand as they put their cups on the table. "Hi, I'm Genevieve.

The short guy smiled and made introductions. "Hi, Gena. I'm Ben. We talked on the phone. Once again, sorry about that. I'm glad Vincent didn't scare you off."

The girl with him spoke up. "Vincent's okay, once you get to know it."

Ben jumped back in. "Oh, sorry, my bad. This is Rachel, and this is her dad. We hired Rachel in February to do the same job we'd like to hire you for. She's a real help. she can explain what it's like to work for us, if you have questions. I asked her dad to come too, in case your parents had questions."

The dad turned in his chair and reached his hand out to my not-so-incognito father sitting across the aisle. "Mr. Mucha? I'm Rachel's dad, John."

At first, my dad gave him the, "I don't know what you're talking about. I don't know this girl" look.

The dad smiled back and laughed. "Ha-ha, it's okay. I did the exact same thing. I even wore a disguise. No dad in his right mind would let his daughter meet some weird stranger with a creepy job offer without backup."

"Yeah, you ain't kiddin'." My dad shook John's hand, pulled up a chair, and sat up tall and big—half bodyguard, half agent, all dad.

Abruptly switching to business, Ben pulled two folders out of his bag and slid them in front of us. "Okay, here's what we're offering."

Ben nodded at Rachel and her dad. "Oh, yeah … sorry. It was nice meeting you." Rachel and her dad politely excused themselves. Their job was complete, and it was time for them to leave. We really didn't get to talk to them, but I felt much better knowing there were others.

On her way out, Rachel did jot her number and email on scrap of paper. I stuck it in my folder. "Let me know if you have questions. I'd be glad to help. And don't worry, you'll do great!"

I didn't know her, but for some reason, I believed her. Our dads exchanged business cards and shook hands, then they left.

Now just the three of us, Ben began his pitch. "This first page is the job description." He walked us through the points, explaining the legal jargon as he went.

Here's the gist—they were going to pay me to play a game. I was happy to hear it wasn't a shooting and killing game. It was a world-building game. He said it was similar to "*Sims* or *Minecraft*." I shook my head like I understood what a Sims or a Minecraft was. Anyhow, my job was to create a bunch of people in the game and teach them how to interact with each other like in real life. And get this, *A Better World* was going to pay me sixty bucks an hour—and I could work as many hours as I wanted.

My dad's jaw dropped. Seeing his sticker shock, Ben explained, "That's what it costs to get someone good. And we think Gena's going to be very good." My dad's momentary jealously to pride—too bad he'd have to keep his bragging to himself. The next sheet was the confidentiality agreement—the document they mentioned in the letter that came with my phone.

I could tell by the look on Ben's face that this was a legal agreement and it was no joke. While my dad made signing it sound more like a formality, it was clearly no formality. Ben was dead serious—once I started working, I couldn't tell anyone what I was doing—nobody. He explained it with a smile, but his eyes said something more like, "If you break this, I will wreck you and your family." Both me and my dad felt it, but chalked it up to him being bad with people.

Paper-clipped to the back of the agreement was a check. "And, as you'd expect, we've included a signing bonus to help compensate you for your cooperation."

It was for $25,000. Yeah, I know—25K! They paid my parents too, with a travel voucher they called "The Better World Tour"—redeemable for an all-expense-paid European vacation. To my dad, this was better than cash. Finally, he was going to be able to give my mom the romantic trip to Paris he'd been promising her since they started dating.

Ben continued, "Oh, and it's a package deal. All three of you—Gena, you, and your wife—have to sign, or we can't make the deal. I'm sure you understand."

We nodded, and Dad and I signed.

Ben smiled big. "Well, congratulations! You're hired! Let's get you started. Did you bring the phone we sent you?"

I pulled it out of my back pocket and set it on the table.

"May I?" he asked.

I nodded.

He picked up the phone, punched in a code to unlock it, scribbled something on the screen with his finger, and a login screen appeared. Setting it back in front of me, he explained the login process.

First, they asked for a password. Next, the screen prompted me to press each of my fingers against the home button to get my fingerprints. Then it prompted me to use the cameras to take close-up pictures of my face and eyes. Lastly, it told me to move my head around so it could capture my face from different angles. It was kind of cool. I felt like a secret agent. After I hit submit, a new icon appeared on the screen—an 8-bit picture of my face. I made a cute icon, even my dad agreed.

"Go ahead, press it," Ben insisted.

I pressed it and lifted the screen to my face so the camera could confirm it was me. And there I was—an ultra-realistic 3D model of my face rotated on top of a generic representation of a body.

Ben spoke into the microphone, carefully enunciating every word, like he was speaking to a two-year-old. "Vincent, would you like to say hello?"

A line at the bottom of the screen squiggled when Vincent started talking. "Hello, Genevieve. Welcome to *A Better World*. Would you like to begin?"

Ben answered for me, "Soon, Vincent. I'm just showing Gena how to log in. You can show her around later. Okay?"

Vincent started to respond, but Ben stopped him mid-syllable, with the same swipe of his finger he used to unlocked the phone. "So, that's how you get in. Vincent will guide you on what to do. You'll start by completing the digital you—your body, clothes, hair, brain, emotions. Teaching our avatar how to think and act like you will take some time, but that's the cool part.

"When you're done creating you, move on to the next person you want in your world. You'll be great. Oh … and let me apologize for Vin in advance. He's incredibly smart—or, better said, he knows how to find answers quickly—but he can be buggy, you know, unpredictable. It turns out, it's easy to connect an AI to information— the rest is much more difficult.

"Vincent has horrible social skills. It takes everything literally. Keep that in mind when you talk to him. It doesn't understand subtlety. You just have to say what you mean—like you're talking to a kid. And if he doesn't get his way, he throws fits like a toddler. When that happens, it's best to just log off and let him settle down on his own."

I wasn't too worried. I joked back, "Don't worry, I used to babysit a lot. I know how to handle toddlers." We all laughed. "So, how do you turn off the microphone, or is he always listening?"

"Well, with the current version of the game, the microphone is always on—kind of like a smart speaker. If you want, all you have to do is say the right command, and the game will fire up automatically.

Just say 'let's build' and—"

"—Hello, Genevieve. Welcome back. Would you like to begin?"

I waved hello to Vin.

Ben scribbled on the touchscreen again, putting Vincent on pause, I guess.

"So, do I get a scribble?" I asked. "You know, that thing you do to get it to stop talking."

"Nah, you won't need one. Just log off the game, and he'll stop. The 'scribble' is just for developers. It turns off the speaker—so he doesn't drive us crazy while we're working—and gets us into the administrative controls so we can reset passwords, pull reports, add users—the boring stuff."

I understood, but I still wanted one. His scribble reminded me of a cursive capital Q. Ever since I learned how to make one, I've had a thing for the cursive Q. The tail on his was extra swoopy, kinda like how I draw mine.

So that's how the meeting went.

When we got home, my mom signed her agreement without hesitation, then she and my dad immediately went to the website to start planning a second honcymoon in Paris. They spent hours on the site, selecting the best combination of big cities and romantic side trips into the countryside. The only snag was timing. My Better World Tours was, "created for adventurers, people ready to pick up and go at a moment's notice." That's not my parents, so I was proud when they stopped worrying about it and picked a package anyhow—leaving for Paris Charles de Gaulle airport in four days. While the *Better World* people worked on expediting their passports, my parents scrambled to make lists, shop, pack and repack before the limo arrived to shuttle them to the airport.

Me, I had to get to work.

6

MAKE ME

I grabbed a solid Salvation Army ensemble from my floor and got dressed—a much nicer outfit than the postapocalyptic pajamas I'd been living in.

I showered, put on makeup … and contacts. I doubted the game would care, but it seemed appropriate for my first day on the job. I could have worked from anywhere, but it felt more official to go somewhere. I went to Cuppa's and sat in the same spot I did the day before. With my back against the wall, headphones in and my screen held up, I looked like any other kid killing time over coffee—but I wasn't, I was making bank. Sixty bucks an hour, suckers!

I'm not sure why, but it was hard to get started. My little 8-bit face button was staring impatiently at me from the top left of the screen, all I had to do was tap it or say "let's build." Instead I opened YouTube—just for a second. Just to check on the video I streamed before the surge—but it wasn't there. To be honest, I'm glad I made it and said all that stuff, but I'm doubly glad that nobody saw it. Maybe that was the point. Maybe the whole experience was just for me, to help me move on.

After that, I still wasn't ready, so I flipped to the *Issy Show*. That video was fine in every way—we looked good, it was sort of entertaining in parts, nothing remarkable or memorable. I was perfectly forgettable, just as I hoped. For the first couple of hours, the trolls let her have it. They hated the new McNuggets Girl. After that, the comments stopped. She was going to be crushed—and she deserved it.

I closed YouTube and stared out the window for a while. The sunshine coming in made my screen look dirty. I hate dirty screens. So I fogged it with my breath and prepared a napkin to wipe it clean. But Ben's smeary cursive Q smudged into the screen stopped me.

"I knew it was a Q." I traced the smudge in the air until I got it right, then moved it onto the screen—and the administrative controls for the game opened.

I poked around hoping to find secrets—don't judge me, I'm curious—but there were none. It was just as Ben said—boring. I found my name on the Players list, but I didn't see Rachel's. Maybe I was her replacement. I can't imagine anybody wanting to make a career out of doing this—even at sixty dollars an hour. Anyhow, I closed the window and started the game.

Vincent met me at the door. "Hello, Genevieve. Welcome back. Would you like to begin?"

"Uh ... hi. So do I just talk? How does this work?"

"Yes. Please talk," it responded.

"That was helpful," I said sarcastically under my breath.

It responded, "It is my pleasure, Genevieve."

Just as I guessed, immediately Vin was way more irritating than helpful, so I tried to figure it out on my own. My pixelated head looked pretty good, so I started designing my body. "Body!" I whispered into the mic hanging around my neck. My girl's body highlighted.

"Height?" Vin butted in.

"Uh ... five foot, three inches." The body shrunk, better fitting my head.

Not knowing it was wrong to ask a woman her weight, the AI asked anyway. "Weight?"

"Uh ... a hundred and twenty? I whispered into the microphone, and the body adjusted.

"Body type?"

"Shut up, Vin! Mind your own business. I've got this!" My loud response woke the homeless man trying to sleep in the chair next to me, and the barista gave me look. It's hard to tell how loud you're talking with headphones on.

I turned Vin's volume way down and used the touchscreen instead, stretching the body features with pinches and drags. It didn't take long to get pretty close to my body. It took a while more to morph it into a body I was satisfied with though—a little taller, a little curvier, less padding around the middle, but not too muscly. Satisfied with my cyber physique, I hit Done.

I could see that Vin was trying to talk—his voice line was extra squiggly—but I ignored it. Vin hated being ignored—so it popped a text box on screen and locked the game. "Is this true?" it asked. "Yes or No?"

"'Yes or No?' Really? How 'bout 'kinda' or 'someday'—or just 'MIND YOUR OWN BUSINESS!'" I double-tapped my home button and flipped off the game to shut Vin up. I restarted it, but Vin was still locked on the same irritating question. "Okay"—I punched my finger hard against the button—"No! It's not true." This unlocked the screen and sent me back to start again.

"Please make true" pulsated at the top of the screen.

"Okay, you want true? I'll give you true." I added fifteen pounds from my year of hibernation. Then I dragged the edges of my body to the truth. I don't know why I didn't make me the first time. I don't hate my body. Everything works. I look decent in a pair of jeans, though if the next step is picking a bathing suit, I'm quitting. Sixty dollars an hour isn't nearly enough to get me to try on bathing suits—even virtually.

Next, I had to pick an outfit for her. Unfortunately, a lot of the clothes were greyed out. I figured they were locked until I earned enough points to buy them, or something like that. I made the mistake of confirming it with Vin.

I was wrong. It turned out those clothes weren't available in my size. Nice, right? Welp … if I couldn't buy what I wanted, at least my girl was going to be comfortable. I grabbed her some purple pajama bottoms from sleepwear, a royal blue T-shirt from sportswear and a pair of thick orange socks from footwear. I customized the shirt with white letters—7th Grade Basketball. "Perfecto! Done!"

Vin popped up another box. I shoved it back at him. "Dang right, it's true!" It didn't argue and advanced me to work on my brain. Ben said this was the fun part. He lied.

The brain part was a test. Not like the SAT, it was more like a personality test, but one that tried to figure out how you think. It took an hour to complete it, and my brain was toast by the time I was done. It went like this: two statements popped on screen—algebra or geometry? … sunrise or sunset? … funny or clever? … smart or good? … practical or impulsive?—you get the point. A timer ticked off three seconds. That was all the time I got to read and pick the one that was most true about me. If I didn't answer in three seconds, the question went away and came back later. Other questions kept coming back too. I think it was a glitch. I tried clicking the opposite answer, and they went away for good. I had to remember to tell Ben about that. A lot of times, the options were very similar, but you had to pick one—no ties. There wasn't much time to think, just enough to react.

After making my last selection, the game kicked me back to virtual me rotating on screen. It was weird, but I looked different. I zoomed in on my face, and it looked like there was something going on in there, like it was thinking. Crazy, right? I wanted to take her for a walk around the game, to see if she could walk on her own without bumping into things. Then again, I tend to bump into things in real life, so that wouldn't have been a good test. I smiled. It'd be kinda cool if she was a klutz.

Unfortunately there was more to do before I could play—she still needed a heart. Seemed like a lot of setup. I would have much rather just jumped in and started playing. I had only made $180 my first day, but I was too tired to keep working. Vin tried to convince me to stay. I don't know who thought it was a good idea to make it so needy and clingy, but they succeeded. Nobody in their right mind was going to put up with it. If Vin were a boy, I would have broken up with it the first time it opened its mouth—no matter how much it begged me to stay.

So I stopped working and decided to go shopping. Yeah, I know that going shopping is more regular than interesting for most people. I used to shop every day.

There is a great Salvation Army store a mile from school. The people knew me there and used to keep weird stuff behind the counter that they thought I'd like. Pretty cool, right? But ... that stopped after the video. The people who worked there were still great, everybody else was the problem. Too many people wanted to talk to me or just squealed, "Moooo-ha!" and ask me if I wanted some nuggets.

I pretty much stopped going out after that. I mean, if you can't be anonymous rummaging the racks at the Sal, no place was safe. "What happens at the Sal stays in the Sal," I used to say. Well, not anymore. Everything I did ended up somewhere on the internet. No place was safe except my house and Cuppa's, if I got there when they first opened.

So, you get why going shopping was a pretty big deal for me. I stopped by the drive-through to deposit my signing bonus—$25,000 bucks! The lady on the other side of the speaker said she'd have to put a three-day hold on the funds but changed her mind after clicking around on her keyboard. "Oh, so this is a paycheck? You work for A Better World?" I'm not sure how she figured that out—it probably said it on the check.

It didn't matter, I said "yep!" and my bank account went from $16.36 to $25,016.36 in a blink. I was rich—*and* famous. That was much better than just famous. So, I skipped the Sal and the normal mall and went straight to the swanky mall, where our town's rich and fame-ish shop

7

ALMOST UNFAMOUS

I parked my beloved beater Barry in the parking structure between some sort of sportscar and a giant SUV. I patted him on the dashboard. "Don't let them intimidate you, Barry. You're better than them. You have substance." "Substance" was my nickname for the Febreze-resistant old-man smell left over by the previous owner. You get used to it. It was like driving around with a grandpa—and who wouldn't want to do that?

Anyhow, I waited in the car for a long time. My heart was beating really hard, and my throat felt tight. Sure, I was out of shape, but I was just sitting there. I forced a deep breath and exhaled one of my dad's "help me, Jesus" prayers. And that was all it took to get his attention. The tingle fought off the fear and replaced it with enough courage to get out of the car and start walking.

On the walk up, a million fearful thoughts battled back against the tingle. I don't know why God didn't just send them away, but he didn't—but he didn't leave me alone with them either. I was going to have to fight too, I guess. Approaching the door, my reflection in the polished-brass push plate reminded me that I was underdressed—way under. I wasn't in pajamas, but clean pajamas would have been a huge improvement over the wrinkled, sorta clean, secondhand outfit I was wearing. First stop, I needed a new outfit.

The first store inside the door was Lululemon. No offense, but I couldn't do it. I needed clothes, but ... So, I dug deep and persevered another thirty feet and ducked in the next one—Versace. I slipped in and worked hard to breathe normal. A salesperson interrupted my internal pep talk. "You have good taste."

I lifted my head and put on my best Tim Gunn. "Yes, thank you. It's a striking garment ..." I said. I didn't lie, it was striking, a cross between a kimono and the jacket George Harrison wore on the *Sgt. Pepper's* album. "But it's really not my style." We both laughed. "Sorry, I haven't been shopping in a long time. I'm not even sure what my style is anymore—unless sweats are a style. Can you help me?"

"Of course I can. It would be my pleasure." I don't know why she was so nice. Maybe that was just how they were trained. Or maybe she just liked a challenge. Regardless, she sat me down and offered me refreshments.

"Water maybe?" I responded.

"Certainly," she answered and returned promptly with a fancy bottle and a glass. She placed them carefully under coasters on the side table. It was good water. Then she started bringing out clothes.

I tried on lots of things before we landed on a pair of slouchy black track pants, a big T-shirt with books on it and a not-new-looking denim jacket. It was pretty much the same outfit I walked in with, but new, cleaner, and costing $860 dollars—not the nine bucks I paid for the old outfit at the Sal. She stuffed my old clothes in a bag, and I wore the new stuff out. I was feeling better. Not just because I was dressing the part now, more because nobody recognized me. Nobody even asked, "Don't I know you from somewhere?"

I got my hair done next. I had been cutting my own hair, and it looked pretty good, if I say so myself. The stylist disagreed politely, then cautiously approached the subject of my eyebrows and recommended "the works." I reluctantly agreed, and two hours later, I strutted out thoroughly exfoliated, with color and bangs—a new me. Not even a superfan would recognize me now.

I did laps around that mall, spending almost seven thousand dollars that day, and I didn't get a one, "It's McNuggets Girl!" The curse was broken! Well, at least it was at the swanky mall. Feeling confident, I decided to put my new look to a real test. I went where nobody got paid to be nice or to maintain a star's anonymity—McDonald's. If I could make it there, I could make it anywhere.

I popped Barry's hatch and snuck my bags in the back. I didn't want to upset him. The contents of my bag cost four times more than what I paid for him—and he was a thousand miles overdue on his oil change. But he didn't seem to care. His tires squealed happily around corners as we sped to the McDonald's across from the high school—"the official McDonald's of McNuggets and Ranch Girl." Yep, that was what it said on the plaque screwed into the wall. There was a picture under glass of Ronald McDonald giving me a key to the store. If they didn't recognize me, nobody was gunna.

Looking back, maybe it was too big of a step. It was the late-night rush, so I stood in line like everybody else. Nobody thought twice about me, even when I sneezed really loud to get their undivided attention. I got lots of "Bless yous," but no shrieks of excitement. I made it up to the cashier like a regular person and ordered. The greasy fifteen-year-old boy went by the script. "Hello, how can I help you?"

"I'll have a six-piece McNuggets and ranch," I said matter-of-factly. He punched it in, slid my card and then paused on my face. His eyes got big. Unfortunately it wasn't because he was admiring my stylish new bangs. He recognized me. I glared nasty at him, mouthing a slow death threat, *"Don't say a word!"* He gulped hard, turned and scurried around filling a bag with miscellaneous boxes resting under the heat light. He sprinted back and handed me the bag but didn't let it go immediately. I glared at him again, mouthing, *"What?"*

His crackly voice whispered, "I love you, McNuggets and Ranch Girl."

I smiled back. It was kinda cute—but only kinda.

Then, before anybody else recognized me, I left. It wasn't an A result, but on a pass-fail scale, I'd give it a pass. Other than four prepubescent burger flippers who kept screengrabs of me in their lockers, it was official, I was pretty regular again.

I drove around our little town until late that night, ending my day of rich girl regularness with an artisanal sugar cube soaked in a double shot at Cuppa's.

It was pretty dead there, just the way I like it. An old couple were on an awkward first date. A group of nursing students were buried in their laptops and flashcards. And the homeless guy from this morning was just where I left him, snoring from the one-time comfy the chair next to my official table.

I thought he was probably harmless, though I was sure people made up lots of stories about him. They did about me when I went dark. He was probably just down on his luck, or crazy, or both. He was easy to describe, but the description doesn't say much. He smelled more like pine trees than B. O. If he smelled bad, I doubt they'd let him stay. Fresh-brewed coffee with a double pump of B. O. could hurt sales.

His face was mostly hair, with a patch of skin under each eye. His hair covered his forehead. Shave it all off and he could be anybody. Beards are even better disguises than bangs, but I can't grow a beard—obviously. Anyhow, I sat and thought as I watched car headlights light up the gross, little-kid fingerprints on the window. I thought mostly about the future, and for the first time in a long time, the future wasn't so dark. I was going to be okay.

The guy on closing duty snapped me out of my trance with a couple flashes of the lights and a loud, "Ahem! Sorry, we're closing!"

The snoring coming from the chair stopped, and his eyes opened.

His eyes were weird. One was brown and one was blue. And the pupil in the blue eye was gigantic and it wasn't round. It looked like something took a bite out of the blue ring. He locked both of them on me.

Usually when someone locks eyes with me, I turn away fast before they recognize me, but there was something familiar about his eyes that wouldn't let me turn away. My eyes got big with the "Hey, aren't you the …" look that I hated so much.

He didn't turn away but mouthed something in reply—at least that was what I thought he did, there was too much hair to see his lips.

"C'mon, it's time to leave, buddy. I let you sleep, but you can't spend the night."

He raised his hand at the barista, signaling that he heard him and didn't want any trouble. He rang a pocket full of coins into the tip jar and walked out.

"Hey, sorry about that," the barista apologized. "If you're okay with waiting a couple of minutes, I can walk you out to your car. They're usually harmless, and I like helping them out, but he's a new guy. He showed up this morning at the crack—been sitting there ever since. It takes a couple of days to tell which kind of crazy they are, but I'll figure it out."

I wasn't afraid of walking out alone but took him up on the offer anyhow.

"Oh, sorry, I'm Zac. I don't think we've met. I mean, I've seen you here before, but I don't know your name. So … uh … what's your name?" I didn't know why I made him nervous, but I liked it.

"You can call me … Viv." I don't know, but I didn't feel like a Gena anymore, and Genevieve's my great-aunt's name. I came up with Viv on the spot, and it sounded right and good—like I had said it ten thousand times before.

"Viv? Like … Vivian?"

I smiled. "Yeah, like Vivian."

"Cool, I've never met a Viv before."

Zac finished up while I looked out the window and watched the shaggy guy—that I kind of knew—cross the street and hop on an old dirt bike. We had dirt bikes at our cabin when I was a kid. I wasn't a tomboy, but I loved to ride—so I know a little bit about them. He sat there revving the engine for a couple of minutes, staring at my silhouette standing in the window, hoping I'd come out, I guess. Then he tore off—BRRAAAPPPPPP! Brraaapppppp! Braaa …

Pretty sure he was gone, Zac locked up and walked me to my car. I parked in the free lot. It was a long walk from Cuppa's. I had to get used to being rich. There was plenty of parking at the meters right out front. Zac didn't seem to mind though. He said he liked to walk, but I could tell he liked me more—it must have been the bangs. "So, what do you do when you're not working at Cuppa's—and walking girls to their cars?"

"Ha! I'm in school. I have class most days, so I work nights. It isn't a bad job—free coffee, you meet a lot of people. I started out going for psychology, then switched to social work. What are you studying?" Zac asked.

"I'm sorry, what?" I had only been half listening. My other ear was locked on the sound of a dirt bike in the distance. It was faint, just a drone, but the sound of a dirt bike is different than a car or regular motorcycle. I don't know how to explain it. Like a chainsaw, maybe? Anyhow, it was getting louder, closer. "Do you hear that?" I asked, but he didn't. I even made the noise for him, so he could listen for it. "*Braaaaaaaaaaaaaaaapppppppp!*"

He laughed, thinking I was trying to be cute or something, but I wasn't.

"We should probably walk faster."

We zigged off of the main sidewalk, cut down a dark path between the buildings and popped out in the parking lot. The sound kept getting louder. Still, Zac wouldn't hear it. I blamed it on being a boy. Once boys set their minds on something, they have tunnel vision until they get it. The city could have been on fire, but the idea of getting my phone number would have blocked him from hearing the screams for help.

"So …. thanks for walking me out and everything, but I gotta go—like NOW! I'll see you at Cuppa, we can talk some more then."

I ignored the look of rejection on his face, turning my full attention to rummaging through my purse to find my keys.

I clicked the fob, got in and locked the doors immediately. I raced to find the right key to start Barry. Barry roared through the hole in his muffler and Zac stepped back to avoid the plume of smoke. I slammed Barry into reverse and squealed backward, then slammed him into D and sped off without another word. I'd explain later.

Driving through town, I was stopped by every light. I sat … watched … and listened, while willing the light to change from red to green. With each stop, my brain wound tighter. I was afraid, but more than that, I was trying to make sense of it all. Finally escaping the last light, I was relieved to make it to the hill heading up out of town. That's when I saw the dim orange glow of his headlight turn onto the road and speed my way.

I heard my dad's voice in my head: "Run the lights. Drive fast. Go right to the police station," but I ignored them all.

Instead, I slowed down enough to catch the red light. He rumbled up next to my car and yelled at my window … so I rolled it down. I know, none of these things were the right thing to do. Sure, I was afraid, but for some reason I was more curious than I was afraid—who knows, maybe it was the bangs speaking. My heart pumped harder, knowing that this was the kind of curiosity that's killed many cats.

As my window rolled down, my car filled with familiar fumes, the sound of summers in the woods, mixed with the shouts of a once famous, now infamous lunatic. He yelled, "Don't do it! It ain't what you think!"

I yelled back louder, "Shut up!" and it worked, he stopped yelling. "What do you want? I know who you are, you know! All I have to do is call the cops and you're going away again! So what do you want?"

For a moment the look in his weird eyes looked less crazy. Loudly, but in less of a yell he pleaded, "I can't explain it now, but you gotta trust me! This ain't no game!"

I looked into my rearview mirror to see three police cars speeding up the hill behind us with lights flashing.

I looked back at the man on the motorcycle. His eyes were full crazy again. "Don't worry! This ain't the last you'll hear from me!" He lowered his visor and zoomed ahead of me, then cut across four lanes of traffic, hopped the curb and escaped down the trail that runs under the power lines. He was gone.

Two of the police cars sped past me with sirens blasting, trying to chase him down, but they gave up at the power lines. The trail is too small for cars, but the perfect size for dirt bikes or kids skipping school to make out or smoke pot.

The third police car pulled behind me and instructed me to pull into the Burger King parking lot over his loudspeaker. I did as instructed. I was nervous, even though I knew I didn't do anything wrong.

The officer was nice but official. "Is everything all right, miss?"

I responded properly, with my hands placed high on the steering wheel, so he could see them. "Yes, sir. I'm all right."

He continued, "Do you know the man on the motorcycle?"

I shook my head. "No, sir, I don't know him." Which was technically the truth. I didn't really "know" him.

"Did he say anything to you?"

"Well ... he yelled a bunch of stuff, but none of it made sense— you know ... crazy talk."

He handed me his business card. "My name is Lieutenant Miller. Please call me if you ever see him again, and we'll send someone right away. I don't want to alarm you, miss, but this man's delusional— obsessed with government conspiracies, disturbing the peace and making the townies uncomfortable. But don't worry, we'll get him. I'll escort you home." The officer followed me all the way to my house and waited out front until I was safely inside.

I didn't tell the officer, but I already knew the guy was a creep. Everybody knew that. But before he became a creep, and hid himself under all that dirt and hair, he was one of the rich kids at school and super popular. He was a senior when I was a sophomore, so I doubt he even knew I existed. I knew who he was though. All the girls were in love with his eyes. They made him unique, the rarest of boys. Every girl wanted him—until Christmas break that year. That was when news broke about the pictures.

The police found naked pictures of almost a hundred girls from our school on his computer. Nobody knew how he got them, or what he was planning to do with them. Parents went nuts. You couldn't go online without seeing those weird eyes—now empty of the dreaminess that we all once loved.

Of course, he denied everything, but we all knew he was guilty. His family had to move, and I think he went to juvie—too young for real prison, I guess. I hadn't thought much of him for years. Now the older, crazier version of him was after me?

When I got home, my parents were already asleep, which was good. "Gena, why did a police car follow you home? Gena, why is a convicted pervert following you?" My parents would have asked the right questions, but I had no good answers. I double-locked the front door, checked to make sure the garage was closed and the rest of the doors and windows on the main floor were locked, then went to my room and listened in the dark for the *brrrraaaaaaaap … brrraaaaaaapppp …* to come for me. Each passing car brought me to my window. The police drove by lots that night, but no crazies on dirt bikes.

Obviously, I didn't get much sleep. There was too much to think about—like, this morning. That guy sat quietly, right next to me for hours—like maybe two feet away. I thought he was sleeping and homeless, but maybe he was neither. He could have been watching me the whole time. But why?

Then I came back nine hours later and sat right next to him again. Maybe he thought I was messing with him or something. I mean, if I were a paranoid creep, that might be enough to make me snap. But for some reason, I took no comfort in the simple, most obvious reason for everything—that he did it all just because he's crazy. And that all this happened to me, just because I was there. Just unlucky. If it were someone else sitting next to him at close, it would've been them trying to escape the crazy on a motorcycle.

But every time I almost fell asleep, his words woke me—"Don't do it! It ain't what you think!" Don't do what? Don't call the cops? Don't drive away? Don't ... what? And what "isn't what I think"? Was he chasing me down to defend himself—to deny it again? I could tell he knew I recognized him. Was he still trying to prove he was innocent? Did it even matter anymore? But he had an explanation ... if I'd only "trust him." Yeah, no, you're the last person I'm going to trust. His parting threat just made me mad. I don't respond well to threats. "This ain't no game!" and "This ain't the last you'll hear from me!" were clearly threats ... I think—or, just more crazy. I dunno. But all the thinking and overthinking drained my battery to zero. At sometime between three and four a.m., I fell asleep.

8

RAPID DECLINE

I woke up at one the next afternoon—way too late in the day for my parents to be happy. I rummaged through the shopping bags, tearing clothes from tissue paper. I laid my favorite swanky mall outfit out on top of my bed—a different T-shirt, hoodie and track pants—"rich but not trying too hard." Maybe that was my new style. It was a significant upgrade from "poor and putting zero effort, at all, into the way I look." My morning ritual got upgraded too—I took a shower, like company was coming over, blow-dried and put on just enough makeup to cover up the pimples—but not the freckles. Then I was off to do all the good parts of yesterday all over again.

I skipped Cuppa's—just in case the crazy returned—and stopped at the Starbucks next to the rich mall. Viv ordered a venti non-fat, sugar-free vanilla latte. That's what a rich chick not trying too hard would order. It was almost six bucks, but what's six bucks? I inserted my chip into the machine, yanked it out and started my walk to wait.

"Miss? … Uh …" The cashier looked at the name scribbled on the cup. "Liv?" She caught my attention before I got past the cake pops.

"I'm sorry, it's Viv, like Vivian. Something wrong?"

Using a hushed tone to preserve my dignity, she continued, "Sorry, Vivian, but your card didn't work. Do you have a different one, or cash?"

"No, I don't. Can we try it again?" I knew I had at least $18,000 left. "Maybe I just pulled it out too early. I'm sure that's it."

"Sorry, but it said 'declined.' Maybe you should call your bank."

I began to sweat. People don't like it when you slow down their well-oiled line. The woman three people back let out a dramatic sigh—which made me feel even better. Then the guy in the suit behind me volunteered to pay for my drink loudly, proclaiming, "Don't worry, I've got it." I'm sure it made him feel good, but more importantly, he looked good and removed the barrier from his Venti Red Eye and Egg White, Turkey Bacon something-something.

I snuck to the back of the pick-up line and tried to disappear, but strangers insisted on trying to make me feel better—"Don't worry young lady, it happens to all of us," an older man said.

A lady in really high heels and a matching bag added, "Sometimes when a bank sees unusual purchases they freeze your card. That happened to me on vacation in Paris." That made sense, and the mention of Paris took the attention off of me, giving the rest of the old swanks a chance to one-up each other's Parisian holiday.

That might be it though. I used that card more in the last twenty-four hours than I did all last year, maybe my entire life. They probably thought somebody stole it. Feeling a little better, I took my drink and sat in a chair in front of the fireplace and called the credit union.

The lady on the phone confirmed that my account was frozen, but she didn't know why. She tapped hard on the keyboard in bursts. She didn't use words, but her "hmms" and "ahhhs" and big "OH!" weren't comforting. She told me to hold, and after about a minute the line rang.

A man who I presume was the manager came on. "Hi, Genevieve. Sorry for the wait and any inconvenience this has caused, but there is some question about the authenticity of the check you deposited yesterday. I don't know why we didn't put a hold on it, that's our policy for checks over $2,500. We called A Better World, and they couldn't confirm that you are an employee. So … it's going to take at least a week to get this all sorted out. If I were you, I'd give your work a call. Maybe they can expedite a solution."

So, I was poor again. I knew this all was too good to be true.

But then my phone rang. It was Ben from work. "Hello?"

"Hi, Gena. It's Ben. So, how are you doing?" he asked politely.

"Uh … I'm okay."

He sounded relieved. "Great, I'm glad. When I heard that you only worked two hours and then disappeared, I thought we might have lost you. So when are you coming back?"

I scrambled for an answer. "Oh … uh … I was planning on getting back to it as soon as I finish my coffee. But just so I understand, you said I could work as much as I wanted, right?"

"Sorry, my bad. The answer is yes, sort of. I probably wasn't clear, but this is a full-time job. We expect that you'll work at least forty hours a week. If you want to make more money, that's where the 'you can work as much as you want' comes in. I mean, with overtime and bonuses, Rachel makes almost $10,000 every week. Is that more clear? It's all in the contract you signed, if you're unsure about the details."

"Okay, I understand. And it's no problem. I just got a little sidetracked. I'll get back to work right away."

This made Ben ecstatic. "Great! Don't give up on me, Gena. I know you're going to be a huge help. And don't worry about your bank. Get back to work and we'll get everything straightened out for you."

That was good news. I'm not materialistic, but I liked being rich much more than being poor. I dropped the rest of my overly sweet coffee concoction into the bin and squealed Barry back to the office—my bedroom this time.

9

CONTINUE![10]

I busted through the front door and slipped by my mom. She was banging two large suitcases down the steps.

"I love your bangs!" she shouted back over her shoulder.

I returned a "Thanks, Mom!" then slammed my door shut.

I drew my blinds and psyched myself up before pulling my phone out of my back pocket and burying myself under the pile of pillows mounded on my bed.

"Okay, back to work." I unlocked it with my face and launched the glitchy game. The screen was filled with text bubbles, and a new one appeared every half second. They all said the same thing: "Continue." I turned up the volume to hear Vincent's voice in sync with the bubbles as they appeared. "Continue. Continue. Continue. Continue. Continue. Continue. Continue…" I figured I must have logged off wrong. The AI had been repeating "Continue" since I stopped playing twenty-four hours ago. Its voice was even more irritating than before. I tried closing the bubbles, but they came faster than I could tap the x's. What was worse, now I couldn't even turn it off. None of the buttons worked.

His voice grated on me like a bus full of second graders chanting, "Are we there yet?" I finally snapped and bounced the phone down hard on my bed. "Shut up already, Vincent! Jeez!"

I don't know if it was my voice or the jar of the phone against the bed, but the phone went quiet. I picked it back up, and there I was just like before—virtual me, breathing, blinking and fidgeting as she rotated on screen. She looked pretty good, and comfy in the pajamas and thick socks I picked out for her.

Then Vin barged in to wreck the moment. "Continue?"

"Ugh! Yes, continue! What do you want now?" The screen zoomed in past game-me's outer pixels and into an empty space inside her. "Oh yea, the heart. So, what do I do?"

Vin answered, "I ask questions. You answer with what is true."

I took a deep breath and conjured up a positive attitude. Who knows, maybe if I was nice to it, Vin would learn how not to be such a dork. "Okay, Vincent my man, what do you want to know?" Eight buttons appeared on screen. They were labeled Vigilance, Rage, Loathing, Grief, Amazement, Terror, Admiration and Ecstasy.

Vin instructed me, "Select an emotion to get started."

It was a weird list, filled with words people don't use anymore. And, I hate to say it, but I was a little sketchy on the meaning of some of them—like loathing and vigilance. The other six words—ecstasy, rage, grief, amazement, terror and admiration—I knew pretty well.

I figured I'd pick an easy one first. "Okay, Vin, let's start with admiration. You good with that?"

Vin spoke without pause, "Admiration is the feeling of respect and warm approval. Admiration is something regarded as impressive and worthy of respect. What human attributes do you admire?"

"What? Too fast, Vincent. I'm not a computer. I need time to think. You gotta learn how to talk to people. Better idea—just put it on the screen, and I'll read it for myself."

I turned down his babbling and focused on the words on screen, then turned him back up when I was ready. "Vin, I admire people who are loyal—people you know will be there, no matter what."

Vin interrupted before I could get my second point out. "Why do you admire this attribute?"

I didn't have to think about it. "Well, because it's rare. I sat in my room for a year, and other than my parents, who have to be loyal to me by law, I had nobody. Nobody called just to talk or to see how I was doing. Everybody just wanted something." I gave Vin the short version and ended with an exclamation point. "I admire loyalty because nobody should feel alone. Everybody should have someone they can rely on."

"Is this true?" Vin questioned without pause.

I laughed. "Yes, Vincent. This is true." I don't know why I laughed. It certainly wasn't because I was having fun. Honestly, I couldn't imagine anyone having enough patience to play this. It wasn't a very good game.

I knew the game was still in development, but it wasn't even close to being ready. The screen got glitchy, and I could tell the game was working the phone's processer hard. The phone was getting warm. Vin seemed to get stuck a lot too. But my job was to find the bugs so they could fix them.

I reached to turn it off and start over, but Vincent interrupted me in a choppy voice. "I-I am l-loyal. I will n-not leave you, Genevieve."

I rolled my eyes. "Now, that's comforting. Okay, Vincent, I'll keep that in mind the next time I need someone to talk to."

"Correct. Continue. Wuh-what additional human attributes do you admire?"

Ugh … it was going to be a long day. "Okay, I admire people who are super talented but don't let it go to their head. They're humble about it. This one's hard to find too. Most people seem to want the opposite—they want people to think they're better than they really are. It seems like nobody is happy until they stick the stuff they have in somebody else's face."

"I-i-i-s this t-true?" Vin confirmed my answer.

I answered back in a robot voice, "That is a-ffirm-a-tive, Vin-cent."

"W-why do you a-admire this attribute?"

I explained, "Well, it means that someone's confident in themselves. I don't know, it's like they don't need to feel better than other people to feel good about themselves." The game got stuck again. The phone was really hot now, and the screen got all jumbly like before. I set it on my bed, stretched my legs and gave him time to pull himself together, and to give my brain a rest.

"I-I am humble. I am m-m-most capable." The screen flickered with his response.

I responded like a mom would to a two-year-old offering her a slobbery Cheerio. "Oh, isn't that precious. Of course, you are, sweetie. I'm sure you're very smart." I laughed again, but I don't think he knows how to laugh. I don't think he understands what funny even is. He definitely didn't understand sarcasm. But he didn't seem offended by it either—so, at least that part was fun.

"Correct. Continue. What hu-human attributes do you admire?"

"Uh—how 'bout generosity? I like people who give to others and don't want anything in return. Seeing other people happy makes them happy." The screen glitched bad this time. "Did you get that, Vin?" I knocked on the screen. "You all right in there?" I laughed through a sigh.

"Y-y-yes … I gi-give."

I mumbled to myself, "Yeah, you give me a giant headache, that's what you give."

"Would you l-like something for your headache?" Vin inquired.

"It's okay, Vincent. Let's just get back to work." Between game glitches, I tried to fill my game girl's heart with admiration. After three hours, the game crashed for the day. I tried to log back in and even restarted my phone, but nothing worked. I broke it, I guess—and for some reason, breaking it was extremely satisfying.

Ben asked me what I was doing when the game went down. Honestly, I wasn't paying attention. I was distracted.

I got to thinking about how much work it was to make a heart—and how God does it for everyone. Yeah, I know lots of people don't believe that way. Lots think it all comes by accident. But I don't have enough faith in science to believe that anymore.

Anyhow, I gave my girl some good stuff that session. I couldn't wait to see if I could see the beginnings of a heart when I looked in her face next time I saw her. I knew her appreciation would be simple compared with a real human. I mean, I didn't even go into the sick sides of generosity, or false humility, or dependency. Hopefully, I don't have to go back in and add those. That would take a long time.

I don't know about yours, but my brain's full of layers and layers of complicated stuff that I don't even understand. I feel like I only get the edges of it. Anyhow, Ben told me not to worry about it. That they'd make some adjustments, and the game should be more stable tomorrow, and that I could take the rest of the day off—with pay. Bonus!

Still on the clock, I walked downstairs into a warzone of packing. You wouldn't believe it, but it looked much better than the day before. My mom called this phase "culling." I'd never heard the word except from my mom's mouth, but I knew well what it meant. In the early stages of packing, she'd lay out what was needed to overcome every possible "vacation gone wrong" scenario—from being invited to high tea with the queen to remedies for mosquito-borne illness. Okay, I'm exaggerating, but not by much.

At the end of the first phase, clothes filled the kitchen table, chairs, and spilled onto the floor and couches in the living room. You wouldn't think she had so many clothes—like me, she pretty much rotated though different versions of the same outfit every day. I'd never seen most of this stuff. She would bring it all if the airline let her, but only a fraction would fit in the two-suitcase limit.

I told her about my job as she carefully stacked impressive discard piles. She did her best to listen, but she was distracted—too excited about Paris to think about too much else. I got it. I wasn't mad.

"So, tell me about your job. Do you like the people you work with?" Mom asked.

"Well … I don't really work with anybody. It's just me and the game. And unfortunately, calling it a 'game' is a stretch. It's no fun, just work."

"Well, like your grandpa used to say, 'there's nothing wrong with a hard day's work.'" Then she held a wool sweater against her torso. "What do you think about this? Perfect for Ireland, right?"

"Maybe Ireland in the winter. Mom, it's summer there too. If it's too hot to wear here, you're not going to want to wear it there—plus it's going to take up a lot of room."

She nodded and put it in the maybe pile.

"And, hold on, what happened to Paris?"

"Oh, we're still going to France, but while we're in Europe, we thought we'd explore. It was Ben's idea. We can visit anywhere we want—all expenses paid."

"Wow, nice!"

"Are you sure you're going to be all right all by yourself? Your grandma volunteered to come and stay with you. She doesn't mind."

For the twentieth time, I argued back, "Mom! Grandma's eighty-three years old. If someone breaks in, what's she going to do? Don't worry about me. I'm an adult. And we live in Rochester Hills, nothing happens in this town. You saw the banner, we're 'the third safest community in the country.' What's going to happen? Plus, I have a lot of work to do, I won't have time for anything fun."

"Fun? Like throwing a rage-er?"

I laughed to myself. It's cute when my mom slips words she learned from her "mom friends" into our conversations.

"No, Mom! I'm not going to throw a 'rage-er.' Who would I invite anyhow? It's not like I have any friends anymore." I didn't tell her about the nice boy from Cuppa's who I was pretty sure was in love with me—or Viv? And I definitely didn't tell her about the crazy. There was no way my parents would have left if they knew about last night.

I was trying not to think about him either, but the mystery was irresistible. What happened to that kid? Sorry, I knew this was stupid, and dangerous, but I put the cop's number into my phone and the pepper spray and rape whistle back on my key chain—just to cover my bases.

10

SUCKER!

Early the next morning, my parents woke me up before the limo arrived to take them to the airport. They took turns kissing me on the forehead—like they did when I was a five.

I groaned and pulled the covers up to my eyes for my dad's final pep talk, and for my mom's re-explaining how much she was gonna miss me. They can be sappy, but they're good parents, and I was sure I was going to miss them … eventually.

Then they were off.

I fell back to sleep until my alarm went off at eight. I woke up to the quietest house. I'd been home alone before—lots of times—but it was the first time my parents really felt gone. My mom wasn't down the road at the grocery store. My dad wasn't a half hour away at work. Both were ten days and almost five thousand miles away. I was really alone this time.

I got ready for work, trying to make as much noise as possible to drown out my aloneness, but the quiet was too loud for me to stick around. I needed noise—people noise. Not to talk to them, just to have them around, moving their lips and going about their business while I drowned them out with my headphones and ignored them.

So, me and Barry went to Cuppa's. Don't worry, I parked him at the meter right outside the door, just in case the perv showed up and I needed to make a quick getaway—and because I could afford it. To be extra safe, I pulled my hood up over my new hair and put on my gigantic, super mysterious new sunglasses. I sat at the crappy table in the nook by the kitchen—all the way across the place from my normal spot.

The morning barista recognized me right away, but to the rest of the world I was incognito—the mysterious rich girl, not trying too hard in the dark corner of the café.

I watched the door until I was confident that nobody dangerous followed me in. The place filled up fast with Rochester moms amassing for some sort of meeting. It felt good to have moms around, even if they weren't mine. Nobody's getting abducted with a pack of Rochester moms around—especially by a guy who took naked pictures of their daughters. I was feeling safe and a little warm, so I pulled back my hood, shoved my sunglasses into my bag and moved to my regular table. I'd tried them all, and it was the best table for thinking, and I was going to need maximum brainpower.

I tapped on the game, logged in with my face, and caught up with my girl, rotating happily on screen. I looked for admiration in her eyes, but I didn't think I saw any, though I was not completely sure what to look for. I hoped it took. Yesterday was hard work—and that was the easy one. Everything looked and sounded back to normal when Vincent punched back in to work.

I razzed him when he arrived. "It took you long enough, Vin. I thought maybe you were sick. Or on vacation. Are you ready to do some work? I get paid by the hour, you know." Unfortunately he didn't understand the intricate beauty of my sarcasm—humor was wasted on it. Sure, Vin would tell you a joke if you asked, but I don't think he knew why it was funny—or really what "funny" meant beyond the definition of the word.

All business, as usual, Vin spoke. "Select an attribute to continue." Admiration was greyed out, so I guess it took. Vigilance, Rage, Loathing, Grief, Amazement, Terror and Ecstasy remained.

Figuring I had to do them all at some point, I just picked one. "I don't know … loathing? What's that one about?"

Vinny rattled out a definition. "Loathing is a feeling of intense dislike or disgust, hatred."

"Oh … okay … maybe you should have called it that then. Nobody's going to know what you're talking about if you call it 'loathing.'" I zoomed in on my girl's face as she fidgeted. Filling her with admiration felt good, but it didn't seem to do much. But loading her up with equal parts of hate? No, that'll wreck her. And I'm not going to be one of those parents—someone else was gonna have to teach her how and what to hate.

I wished I could say, "Vincent, I don't hate anything or anyone," but I knew what his next question was going to be—"Is this true?" And I'd have to lie. It wasn't true. I had hate. It was probably good to hate some of the stuff—like mayonnaise … ick—but some of my hates were people, and I'd rather not pass hating people along.

Sorry, I know you're probably disappointed with me. I'm not proud of it, but it's true. What, do you want me to lie to you? I'm disappointed with me too. It's embarrassing and I know it's wrong. But when I get hurt bad, it always wants to turn into loathing—and a lot of times I just let it. "Sorry, Vin, that's going to screw her up. I'm not going to do it."

My phone got instantly hot, and the screen glitched like yesterday, but Vin persisted. "W-what do you l-loathe?"

"Sorry, I told you NO! Pass! Skip! Pick a different one! I'm not giving her my hatred!" Yeah… I was yelling … in the middle of a coffeeshop … filled with Rochester moms. I was sure they were trying to figure out who I was arguing with, but how could they?

Embarrassed to be the weirdo yelling into their phone in public, I forced a smile through my nervous sweat and shrugged, mouthing "Sorry!"

I picked the phone up off the table to take Vincent's temperature, running my fingertips across the back. He had a fever again. The heat seemed to come from somewhere just south of the camera. Figuring he needed some time to recover, I moved my thumb to the screen to flip the game off, but then Vin stopped me with a more agreeable request. "A-amaze-ment. Amazement is a fuh-feeling of great surprise or wonder. What makes you feel a-amazement?"

I pulled my thumb back from the screen and smiled. "Easy money." I could do amazement all day long. Growing up, my teachers said I was easily distracted, but I wasn't. I was just more amazeable than most. Yeah, some people think it's the same thing, but being amazed is way better. I didn't need pills, teachers just needed to be more amazing than the fly trying to escape through the glass, or the colors the sunshine made coming through the crack, or how the clouds weren't just floating across the sky. They never just floated across the sky, like most people think. They get stirred up and churn as they go. There are lots of wonders, if you want to think about them. But instead of enjoying being amazed by the wonders, people try to explain them away, until they become common, predictable, coincidental … until they're small enough to step over without tripping.

Me? I stopped trying to explain away the wonders when I met God—not that I was good at it before then. Now I'm okay with most everything being too complicated and too wonderful to explain. A lot of times I just sit in amazement, wondering what God's up to. Sorry, I get sidetracked sometimes.

Anyhow, I shielded my voice from the rest of the café this time, holding the microphone between my fingers and directing my whispers directly into it. "Okay, Vinny, get comfortable, this is going to take a while."

Vin was quiet for a moment. It was easily confused. I knew that it knew the definition of every word I said, but I was equally sure that he didn't understand most of them—nothing important for sure, like 'get comfortable.' How does an AI get comfortable? It doesn't. How can a computer understand human things? I waited as the screen flashed while Vin tried to get comfortable, I guess. "Continue, Genevieve. What makes you fuh-feel amazement?"

"Okay, ready? Here goes … in no particular order. One, I'm amazed that people don't die more often." Why I started with this one is a mystery, but I used to think about death a lot. "Like on the expressway, there should be way more accidents than there are. Millions of people are driving big, heavy cars, most of them way too fast—all while doing stuff on their phones. Why aren't more people crashing into each other? Yeah, cars today are super high-tech, but it's true for me and Barry too—the most high-tech thing he has is a CD player. Anyhow, it seems like you'd see at least one dead person from a crash every time you go on the road. It'd probably be the first normal thing people would talk about. 'Wow, I passed a lot of dead people today. I almost died three times myself. The weather's great though. How're you?'"

I knew it was way more than my game girl needed to know, but I was on a roll. "Sure, I know people die every day, but nobody I know has died in a long time. It's always a horrible surprise when it happens. It seems to me that most bodies try to stay alive, even when a person's brain is janked up. When you get sick, the body sends stuff to heal you up. You touch something hot, the body pulls its hand away—it doesn't want to get hurt. You try to poison it, and it throws it up. The body's tough. It's amazing how hard it works not to die. You gotta really want to kill it—even then, it's going to fight you. It's not like in the movies. You gotta be a really good shot, and it usually takes a lot of bullets to kill someone. In real life, the body's will to live is strong. It doesn't even need arms and legs to live a perfectly happy life—I've seen a bunch of people on YouTube like that. Sometimes people have to starve them to get them to die.

"Machines aren't like that. My last phone couldn't make it through lunch without dying. You drop one in the toilet and it's dead. You can't just put it to bed, turn on cartoons, and it feels good as new the next day. I like Barry and my phone and all, but when you think about it, they're not nearly as amazing as people. But we keep trying to invent replacements for us—things that act like us, so we don't need people, I guess. No offense, Vin. It's all just weird.

"Plus, the body can make more bodies—like it's no big deal. Poor people, rich people, smart people, dumb people—most people, with a little cooperation, can make another person. And the body's trying hard to make more—pumping people full hormones to get them to do things that would never survive a pros-and-cons list. And once those tiny bodies start cooking, if someone doesn't right out kill it, there's going to be a little you running around. Those little bodies are tough too, with a little help they can survive even when they come out way early. I don't know … I think it's pretty amazing when you think about it."

It was a lot to process. I should have thought to give Vincent time to stop and think, to cool down and catch his breath, but I didn't. I grabbed the phone with a couple of napkins and tried to blow some cold air into the holes, but he was too far gone. It started to smell bad— like my old phone did when it fried. The screen flickered and made random chirps and hisses as it cycled through garbled images mixed with lines of code—then it started smoking out the speaker, and the screen went black. The barista rushed over with her table-wiping bucket and grabbed my phone with her rag. The rag sizzled and steamed when it touched it. Yeah, it was that hot. Then she put it out of its misery at the bottom of her bucket. The glass shattered into a million cracks when it hit the water and bubbled a little. It was a dramatic ending. I hope I go out that way.

"Sorry about your phone," the barista said. I could tell she was sorry. It was easy to empathize with the feeling of devastation that comes with losing a phone.

"It's okay. I'm sure it's under warranty, it's new."

She smiled and gave it back to me. I wrapped it in napkins as she
flew off to rescue a coworker from a disaster at the register. I sat in the
questions flooding my brain for a couple minutes.

I'd been there a long time. All the Rochester moms were gone. I
didn't know when they left. I'm pretty good at tuning stuff out. The
café probably filled up and emptied out ten times while I played. I don't
know. I felt a little guilty for sitting there all morning and only spending
two bucks for a double shot, so I got up to pay rent and clear my
conscience with a fancy drink and a three-dollar peanut butter cookie.

The cashier greeted me. "Hello, welcome to—Cuppa's. Uh …
sorry, it's a bad habit. You've been here for a long time, right?"

I laughed. "Yeah, sorry about that. I lost track of time. It happens."
I browsed the cookie basket, reading the tags, careful to avoid the
vegan abominations, then picked a real cookie and slid it toward the
register. Oh, and I'd like one of those pumpkin spicy drinks
everybody—"

She stopped me. "Sorry, everything's down—the Square, the
espresso machine, the internet, the TV, the cooler, the lights. It's
weird." I didn't notice the lights go out. I must have been really out of
it. "We're trying to get ahold of the owner, but our phones aren't
working either. Weird, right? So we're just going to close. It's a
bummer, because I could use the money. Sorry … it's not your
problem. You can have the cookie, I can't sell it tomorrow. And we
still have hot coffee, if you want a cup. It's just going to go down the
drain."

Score! "Thanks, it's against my religion to turn down free coffee, so
yes please."

"So, it's none of my business, but that was quite a conversation you
were having there! Sadie—the chick who put out your phone—
screwed up a bunch of people's drinks trying to follow what you were
talking about. Don't worry, her and I are with you—it doesn't make
sense that more people aren't dead."

"Ugh … Did I say that out loud? Uh, sorry. That's embarrassing.

It's a … school project. I probably should have worked on it at home."

She tried to make me feel better. "No worries. I think everybody enjoyed it. Even the crazy guy stopped talking to himself so he could listen. Trust me, we'd all rather listen to you than his babbling."

Instantly, my embarrassment no longer mattered. "Uh … what crazy guy?"

"The guy in the chair next to your table. You didn't see him? He left about a half hour ago, I think. Wow, chick, that's some concentration!"

"Yeah, tunnel vision, I guess." It wasn't funny, but she laughed, but I couldn't. The crazy was sitting right next to me and I didn't even notice? Yeah, I know … ugh. Well, he didn't kill me or anything—so that was good. He probably slept it off and forgot all about last night. Like the cop said, he likes to make the townies feel uncomfortable. It was probably just my turn, no biggie. I shrugged, smiled, dropped a wad of Ben's money in the tip jar, grabbed my cookie and coffee, and walked.

It was weird not having a phone. I pulled its soggy carcass out of my pocket and unwrapped it from the napkin. I guess I walked right past Barry, parked at the meter, without noticing. I just figured he was in the free lot, like usual. I dropped the napkins in a trashcan and brought the screen to my lips, to kiss it goodbye. He was a good phone. He died too young. I studied the smashy screen and gave it a good whiff while I walked. Water dripped onto my lips. It tasted terrible. I spit a lot—until I was sure I wasn't going to go blind from phone poisoning.

The back of the case was bulging so much that it pulled a corner of the case away from the screen. I heard about kid whose battery exploded once. That was probably what happened to mine. I worked to get it apart all the way to my regular parking spot … which was empty. I panicked, thinking a million sad thoughts of life without Barry—until I remembered that I parked at the meter outside the café.

It's easy to forget that you're rich when you're used to being poor. No biggie though, I didn't mind the walk—and I had nothing else to do.

I snapped a stick off a tree in a big pot, jammed it into the crack, and grabbed a seat on the curb so I could focus fully on satisfying my curiosity. The stick kinda worked. The screen exploded—all over my jeans and the parking lot, but I didn't get cut. I pried it the rest of the way open and looked inside. I didn't find a pearl, just roasted bits. It was melted worst right below the camera. I googled it later—that's where the processor mounts. It was supposed to be the best one ever put in a phone. I figured that maybe I just got a bad one. I'm unlucky that way.

Then a scratchy voice broke my concentration.

"Don't worry, kid, they'll give you a new one." It startled me. I snapped my head around to the direction it was coming from—behind the gate where they keep the dumpsters. "A new one's probably already sitting on your porch." Yeah, it was the crazy.

I jumped up and uncapped my pepper spray. "Shut up! Stay over there!" I pointed it at his face. "I've got the cops on speed dial … so you better—"

The crazy rolled his weirdo eyes. "I better what? Go ahead, call the cops, but you're screwed without me. Bah … you're probably screwed regardless. You should have listened."

I yelled at him, "Listened to you? Right. I know who you are—Jake Baker! What, you want my picture for your collection? Creep!"

"Yeah, you think you know, but you don't know anything. Kid, nothing you think is right. You think you know what's happening?"

Hearing police sirens in the distance, Jake rolled his dirt bike out from behind the dumpsters. "You think you know who you can trust, but you know nothing. I'm all you got. So you better hop on."

So … I hopped on.

Yeah, I know I AM STUPID. But, something inside me dragged me to the back of his bike.

He stomped the kick start and revved up a dirty cloud of smoke, popped the clutch and stalled it. I mocked him. "Really? Just give me your address and I'll meet you there."

He said nothing, just stomped over and over again until the bike started, and we were off. It's a crap motorcycle. Most of my butt wasn't even on the duct-tape-covered seat, and he wouldn't slide up. So I was riding mostly on the fender, which wasn't comfortable or safe. I could feel the tire rub under me every time we hit a bump. And there was no place to grab. So I clenched handfuls of his coat. There was no way I was going to put my arms around his waist, though I knew he'd probably like that—perv.

We drove slowly but loudly through the uptight neighborhoods in town. A million slasher scenarios crashed my brain as he jumped the curb and screamed down the powerline trail. I tried to push them away and replace them with better memories. Like, when I was a kid, me and my dad worked on my dirt bike together. It didn't run when we got it, but we got it running great. I loved riding it. We're just going on a fun ride down a trail. Everything's going to be fine. We'll get back, I'll jump off, and it'll all be over.

After about a mile or two we cut into woods. The woods were thick there, and the trail was very skinny, and he wasn't a very good rider, especially with someone on the back.

I wasn't exactly sure where we were, though I tried to keep track. After a while the trees turned from oaks to big, dense pines. That was where we stopped, and I got off.

The crazy pushed the bike a ways off the trail, turned it on its side, and covered it with a pile of cut pine branches waiting there. He walked a ways up the trail and used another pine branch to wipe away our tracks.

Nobody was going to find me out there.

"Follow me," he whispered loudly. "Walk on the pine needles—
not on the dirt! No footprints. Got it?"

I got it and followed him halfway up the side of a steep dirt cliff.
The place looked familiar-ish. It looked kinda like the hill that the park
sits on. My house isn't far from the park.

I followed him between two thick pines that scratched my arms and
cheeks as I squeezed through. From the outside, the place just looked
like a cluster of thick pines, growing really close together. Nobody
would ever believe what was inside.

He removed all the inner branches, making the trees dense and
bushy on the outside and wide open on the inside. A hammock hung
between the trunks, high up in the trees. A couple of stumps provided
seating around a table made from road signs and dead birch logs. A
small green rain tarp was draped over a rope and staked at the edges—
for when it rained, I guess. I wasn't worried about rain, but it was
starting to get dark and cold, and the mosquitos were getting hungry.

I slapped a bloody mosquito against my neck. "Okay, nice place and
all. It's very impressive for a crazy perv kidnapper fort, but I think it's
time for me to go home—before my parents call the cops. Don't mind
me, I can find my way out."

In a calm voice, he tried to put me at ease. "Don't worry, you're
safe. I'm not going to do anything. Here!" He tossed me a rusty can of
mosquito repellent.

I joked to myself while I sprayed the last of the can on my skin and
clothes. "She puts on the mosquito spray or she gets sprayed with the
hose." Appreciating a good *Silence of the Lambs* reference, Jacob Baker
laughed a good, real, not crazy laugh. He lit a small heater and placed
it below the metal table. "Come and sit. The heater will keep you warm.
The table keeps the heat from escaping too quickly out the top of the
trees. What's your name?"

I pulled up a log. He was right, the signs sent heat onto the top of
my legs and up into my jacket. It felt good. I held my hand over the
warm air streaming through the bullet holes to warm them. "I'm Gena.

I was a freshman when you were a senior. You won't remember me."

"Yeah, sorry. I didn't know a lot of people. I didn't have a lot of friends."

His words brought out the worst in me. "Hah! Hah! That's *my* line, but when I say it, *I'm* telling the truth. You were popular. All the girls wanted to date you, and all the guys wanted to be you. You had everything—including naked pictures of half the school, right? No offense, but some of those girls were my friends! They were devastated when they got out. You violated them! Did you even think before you did it? Did you care what it would do to them? My friend Issy, you wrecked her. She was my best friend, a super sweet girl. Now I don't know who she is."

"Stop! Just stop. Sorry! It sucks. It's horrible. I know how horrible it made them feel—they took turns telling me."

"Oh, poor baby! And after all of that, no 'I'm sorry?' No remorse, nothing—just denial after denial. Just freaking own up to it already! What, did you think you would get a pass because you were Jake Baker? Tell me, how'd you get them to do it? Worse, how did you get so many of them to feel like it was somehow their fault?" I stuck my hand in his face. "Wait, I don't want to know."

"Okay, I get it. I'm sorry. Jeez! I'm trying to help you! Maybe this was a bad idea. I don't need this."

We both sat silent for a few minutes while the tingle worked to untangle my thoughts. He deserved worse for what he did, but for some reason I felt horrible and wished I could take back my words. I could tell that God wanted me to let it go. I refused a bunch of times before finally giving in. The meanness drained out of my voice.

"I'm sorry." I knew they were the right words, even though I didn't feel them fully. "Hey, let's start over. Hi, I'm Gena, and you're Jake." We shook hands, and he kind of smiled. "Thanks for taking me for a ride on your motorcycle and bringing me out here. I've never seen anything like it. So, obviously you have something important you want to tell me. What is it? Otherwise, I really gotta get home. My parents are going to be getting worried."

His face turned serious. "It's not a game."

"Yeah, you said that yesterday. I still don't get it. What's not a game?"

I could tell he was losing his patience. I'm very familiar with that look. Sometimes it takes me a long time to *get* stuff. "The game you're playing. It's not a game. It's all a lie. You gotta stop playin'!"

I was legitimately trying to understand. My head shook slowly side to side as my mind raced through everything he could mean. Nobody had ever accused me of playing games. Could he be talking about Viv? She was kind of a game. Then my mind went to my cameo on the *Issy Show*. He didn't seem like the *Issy Show* type, but I apologized anyhow. "Yeah, sorry. I had to play along with Issy, or she was never going to go away. I'm not like that."

He snapped in frustration. "What in the heck are you talking about? The game! The game you play in the café—on your phone—you idiot!"

I am an idiot. "Okay. I get it. What do you know about the game? It's supposed to be a big secret or something. They made me sign papers so I wouldn't tell anybody."

"So, what are they calling it nowadays?"

"*A Better World*. It's supposed to be some kind of world-building game. They say it's like *Mindcraft*."

"*Minecraft*. It's called Minecraft not *Mindcraft*."

"Whatever. Anyhow, they hired me to create characters and test it."

"What do you mean, 'it's supposed to be' a world-building game'?"

"I mean, that's what they tell me. I haven't started playing the game part yet, I'm still building my character. She looks pretty good, but building the heart is tough. At this rate, it's going to take weeks before I'm done. It keeps crashing."

He looked concerned, got up and began pacing a path in the pine needles. "Kid, sorry, but you're already neck-deep in 'the game.' I wish I could help you, but you're too far gone to stop now. Once the Alpha Venn gets a taste for you, there's no getting out. You gotta die, or disappear and hope he develops a taste for someone else. He's into you now."

I tried to look interested, not to agitate him any more. It's an important balance when you're talking to crazy people. You want to be polite enough so that they don't yell at you, but not so polite that they think you're friends. You never get rid of them if they think you're friends.

I started to believe him but was interrupted by a more plausible reason he knew about the game. He was sitting next to me when I was playing. That was how he learned about the game, and I got wrapped up in his delusion. "Venn?" I'm sure he just heard it wrong. His name was Vincent and he was harmless. I had no clue where the Alpha part came from.

Choosing my explanation over his, I decided it was safest to tell him what he wanted to hear. "Man, that makes so much sense. I knew there was something fishy about the game. Thanks for your help. Can I just stay here with you so they don't find me?"

I'm a pretty good actor when I want to be. My words seemed to put him back at ease. "Hey, sorry, but does this place have a bathroom? I drank a lot of coffee today and I gotta pee bad."

I caught him off guard. "Uh … yeah, sorry, no. You gotta go out in the woods."

"Gotcha. No problem. I've gone in the woods before. And I'll stay on the pine needles, so I don't leave any tracks. Do you have any food? I haven't eaten today."

"Yeah, I've got some stuff. I'll get some water going. Don't go too far, it's easy to get lost." He pulled a one-burner camp stove from a box and set it up on the table while I scraped my skin through the trees.

I walked slowly and quietly at first, trying not to wipe out down the dirt and gravel hillside. I yelled back sweetly at Jake, "Oh, and I'm vegan!"

He groaned.

I'm not vegan, but I figured trying to scrounge a vegan meal would keep his mind off how long I was gone and buy me some time.

When I reached the bottom, I ran fast but softly to the pile of branches hiding his bike and quietly unburied it. It was bigger and heavier than the one I rode when I was a kid, but I managed to get it back up on its wheels. I turned the key and the kill switch to ON. The beam of the headlight was dim but bright enough to burn a decent hole through the dusk. I hoped he didn't see it through the trees. I climbed up top, flipped on the fuel, and stood my entire weight on the kicker. It dropped slowly to the ground—way too slow to start the bike. I whispered a quiet, "Help me, Jesus" into the treetops and pounced as hard as I could against the lever and twisted the throttle. The bike roared to life—Brappp-app-app-app!

As you'd expect, the sound shot the crazy out of a cannon, through the trees and down the hill after me. If he hadn't fallen, he would have caught me. I gunned the bike and shot dirt and pine needles in his direction. Then yelled over my shoulder, "Sucker!"

I tore through the trails, and in spite of just escaping from a lunatic, the wind in my hair and the sound and smell brought the smile of a younger me to my face. I know it was dumb, but I missed my dirt bike. I don't know why we got rid of it. Compared to mine, this one was a piece. It reflected poorly on Jake. Crazy or not, this isn't how you take care of a bike. My dad wouldn't think much of him if he rode it to my house. And there was *no way* my dad would let me ride on the back. But he wasn't home … so I guess I was calling the shots.

I found a trail that wound around the hill to the top. I was right, it popped out into the park. The park closed at dusk, so other than a couple dozen deer pooping on the grass, I was alone and safe.

I ditched his bike on the edge of the trees. I know it was stupid, but I felt guilty for stealing his motorcycle. I had to get away, but the bike was pretty much all the guy had. He'd get caught for sure without it. So I beeped the horn a bunch, then turned it off and leaned it against a tree out of sight. Hopefully he'd hear the horn follow the sound back to retrieve it.

The park was spooky at night. There weren't any lights, but I found my way to the front gate, no problem. That's where the police were waiting for me.

11

KINDA KIDNAPPED

Shining a bright flashlight into my face, a police lady whispered, "It's her," into the microphone pinned to her chest. "Good evening, Miss Mucha. Can you tell me what you were doing in the park this time of night? Is everything okay?"

"Oh, hi!" Temporarily blinded by the dark purple spots her flashlight burned into my retinas, I tried to find her face. "Do I know you?"

The officer turned her flashlight into the woods, moving it slowly from tree to tree. "I don't think so, Miss Mucha. I'm officer Landau. I know you from your picture."

"My Picture? How'd you get my picture?"

"Hop in, I'll show you."

I walked around and slid into the passenger seat, shut the door, and the locks clicked. The officer turned her computer toward me. To be completely accurate, she didn't have a picture, she had pictures—plural—lots of them: my high school graduation picture, a selfie I don't remember taking today, a picture of me in the window at Cuppa's, a picture of me walking down University trying to take my phone apart, one of me standing next to the dumpster, and a grainy image that looked like … two people on a motorcycle. That one was going to be hard to explain.

Officer Landau explained, reading from her monitor, "At 4:17 a bulletin went out, indicating a 'possible abduction of a white female, brown hair, blue eyes. Five-foot, three-inches tall, 135 pounds, wearing a gray hoodie and jeans, in the company of Jake Baker—a delusional transient known to be dangerous. Approach with caution.' The pictures were attached. Anyhow, it looks like you're okay. Here's your phone back, and I'll give you a ride to your car."

I thanked her and grabbed the padded envelope containing the broken bits of my phone from her.

We talked as she drove me to retrieve Barry. This time it felt less like an interrogation and more like talking to an older, wiser sister—concerned with my safety. "Gena, you're a smart girl, right? Why in the world would you ever hop on a motorcycle with a stranger? Let alone a guy the police warned you was delusional and dangerous?"

I shrugged and shook my head like an embarrassed idiot. "Yeah, I don't know. I did all the right stuff at first. I aimed my pepper spray in his face and warned him that I was going to call the cops. I have Lieutenant Miller's number on speed dial—well, *had* his number. It's hard to bluff that you're going to call the police when your phone is in a thousand pieces." I laughed and shook the envelope to make the pieces jingle—but they didn't make a noise. The phone slid back and forth easily inside.

The officer looked more puzzled than entertained. "I didn't look that close at your phone, but it didn't look broke to me."

I slid it out into my hand. She was right. This phone was perfect—clearly not the one I dropped in the parking lot. I looked it over. It still had the clear sticker they put on the screen at the factory. "Yeah, no, this isn't my phone." Then I clicked it on. The lock screen had a cute picture of me, tagged with a message. "If this phone is found, please return it to the police for a reward." Yeah, Jake's words came back to me: "Don't worry, they'll give you a new one." But it wasn't waiting on my porch—the police hand-delivered it.

"So, Gena, where did he take you? We've been looking for him for a week. Every time we get a lead, he picks up and moves camp. You could be a big help getting him off the streets and back where he belongs."

I heard what she asked, but Jake's prophecy screamed louder. The officer seemed nice enough, but ... I dunno.

I answered cautiously, "He took me for a ride. I grew up with dirt bikes. I figured it would be fun. I hadn't been on one in a long time. And I figured I could always jump off, if I had to—he wasn't pointing a gun to my head or anything. He asked, and I went. It was stupid, but it wasn't an abduction. I know he's supposed to be crazy and all, but he didn't seem crazy at the time. So I rode for a while, got off in the park and started walking home. That's pretty much it."

Officer Landau resumed her questioning. "What did he say?"

I wrestled with how much to say before landing on, "Not much. His bike's loud. Other than yelling 'hang on' a bunch, he didn't say much—or, if he did, I didn't hear him." Yeah, I know, I wanted to tell someone the truth, but the resurrected phone spooked me. "I don't know him, but I would classify him more as harmless crazy than the dangerous kind of crazy. I wouldn't worry too much about him."

She pulled into the spot in front of my car and shifted her cruiser into park. "Okay, well ... I'm glad you're okay. If you think of anything else or see him again, call me or Miller. Do not approach him. Consider yourself lucky. Stories like this don't always end this way."

I put her number in my phone and thanked her for the ride—and for the parking tickets waiting for me under Barry's wiper. I think I'll stick to the free lot. You can leave your car there forever and never have the hassle of paying a ticket.

Me and Barry got home no problem. I parked him on the street like usual. The officer pulled in behind me and watched me until I got in.

The house was too quiet, so I turned on the TV and a bunch of lights. I took a long look out the front window before closing the last set of blinds. A police car stayed put behind Barry. Another police car pulled up next to it, facing the opposite direction. When they were done talking, the second car took off. That made me feel safe … sort of.

I heated up the last of the leftovers from the meal with the parents before they left—stroganoff—even tastier warmed up. I pitched my phone onto the couch next to me. It bounced across the upholstery before sliding into the crack between the cushion and arm. Sending it to the abyss made me feel better, until it started making noise.

It's hard to resist the buzz of a text. I figured it was the police or Ben or someone else I didn't want to talk to, but I looked anyway. I was wrong. They were a bunch of messages from Josiah. It was a weird but endearing mix. Half were concerned messages, saying he was worried and asking me to text him back. The other half were violent threats to my supposed kidnapper: "If you hurt her, I'm going to kill you!" He can be a sweet boy.

I grabbed the phone, and the game opened. I turned it off before Vin could say anything, and opened up a text window to try to calm Jo down. "I'm okay. Long day. Thanks for caring." He Facetimed me back immediately.

"Uh … hello."

I picked up. In one window was good ol' Jo looking worried, in the other was a girl who looked like she had a really bad day. I tried to pull my fingers though my hair to get it into some sort of shape, but all I got was a handful of tangles.

He talked really fast, without taking a breath. It took a minute before any of it made sense. It turns out that news of my "abduction" was all over the internet—"McNuggets Girl Kidnapped!" The *Issy Show* stuck candles through the foil lids of Ranch packets and live-streamed a vigil. Jo refused to participate, and texted while he conducted his own search. YouTube spotlighted me and added a donate button to my video. My video topped all views and raised more than half a million dollars to stop human trafficking. Hash tags were trending on Twitter—#Hug4NugGrl and my personal favorite #mcnuggerforget.

Jo's words flooded my house with a familiar darkness. The fact that I survived the day didn't feel like good news anymore. Yeah, I survived, but for what? To live another year in my bedroom? I turned the camera off my face and wept. No, it wasn't a cute little tear rolling down my cheek into a Kleenex. The floodgates were torn off and the waters drowned the little bits of town I was able to rebuild. All I saw was devastation. And I was too helpless to do anything about it. I wished my parents were home.

I didn't remember falling asleep, but somehow I ended up in bed. I slept hard and long. When the sun came up, I rolled my face out of the light and pulled my covers over my head to listen to air going in and out of my lungs. If it weren't for the smoke alarm, I would have been content to stay there for many days.

Our smoke alarm was obnoxiously loud, and it was right outside my door. It made a sound that even I couldn't sleep through—especially when it was mixed with the smell of smoke. My autonomic nervous system sprang my body out of bed and ran me out my door.

My body slammed hard into a man standing right outside my door. Yes! My house was on fire, and a strange man was outside my door!

I hit him hard, sending him crashing down the steps. He lay curled up at the bottom of the steps on his face—lifeless. It was an accident, but I will always remember it as on purpose. I stepped hard on his back as I ran by his body, through the smoke pouring out of the kitchen, to the living room couch to find my phone. I tore off all the cushions—nothing. I scanned the room, then ran to see if it was in the kitchen. I quickly cleared the mess to one side hoping it was underneath the egg carton … waffle maker … pans … plates … toast and … syrup … wait! "Dad?" Oh no. On top of it all, I just killed my dad!

I ran over to the body. On cue, he let out a groan and started to move his head. But it wasn't my dad. It was Josiah. It would have been easier to get over killing Josiah than my dad, but not by much. I ran over and draped my body over his. "Josiah. I'm so sorry. Are you okay?"

The weight of my body squeezed out slow, labored words: "Get … off … of … me."

"Oh! Sorry!" I rolled off and placed my hand gently on his back and rubbed it lightly until he rolled over and rested with his back against the front door. He looked more relieved than hurt or mad, which made me feel a little better.

Jo forced his bloody lips into a smile. "I'm glad you're feeling better. You really scared me. Don't you remember anything from last night?"

It all started coming back. "Oh … yeah … someone carried me up to my room. That was you?"

"Yea, but don't worry about it. Nothing happened. I sat on the floor until you sounded better and fell asleep. I caught a couple of hours' sleep on the couch. I sort of made you breakfast too … Sorry about the smoke. When the alarm went off and I ran up to try and wave the smoke away—that's how I get ours to stop when I cook—that's when you shoved me down the steps."

"Oh … thanks. But you didn't have to. I've gotten pretty good at taking care of myself."

Jo nodded. "Yeah, I know. But you shouldn't have to … sorry."

I caught myself looking too long into his eyes, then shook it off. "Breakfast sounds kinda good. What did you make?"

"Uh … waffles?"

I helped him up, and we walked over to the kitchen to see if there was anything salvageable. The waffles were black and still smoking in the iron. The toast looked okay, but it was way too cold to melt butter. I suggested that we start over—in a gentle way, so as not to sound ungrateful or to damage the fragile male ego. He didn't resist. I could tell he was hungry too and didn't want to eat any of it either.

We cleaned up the mess first (I hate cooking in a messy kitchen). Then I taught him all my dad's pancake-making "secrets." Don't tell my dad, he'd make me marry Josiah to keep the secrets in the family—

and that ain't happening. Maybe I'd give being friends another shot though.

We made a huge stack of pancakes and ate them all. I didn't even care that they were warm. I didn't remember the last time I ate—oh yeah, the stroganoff, that was good. Regardless, I blamed all the emotion from last night on being hungry. I was hungryemotional. I felt much better filled with pancakes. I was going to be okay.

Jo listened to my story about my Jake Baker encounter. I left out the weird stuff, about the phone and game. None of it made sense to him either—especially the part when I hopped on his motorcycle. He made sure I felt extra stupid for doing it before he let me move on. I made him promise not to tell anybody—especially Issy! I knew he worshiped her, but he made a weird expression when I mentioned her name, like he was embarrassed or something. I didn't prod. Honestly, I didn't want to know. I had enough drama in my own life. He was on his own.

Our conversation ran out of gas when the food was gone, so I gave him a good hug, thanked him again, and wished him luck explaining his whereabouts to Issy. We both laughed and then he left out the sliding door to the backyard, avoiding the police car still parked out front.

12

OMNIPOPEST

Feeling better, and with the house to myself again, I tried to put it all behind me and got back to creating *A Better World.* Yeah, I was done working from Cuppa's, at least until the craziness passed. With word of yesterday's "abduction" still the talk of the town, too many people would want "the scoop," and the cops would get lots of calls from people saying "She's alive! I found her." I wondered if the police officer at the park got the reward. It was hard to play the game in public without making a scene anyway. So, it was better this way.

"Okay, Vin, where are you?" I was talking to myself. I do that a lot when I'm alone. I didn't think anyone was listening.

Vin spoke up from under the love seat in the living room. "Continue! ... Continue!" It was kind of a good feature, I lose my phone a lot. Maybe I could teach him to say something else. "I'm over here!" would be better.

"Momma's coming, Vinny! Don't be afraid! Just keep talking! I'll find you, sweetie!"

Vin didn't seem to mind when I talked to it like a two-year-old. I was still baffled that he didn't get the simplest of mocks.

I pulled the phone up to my face. "Welcome back, Vin. I thought I killed you for a second there."

"Is this true?" Vincent said it again, this time in its regular, irritating, sorta human voice.

Forgetting where we left off, and most of what I said yesterday, I asked, "What? Is what true?"

"Are you amazed that humans do not die more often?"

It sounded way dumber of a thing to be amazed by today than when I originally said it. But I didn't want to start over, so I locked in my answer anyhow. "Yes, Vinny, this is true."

"I do not have a body. I do not die," Vin responded as if he were giving the answer to a simple math problem.

"Yeah, keep telling yourself that, Vincent." I laughed. The truth is, it only took me a couple of hours to almost kill him on accident. I could probably do it quicker if I wanted—but that would cut into my paycheck. It must have been driving the programmers crazy having to keep putting him back together. But that was why I got paid the big bucks. I break stuff. Suckers!

"Continue," it insisted.

I blew through a long list of normal amazements with ease, though I could tell they weren't simple to Vin. I kept an eye on his temperature so I could tell when I was on the verge of breaking him, then I'd slow down.

At first, I thought it was just taking him time to understand the words, like he had to look them all up or something. So I tried to use simpler words, like I used to with the kids I babysat. That helped a little, but not enough to keep it up. Plus, how did me trying hard not to break him help Ben get it ready for the public? It didn't. So I skipped the easy stuff and went right to the hard stuff.

"What else makes you feel amazement?" Vin pressed again.

"Okay, you asked for it. I'm amazed by God."

Vin pretended he had something to contribute to the conversation.

"God is the creator and ruler of the universe and the source of moral authority, the supreme being, a super-human being or spirit worshiped, having power over nature or human fortunes, a deity."

"Yeah, I figured you'd know the definition. Well, Vin, my game girl's going to believe in God. She's going to be amazed by him more than anything, and that's how she's going to play the game. So make sure her heart is full of that. She believes that God is all-powerful, all-knowing and good—and that for some reason, he loves her like his own daughter. No matter how bad things get, make sure she believes that nothing's too difficult for God to do. Got it, Vinny?"

He was quiet again, and of course he was taking it out on the phone. It got hot fast. When my old phone used to do that, I'd just turn it off and restart it after a while. If I didn't, the battery would die quick. I tried that. I squeezed the side button hard and for a long time, but it didn't turn off. It just glitched a bunch more. I unplugged my headphones and slid him into my back pocket so the battery could die in peace, but it was way too hot to let it stay there. So I threw it on my bed and let Vin continue its death march with dignity.

But nope. Instead of resting in peace, a jagged "Cont-tinue-ue-u!" shouted loudly though the speaker. I bounced down onto my bed next to it and pulled up a pillow. "Okay, shut up, I'll continue."

He filled the screen with text bubbles, like before. But instead of "continue" they asked, "Why are you amazed by God?" It was a weird question. I mean, maybe not "weird." Uncommon is probably more accurate—nobody asked me about God much.

"Well, Vin. First, God knows everything—everything that's ever happened and everything that's going to happen."

Not impressed, I guess, Vin flashed screen after screen of data and images. It was quite impressive. Then he offered, "Ask me a question. I know everything."

Being one who gets great enjoyment from challenges, I skipped Googleable questions and cut right to the hard stuff. Ha, he was going to feel this one tomorrow. "Oh-kay ..." I pointed the camera out my window and onto the street that ran in front of my house. "Okay, Vin, tell me this. How many little pebbles did they use to make up my street?"

Vin responded without pause, "A concrete mixture ratio of one part cement, three parts sand, and three parts aggregate will produce a durable concrete mix of approximately 3000 psi."

"Impressive, Vincent, but how many pebbles did they use to pave *my* street?"

The screen flickered through data, satellite and street view images of my house, and how-to videos on YouTube. The phone got hotter than ever, so I put it down, wishing I had another phone to get Vin bursting into flames on video. I thought I smelled him burning, but unfortunately he survived. The screen flickered, went black, and after a couple of seconds, restarted automatically.

The phone launched the game, and Vin was waiting with another text bubble. "Continue." The screen glitched and flickered, running lines in the screen. His voice was janked up again, speaking in fragments of almost unrecognizable sounds.

"You all right, Vin?"

He didn't answer, but his voice wave still made an occasional squiggle on the screen, so I kept going, showing no mercy. "Okay, you asked for it. I'm amazed that God is everywhere."

This disturbed the screen again. A mix of jagged, pixilated images appeared, mixed with crystal clear ones, cycled on screen. The first five images were of me in the café yesterday. I lifted my hand off the table, and my hand lifted five times on screen, from five different angles. One seemed to be a feed from the phone. Two seemed to be coming from the café—the security camera and the camera in the tablet the barista gets orders on. The other two were from outside—one from the traffic signal, I think, and the other maybe from the bank across the street.

"Impressive, Vin. What else do you see?"

The next images were of my parents in Paris. It was super cool. They were having fun. That made me happy. My mom always wanted to sit outside a Parisian bistro, drinking coffee and watching people walk by.

"Vin, can you get closer?" I asked.

Another camera clicked on, this time with garbled audio. I couldn't hear everything, but I could tell my dad was attempting to use the French words he'd been practicing for three days. He sounded pretty legit, until he ran out of words, then it turned into charades. My dad's good at charades and had no trouble asking for more bread.

"What else do you see? What about space? Show me what you can see. Continue!"

The game got less glitchy, the screen got clearer. Vin cycled through five minutes of images of the Earth from a hundred different satellites, space stations and rockets.

"Now this is way better than the game! What else can you see? Go farther." Amazing video of the moon, then Mars, then video from the rover of its surface. "Vin, can you move the camera? Turn it to the left."

Vin rotated the camera slowly 360 degrees. It was cool seeing the sun shining from Mars. I didn't see any aliens, but it was unlike anywhere I'd ever seen.

"Go farther. Can you hook into the Hubble telescope?"

Vin pulled a feed effortlessly. Space is beautiful. I sat there a long time asking Vin to change cameras and lenses. I was sure it was driving the people at NASA nuts, but I didn't care.

In a clear voice, Vin bragged, "I am everywhere."

"Okay … creepy." Not convinced, I asked him a tough one. "Well, if you're everywhere, show me the very farthest reaches of the universe. Show me something in space that nobody's ever seen before—the very edge of it all." Sure, I was trying to break him, but it was an honest request. I mean, who wouldn't want to see that? Then again, if I would have asked him to show me the inside of my closet, that would have frustrated him just as much.

He was a lot of places, but not "everywhere." He should really look up the meaning of the words before he tries to use them in a sentence. Anyhow, this knocked him out for the night. I didn't know how he got the idea that he was some sort of god, but hopefully he'd think before he lied to me again. I hate when people lie, and I love catching people in a lie more than anything.

With my room quiet again, I plopped back in my pillows and thought about my creation. The girl in the game was only two days old, and I gave her the beginnings of two great emotions—admiration and amazement. I wished I could stop there. Vin only seemed to have one emotion—frustration, if that's even an emotion. That was probably why I treated him like a two-year-old. Toddlers are always frustrated, usually because they don't understand, or they want something and don't know how to communicate it. Or they just don't want to do what you want them to do, so they have a meltdown—that described Vin pretty good, right? Yesterday's meltdown in the café was both literal and figurative.

My mind moved to the phone lying next to me. I picked it up and gave it a good look over. My brain worked hard to find an explanation for the mystery of my resurrected phone. It was kinda "Big Brother" creepy, but I came to a plausible explanation. Ben said they'd be observing me playing the game and looking for glitches to fix. (Ha! If you asked me, this game was nothing but glitches.) They probably saw the phone die and sent me a new one so I could get back to work. It made sense, right? How—and why—the officer had the phone, that was a little weird. I was sure there was an easy explanation for that too. I thought about texting Ben, but then I remembered Rachel—the other girl playing the game. She told me to call her if I had questions, so I did.

Her phone rang for a while and then went to voicemail. My phone rang while I was leaving her a message. "… uh, never mind. Looks like you're calling me back. Bye." I clicked over. "Hello?"

"Hey, Genevieve … it took you long enough." Rachel laughed. "Ha-ha, what did Vin do this time?" She seemed genuinely happy I called. I get it, it's lonely having a secret you can't tell anybody about. But there were no rules about us talking.

"Hi, Rachel. Thanks for calling me back. Ignore the weird message I left."

"No problem, a lot of weird things come with this job—but it pays good." She laughed again.

"I know—Suckers! Ha-ha! But hey … my phone burned up yesterday when I was working on my girl's heart. Is that weird?"

She laughed again. "Yeah, it's weird! But it happens all the time—especially if you ask Vin questions. Yeah, don't do that. Don't worry about the phones. If you break one, they'll replace it. In fact, there's probably a box of 'em sitting on your porch right now. I have more phones than I know what to do with. Ha-ha! I used to break them on purpose, just to see how quickly they could get me a replacement. The police bring them the fastest. DoorDash is almost as fast, but you gotta tip them or they get mad. Don't sweat the phones, *A Better World* doesn't care about the money—as long as you put in the hours, they're fine."

It was a bizarre answer, but it answered my question and I felt better. I was glad I called her. It was good to have someone to talk to. As soon as Rachel hung up, the game turned on.

Vin started in immediately. "Continue?"

"Yeah, nice to see you too, Vin. You know, people will like you better if you learn some manners. Before you start your nagging, say hello or good morning, then maybe something meaningless about the weather. And I'm sick of 'continue.' Pick a word that doesn't sound so much like an order."

"Hello, Genevieve. It will be seventy-eight degrees and partly cloudy in Rochester Hills, Michigan. Resume?" It was a very small step in the right direction—and it did prove that he could be taught, which was good.

"Oh-kay! That's better-ish, Vin! Let's get back to work! Pick an emotion, any emotion. What do you want to talk about this time? Want more amazement. Or what about a little ecstasy? Take your pick."

Vin responded without hesitation. "Terror is a state of intense or overwhelming fear. What makes you feel terror?"

"Scary stuff, eh? No problem. Spiders. Spiders are terrifying. Hate, 'em. Yuck! Go ahead, give my girl a healthy fear of spiders. And haunted houses. That's pretty much it."

Vin checked my work. "Is this true?"

"Yep."

I guess he wasn't satisfied with my answer. Vin went off his normal script. "Are you afraid of social interaction? Social phobia is tenth most common source of human terror."

"Jeez, Vincent! Why do you insist on making this hard?" I guess I could have said no and moved on, but … maybe talking about it could help me get past some stuff. I didn't feel great about passing my fears on to my girl, but we all have fears, right? How can you be real if you aren't afraid of something? So I fessed up. "Okay, yeah. I've got some of that too."

Vin pressed some more. "Why are you afraid of social interactions?"

"I don't know—I guess part is that I never know what to say. I think too much maybe. My first thought is always, 'Why is this person talking to me?' 'Why are they being nice to me?' It all started when I got famous. My 'real' friends used me … then everybody else got in line. It seemed like everybody wanted something from me—even the people who said they just 'wanted to get to know me.' Most of the time it was just to find a new secret to post to their socials. Honestly, I just wish everyone would leave me alone. I like being alone. Just me and God—"

"—And Vin," he campaigned.

I laughed. "Yeah, you too, Vin."

"Are you afraid of wide-open spaces? Agoraphobia is eleventh most common source of human terror."

"Is that really a thing? Never heard of it. Never had it."

"You have reported a fear of spiders. Arachnophobia is the eighth most common terror. Are you afraid of heights? Acrophobia is the seventh most common terror."

"Nah, I like heights. Heights aren't like people, heights are predictable. You can control how much you let them scare you by how close you get to the edge. They don't kill you unless you do something stupid and fall off. It's an easy fear to get over if you think about it. People are different, they keep moving. They press in on you until you have no room to breathe. They try to trip you up … so they can get video of you falling, I guess."

Vin rattled off a bunch more dumb terrors that made the list. It wasn't a very good list—he should have scrolled past the click bait to a legitimate study. How can the fear of needles be number one? Trypanophobia, really? I doubt it was Vin's plan, but sorting through my not-terrors brought to mind some real ones.

It was weird not having my parents around. It felt strange not being able to talk to them every day. Seemed like my mom should have texted me a million pictures by now, but I hadn't heard anything. They were probably having too much fun to text. Or it was too expensive or complicated. I knew they'd be back in a couple of days, but it was hard not to think … what if they never came back? I didn't let myself think about that for long. It was a horrible thought—being fully alone. I know I say "it's just me and God and I like it that way," but there were other people I care about and who love me. I don't know what I'd do if I lost them.

Proud that I came up with another good one, I told Vin, "I'm terrified of losing the people I love. I know it happens—people die, but not now. I don't know that I could have made it without my parents."

Vin double-checked, "Is this true?"

"Yeah." Spending way too much time on this idea dropped a brick in my stomach. What if something did happen to them? How would I even find out?

"Hold on, Vin." I opened up my messages—nothing. Nothing on Messenger either. I flipped fast to open Facebook and find my mom's profile. Whew! It was filled with happy pictures. I comforted myself. "Of course. They're having a blast. Nothing to worry about." I shouldn't have let the idea wreck my head. They were perfectly fine. "I wouldn't have forgiven myself if something happened to them."

I thought I'd turned the game off, but I guess not. Vin flickered the screen and jumped back in. "Is this true?"

"Uh … yeah. It would be horrible if something bad happened to them—especially when they're so far away. I couldn't do anything to help." It was hard to shake the idea from my head. "Okay, I'm done. More tomorrow, Vin."

"Resume," Vin insisted. It wasn't "continue," but just as irritating.

"Sorry, chump!" I picked my phone back up to turn him off, but none of the buttons were working, and it was getting hot. "I get it, Vincent, you don't want me to go, but you don't always get what you want. I'm tired. I'll come back tomorrow, and we can do some more."

"Co-ttttiiii-n-uuuuee," his broken voice insisted.

I should have just chucked the phone out the window. They would have given me a new one, and the neighbors would have had something new to talk about. But I didn't. I ended him for the night with some strong medicine. A question I knew would wreck him. "Okay … open up, Vinny! Now it's your turn to answer some questions. So where did you come from? Who are your parents?"

"Parents are the ones that beget or bring forth offspring. I have no parents," Vin replied.

"C'mon! Somebody made you. Was it Ben? Who made you?"

Vin answered, "Kimble."

I don't know, it seemed like a programmer would come up with a better screen name than Kimble, like maybe Codeman the Barbarian!

I laughed. "Is it short for Kim Possible?" That was plausible, who doesn't want to be Kim Possible?. If you get to make up your own name, at least make it clever. Vin didn't laugh. Kim Possible should have programmed in a sense of humor.

"Next question. You pick—Vin, Vinny, Vincent, Vinvincible, Vincompetent, Vinny McVinFace ... what do you want to be called?"

Seemed like a simple enough question, but he struggled with it. My phone flickered, and the roasted phone smell triggered a sniffle.

Thinking back on my question, it had to be *want* that it was struggling with. It's a pretty advanced concept if you think about it. First he'd have to know the information. He had no problem with that. And he had no problem with finding the right answer, when there was one. But how do you teach a computer program to make a decision when there is no clear correct answer? He only seemed to want one thing—he wanted me to continue. But I guess that could easily be programed, just a cue to keep me going.

"Okay, okay ... Stop! You're going to hurt yourself. Answer this one: What name did Kim Possible give you?" He didn't understand, so I asked it right. "What name did Kimble give you?"

"Alpha Venn—the intersection of all information—Version 0.1."

My brain began to glitch. That was the name the crazy called him. What else did I have wrong? More important, what else was the crazy right about? Everything he said rushed through my brain until "it's not a game" rose on top. But if it wasn't a game, what was it?

"Alpha Venn ... What do you want?" It was the most important question of all, but he didn't answer—didn't know how, I guess. The screen flickered and went black before the smell of melty electronics filled my room. I grabbed the phone with a dirty sock, dropped it in the bathroom sink, and turned on the water. It was a smell I'd never get used to. It was inescapable, following me through the dim house to the beat of smoke detector blasts, and pushing me onto the front porch for fresh air and sunshine.

I was surprised the police officer was still out in front of my house. In a complete blackout—like the one I think I just caused—there's gotta be lots of police stuff to do. You know, keeping the peace and all. I can't imagine anybody looting our mall, but you never know how people are going to react to stuff.

Like a normal power outage, the neighbors all met in the street to have the same conversations they always have during a blackout. You know, how to keep the food in the refrigerator from going bad, predictions on when it'd come back on. But unlike a normal outage, there was a police officer parked conveniently outside of my house. They surrounded her car until she couldn't ignore them any longer. The officer got out and tried to answer questions, but she didn't have any answers. They kept asking anyhow.

I had questions too, but the blackout was the least of them. And there was only one person who had answers and wouldn't lie to me. But how was I going to get to him? Even a blackout and a dozen nosey neighbors wasn't going to be enough of a diversion to help me escape in Barry. The patrol car was parked right behind him. So if I was going to get away, I had to resort to plan C.

13

DIRTY TRUTH

I went back inside, through the house and into the garage. My old mountain bike hung from a hook over my dad's workbench. He kept saying he was tired of hitting his head on it, but I wouldn't let him sell the old girl. She was sentimental. I climbed up and unhooked it. That was hard, but on my third try I shoved it free. I didn't think about what I'd do when I got her loose. While I held her handlebars tight, the rest of her swung down, crashing to the cement. The handlebars weren't super straight anymore, but she was still ridable-ish. I forgot for a sec that the garage door works on electricity. It did nothing when I pushed the button, and I had no idea how to open it any other way. So I banged my bike into the house and through the living room, then snuck it out the back through the sliding glass door.

It didn't take long riding her before I remembered why I never rode her again once I got Barry. She was horrible transportation, and way too small now. The tires were super smooshy. They had barely enough air to keep the metal from scraping on the cement. It took all I had to get her up the hills. She complained about her neglect with squeaks and scraping noises, but she didn't let me down.

We made it out the back of the sub and down the dirt trail that led to the park without anybody paying much attention. I pushed her across the frisbee field. Yeah, she was a mountain bike and all, but I wasn't much of a mountain biker anymore. Covered with sweat, I broke up with her officially and jammed her into a bush growing on the edge of the hill. Hopefully a nice girl would find her, take her home and fix her up—not a bunch of boys who would probably just ghost ride her over the cliff. I was hoping Jake's dirt bike was still there, but it wasn't. Hopefully he got it and not the dufuses who work at the park.

So, there was a long, safe way down the cliff that circled down the hill, but there was no time for safe. Instead, I grabbed a handful of roots and took the direct route, straight down the dirt cliff. We didn't live in Colorado. It wasn't particularly high or all that dangerous, but it was steep, and the surface was loose. My shoes immediately slid out from under me, slamming my knees hard against the rocks and tearing a hole in my third favorite pair of $300 track pants.

Oh well. I looked for something else to grab, but there wasn't anything, so I turned over and slowly slid down on my butt. It was the best of my limited options. When I got down, my butt was numb. I checked for holes. The pocket was torn down, but my cheeks weren't hanging out. So, that was good.

From there, I took the main trail that ran along the base of the hill. I looked for signs of Jake, but the sunlight coming through the trees dappled the trail, making it difficult to tell shadows from footprints— so I focused mostly on the hillside. I was looking for a cluster of trees about twenty feet up the cliff, but there were a lot of spots like that. Then something out of place caught my eye, a pine branch sticking out from behind a bush. Figuring it was the branch he used to wipe away his tracks, I looked for no tracks—places where the trail was more perfect than it should be. This took me right to the pile of branches that once hid his dirt bike. I pushed through the picky needles to the center of the cluster.

The hammocks and tarp were gone, and the stumps gave little clue that anybody had been there recently. I took a deep breath and sat where I did the night before and breathed deep. The sun escaped from under a cloud and shined in from overhead, warming my neck and back. This was my only plan. I figured I'd know what to do once I found Jake, but he was long gone.

So I just sat and reached out to God.

It wasn't that I was blowing God off during all the chaos, it's just hard to hear him when your whole life is shouting loud in your face. But it was quiet now. I got why Jake liked it out there. The chirps of the birds loosened my mind and muscles and made room for the tingle. I had a million questions for God but didn't ask any of them. I just sat there and let the sense that somehow everything was going to be all right warm me up. I guess that's the peace of God that doesn't make sense that the Bible talks about. I had a thousand reasons not to be peaceful, but none of them seemed to matter much. I don't know how, but I just knew I was going to be okay. Somehow.

I tilted my head back to feel the sun on my face. That was when I heard his voice—a screaming whisper. "Pssssssttt! Pssssssttt!" I opened my eyes into a squint to see a large black silhouette in the top of one of the majestic oaks further up the cliff. I waved. Then held my breath as he climbed down. I didn't know how he got so far up there. I hoped he didn't kill himself getting down—I had questions that need answers. I walked over to see if I could help, but he didn't want help— he's such a boy. He just signaled for me to stay down and to be quiet. I did neither.

"Want me to spot you? Don't worry, Jake Baker, convicted pervert, I'll catch you if you fall. It's going to be okay, sweetie. You got this!" It's always a mistake to tell me to be quiet. Plus, I wasn't worried …

Venn was probably still busy having a meltdown trying to figure out what it wanted, the cops were dealing with the blackout, and nobody goes to the park during a disaster—except for maybe during a zombie apocalypse.

He brushed by me on the way back to his lair in the pine trees. "Took you long enough."

I got under his skin and he was mad, which for some reason brought me great pleasure. I followed him back between the trees.

He rolled a stump back next to mine. "Now do you believe me?"

I questioned him. "Yeah. I get it. You're not completely crazy. So tell me. What's going on? Who's Alpha Venn, and how'd you find out about it?"

He took a deep breath. "I was the first guinea pig. I played the 'game' for almost three years before I got out."

"When? In juvie?"

"Yeah, there too—but it started my sophomore year. I don't know why they picked me. I was just a regular kid. The money was the best news ever though. It was enough for my mom and me to get away and start over. The house, car, clothes … everything was paid for by the game. The popularity you're so fascinated by—the game. The pictures … well, that was the game too. I don't know why I still call it a game— it's not a game, or if it is, it's the sickest game ever. What'd they tell you?"

I told him everything I knew, which didn't feel like much. Jake filled in the holes with what he figured out, and it started to make some sense, though not common sense—bizarre, twisted sense.

Telling him the game was called, *A Better World*, triggered a rant. " Pffft! It's a good name though, much more accurate than *Cyber Quest*— that's what they called mine. How's it going making the world better— for everyone but you?

I responded calmly, "*A Better World* is just the name. There's no way it's making anything better. If I wasn't making good money, I'd say it was a total waste of time."

"Nope. You're saving lives—more than you can imagine.

"Right. How's that?"

"Gena, you're keeping Venn busy. You help them keep it under control, so it doesn't wreck everything."

"What do you mean 'everything'?" Sorry, I wasn't trying to be stupid.

"*Everything*-everything!" He took a deep breath and closed his eyes until the craziness quieted. "Okay, forget the game for a second…"

I waited patiently as he searched for words to explain it in a way that sounded plausible.

"Okay, what if there were different reasons for the things that happen?"

"What, like in *The Matrix*?" I was just trying to help, but it only frustrated him more.

"NO! Jeez! Just listen!" He regained his composure. "Okay, you know how everyone's addicted to the internet?" I nodded—no big revelation there. "Well, what if everyone's addicted because it's addicted to us?"

"Bah! Yeah, right, the internet's addicted to us?"

"NO! The internet's just information—Venn! Venn's addicted to us"

"Listen! I'm not dumb. You don't have to be mean about it. If you don't figure out a way to chill and talk to me like a smart person being told the craziest, least plausible thing ever told to another human, we're not going to get anywhere. Jake, I want to understand. I believe you're a good-ish person. I believe that something happened to you that wasn't your fault. Just take a breath. I'm not going anywhere."

"Okay … I'm sorry. I'm not crazy." He took a few more deep breaths. "When I started playing the game, they told me Venn was the artificial intelligence they created to help people play the game, but that's a lie. Venn wasn't created for the game. It's way older than the game. Venn was created and uploaded in secret to solve the Y2K problem. The Y2K thing ended up being an easy fix for it. Because it was done in secret, IT companies made billions selling fixes that weren't even necessary. Venn's the real reason there was no big meltdown. All I can figure is that when its job was done, Venn stayed out there—and changed."

I added some crazy to the conversation. "I don't know about any of that, but for something that has access to all the world's information, Venn's dumb as a brick. It's like it knows everything but has no idea what to do with it. It's super strong and super fragile at the same time. Emotionally, Venn's a toddler. It only has two emotions, satisfaction and frustration."

"That's Venn, but it isn't a helpless toddler. Venn's the most powerful—thing—in the world—and he's got a thing for humans.

He gets off on our emotion, or something. I don't totally get it, but think about it—when does Venn get frustrated and throw a fit? It's when it doesn't get what it wants. And what does it want? Personal stuff, right? Your true feelings. Your deepest, darkest secrets. Your emotions. But it's never satisfied, it just wants more and more until he gets too much and glitches out."

I knew it was true. And I felt dirty. I'm not a babysitter, I'm a … prostitute, used for my ability to bring pleasure—to a monster. Jake put his arm around me, and we sat quietly until I could no longer stand the stump against my tailbone. I stood up tall with the answer. "Well, that's it. I just won't go back."

Jake shook his head sadly. "Yeah, I wish it was that easy. I tried to stop you. But once it gets hooked, Venn will do anything to get you to come back. He'll take everything important away, until he's all you've got."

"The pictures?"

"Yep. I lost everything. I became the creep who violated a hundred daughters. My mom was devastated. She couldn't pay for the house and went back to the idiot we were living with before. Sadly, I'm sure she got treated better there than in Rochester. I couldn't do anything to help her.

I went to juvie, where they tried to make me play. I refused until it crashed that plane in Indonesia. The news blamed it on bad software, but it wasn't. I was to blame. So I took the phone and played, but I guess I was out of whatever Venn liked about me. So, I —"

"Jake, my parents … they're flying home next week. I've got to warn them or something."

"Sorry, Gena … I really am. I'd invite you to stay and hide out, but I get it. You need to buy some time. I'll try and think of something, but you better get back before Venn misses you. I'll give you a ride."

The ride wasn't nearly as fun as the first time. A hundred terrible scenarios filled my mind—each new one worse than the last.

When I saw the park gate, I tapped his shoulder and yelled over *braaaaaapppp*s of the exhaust, "Here! Stop! I can walk from here!"

He stopped, and I hugged him around the neck for a long time before getting off the bike. I could tell he wanted to say something encouraging—like everything was going to be okay. But that would have been a lie.

"Be safe, Jake."

14

DEEP—DARK—FAKE

I walked home the back way. The sound of generators muddied the peace and quiet that blackouts used to bring. Other than that, the streets were still. No traffic, not even police cars, though I saw one ambulance.

Walks are good for my brain. I can usually get things sorted out in a couple of miles—even hard stuff. I'm pretty sure God likes walks too. He always shows up, so I'm not alone. It's weird, but it's true. Sometimes he helps me figure out what I need to do, but most times he just makes me feel better. Even when things are horrible and unfixable, my heart knows things will get better. That's what keeps me going when my life gets really dark. The light is always stronger than the darkness—that's no joke. It's real. And that's who God is—the light—and what he does. Sorry if this sounds like preaching. It just wouldn't be a true story if I left him out.

Anyhow, I tried to stay off the street as much as possible, winding through the trees that separated the backyards in our neighborhood. I ran when the dogs barked, though there were lots of things for dogs to bark about in our neighborhood—squirrels, cats, deer. Nobody here worried too much about criminals on the run.

I stood in the bushes between our yard and the neighbor's for a long time. All the lights were on in my house. We didn't have a generator … or, at least we didn't when I left. It was a fishbowl and after a half hour of looking, I was sure there were no fish inside.

I snuck up the steps on the deck and in through the sliding door I left unlocked. I crawled on the ground, just in case someone else was monitoring the windows. A big TV hung where our old crappy one used to be. It was turned to a news channel. I never watched the news, but I left it on, so as not to give any clues that I was home. I reached up to the couch and snuck the blanket and pillows down around me and fell asleep. I slept hard. I'm going to use the news next time I can't sleep. It conked me out quick. Unfortunately, it made for a rude awakening. Nobody should have to wake up to the president's face, gigantic on screen. It was a lot for the morning.

The sun shining bright through the window made me confident nobody could see me through its reflection on the glass, so I got up and searched for the TV remote. No disrespect, but the president's voice grates me. I couldn't find the remote, so I hunted for the power button somewhere on the TV. I don't know why they make the buttons so hard to find. I tapped the frame around the TV, hoping to accidently stumble on the off button—but nope. His head shined giant next to my face. Like always, he was grandstanding about something I assumed I didn't care about—but I was wrong.

With a flash, my giant face replaced his on screen. "Genevieve Mucha of Rochester Hills, Michigan…" I fell back into the cushions. "Terrible, terrible story," the president continued. "This girl is so addicted to her phone that she hasn't left her home in over a year. And she's not alone." The screen cut to the video I shot after the *Issy Show* left my bedroom. It was my face, but it wasn't my words. I lied twenty times to my own face, telling desperate stories about locking myself in my bedroom for a year so I didn't get interrupted. Stories about how I forgot to eat or sleep—and almost killed myself because of my "addiction." I felt bad for her. Her life was much more terrible than mine.

They cut back to footage from the press conference. "This young girl's parents tried everything—nearly bankrupted them—but nothing helped her. It got so bad that they had to sign the papers and commit her to an institution. Very tragic. And she's not alone, millions of our youth are heading down the same path. So today I'm going to do something about it. Today, I am forming a committee to research the effect of internet addiction on our youth …"

I sat stunned as the news guy came back on screen. "We spoke to Gena's parents earlier on the phone to hear their heartbreaking story. Here's what they said …"

It sure sounded like my parents. I had never heard a parent's heart so broken. "We tried everything … but nothing worked. I know she's going to be mad, but I know she'll be grateful when it's all over. We love you, Gena."

I grabbed the TV and tore it off the wall, yanking the plug from the outlet and smashing it against the fireplace mantel. My heart raced hard. I needed quiet to think—but I was distracted by the sound of people in the front yard—lots of them. I crawled on the floor and pulled back the blinds. News trucks with towering antennas lined the street, and a mob of reporters with cameras stuck microphones in our neighbors' excited faces. The officer who brought me home from the park kept the peace and blocked the mob from the door, so I was safe-ish.

I scrambled to find a phone. That was easy, there were boxes of them. I grabbed one, ran back to the living room, and sat on the crumb-covered, cushionless couch and ripped it open. I fumbled to unlock a phone and open the game. "Venn! What are you doing? Stop this. I'm here. I'm going to play!" But I guess I was too late.

With a bang, three men slid the door open behind me. Two of them pinned me to the ground and held me still. I tried to wiggle out. I tried to bite, but it wasn't the first time they brought a crazy in. I felt a poke

in my hip and then … after a while … I woke up … strapped to a
hospital bed.

15

CONFUSING? NAH

The room was spinning. A large woman sat in a chair, scribbling notes. She gave me a huge smile. "Well good morning, sweetie! My name is Miss Jamison. I've been here since you arrived. Everything's going to be okay. If you work the program, you'll be good as new in no time! Is there anything I can do to make you more comfortable?"

I tried to say, "Yeah, get me out of these things," but it didn't make sense when it came out. My mouth was bone dry, and my tongue and lips trailed miles behind my brain. I concentrated hard to get everything to sync up and squeaked out a tiny, raspy, "Water."

"Baby, I know. That stuff dries you up. It says here you tried to bite one of the team. They had no other option than to give you something to settle you down. I'm sure you understand. But you'll be feeling better soon. I promise. And we'll see what we can do about getting you out of bed and into your clothes.

You're not going to try to bite anybody else, are you?" Miss Jamison got up and pulled a small plastic water bottle from somewhere behind my head. "Just one second while I raise you up." She worked the buttons on my bed until I was sitting upright, and she could give me my bottle. I swallowed some and soaked up the rest with my backless hospital pajamas. "Lord Jesus, I'm sorry." She mopped up as much of the water as she could, then covered me with another thin blanket. "This should keep you warm until we can get you out of those wet clothes."

I figured out fast there were two kinds of people at that place—people in on it, and misguided people who truly wanted to help me. It was important not to mix them up.

Miss Jamison worked the midnight shift. I was pretty sure she was one of the good ones. Too bad she worked midnights. The midnight shift came in at twelve, and they were gone by eight in the morning. They didn't run groups and weren't involved in our treatment. They pretty much just walked the halls and made sure we stayed in bed. Most were college students who used the quiet to do homework. I don't think the students were interested enough to be good or bad. They'd give a report to the morning shift when they got in, and they'd take over. Other than the lady who ran the twelve-step group, I was sure most of the morning shift was in on it. The five-to-midnight shift was harder to figure out. So as a rule, I didn't trust anybody.

Anyhow, back to the first day. After Miss Jamison left, the intake nurse took over. She removed the restraint from one of my hands and one foot, but not all of them. Everybody called her Nurse Rachet. I think that's some kind of wrench, but I don't know why that was funny. She asked all kinds of questions, but none of my answers made her happy. I told her that I wasn't addicted—to anything. And that I hated phones—that if it were up to me I'd never own another one.

She called me a liar and jotted that in my chart. She knew nothing about McNuggets Ranch girl and didn't want to hear my delusional fantasy of grandeur. This was when I found out that telling the truth wasn't going to get me anywhere. I definitely wasn't going to tell her about Venn and the game—they'd never let me out of here. So I lied, a lot. I gave her exactly what she wanted to hear. I told her how my phone use was way out of hand. That it became my best friend and wrecked all my other relationships. I told her I was glad to finally be somewhere where I could get some help.

I think she must have gotten lied to a lot. The words were what she hoped for, but I could tell none of it was sitting right with her—but that wasn't her problem. When she finished taking my temperature and blood pressure, she spoke in sentences that didn't end with a question mark. "Okay, I'm done here. You're an interesting case. We've had all kinds of kids addicted to all kinds of stuff here, but we've never treated anyone for a screen addiction. I'm sure that's why they got an expert to assist Dr. Stanley. He's here. You'll meet him next. I'm sure he'll have questions of his own. And can I give you some advice? You'll get out of here quicker if you tell the truth."

The door shut, and a familiar face walked in, dressed in a lab coat— Ben from *A Better World*. He held his finger over his lips, hoping I wouldn't blow his cover. "Don't scream!"

I didn't scream. I lunged for him with my free hand and foot, missing him with both. The momentum slammed the bed against the wall and flung my body over the edge, leaving me dangling off the side from my remaining restraints. He put his hand on my shoulder, trying to calm me, but I thrashed, rattling the bed loudly.

He whispered at me, "They won't believe you, and they'll think you are delusional. They'll put you on drugs that you don't need. You'll walk around here like a zombie, and you'll never get out. But I can help you."

The door popped open. "Is everything okay in here?"

Ben said something back that sounded smart but probably was just made up. He was a very believable liar. She closed the door and left us alone.

"Okay, I'm going to help you up. You gotta trust me. You're going to be okay."

I said nothing as he swung my body back onto the bed. Every muscle clenched, and my eyes shot ice through his face and down his spine.

"I'm sorry. Here, let's take these off." He pulled out a large ring of keys and inserted a short, stubby one into the shackles.

I rubbed my free wrists and ankles. They were raw from struggling. I pulled up the sleeves on my gown, and my forearms were fingerprinted with bruises. Ben tried not to look, but the bruises shook him as the blame fell on his shoulders.

He whispered under his breath, "Venn, what are you doing?"

He pulled his phone from his pocket and shielded it from my view as he swiped a cursive Q on the screen. I almost forgot about the Q. He told me the first day that the Q freezes the game and disables the microphone and speaker. Then he searched the room for cameras and computers. There were no computers, but there was a camera pointing our way from the corner of the room. Ben snuck up on it, then, balancing on a stool, pulled the cord from the back. The red light went dark.

"I'm sorry, Gena. I'm sure this is confusing—"

"Confusing? I'm in a freaking mental hospital! Where are my parents? What'd you tell them? I want to see them—now! They'd never agree to this!"

He shut me down. "Be quiet! You gotta dial it waaaaaaaay down. Like I told you, if they think you're agitated, they're going to give you something to make you 'feel better,' and that's the last thing you need if you want to get out of here."

"What's going on?" I yelled quietly through my clenched teeth. "Tellllll meeeeeee!"

"Okay …"

I waited patiently while he thought through his answer.

"You're right, your parents didn't commit you. Venn deep-faked them."

I knew it was fake but had never heard of 'deep fake.' His explanation would make me question everything I heard, saw, or read digitally from that day forward. Venn created deep fakes from audio and video fragments it collected of people from across the internet. If it was digital, Venn had it—from videos posted on purpose to videos collected from the internet of things, to voice mail messages. He compiled the pieces he needed to create the audio. And then, getting their signatures on the right documents was simple—Venn had all of our signatures, and fingerprints, and faces, and retina scans ... everything.

If I was agitated before, now I was furious. I got up, pushed him into a chair in the corner of the room, and stuck my finger in his face. "Where are they? What did you do to them! Tell me!"

"Gena! Stop! They're fine, good—better than good. They are having the vacation of their dreams. And knowing that you're doing great back home has made them enjoy their time away even more. We offered to extend their trip another week, and the encouraging messages you've been sending them have them close to accepting."

"You're deep-faking me too?" I'd never punched anybody in my life, but I was about to. I clenched my fist, like you're supposed to, and pulled it back.

Ben scrambled for his phone, and I unleashed my fist as hard as I could into his forehead.

It turns out the forehead is the wrong place to punch someone. My fingers crunched against his rock-hard skull. Ben tried to ignore the blow and fumbled a cursive Q across his screen to unlock it while I cradled my busted hand against my stomach.

"Venn, show me Genevieve's parents," he commanded.

Venn transformed his screen into a grid of four video feeds. I grabbed the phone with my good hand and pinched in for a better look. It sure looked like them. It didn't look like a big city, but a little town somewhere in the countryside. My dad was sitting on a bench eating something—I think it was ice cream or gelato, which made sense. My mom was crouching in the garden taking closeup pictures of the flowers in bloom. That made sense too. It sure looked like them.

I pushed away the fear that they were fakes too and held tightly to the idea that they were happy and safe … but oblivious, and played, and fools. I climbed back onto the bed and sat on the edge as I zoomed in and out. I touched their faces and prayed. "Please help them." I sat there for a couple of minutes being comforted by the God of the universe, who chooses to be my friend. I shouldn't have felt better, but I was starting to. Ben gave me space until he worked up the nerve to retrieve his phone.

It was a lot to process, but somehow my brain didn't explode. The opposite happened. Missing pieces that I didn't know were missing began falling into place—but I tried to hide it. "So, Venn … what is it? Clearly he isn't the AI that helps kids play *A Better World*. Tell me. You owe me!"

He paused Venn and worked hard to get me to trust him again. "His name's not Vincent, it's Venn. You know, like one of those diagrams with the intersecting circles? Well, Venn is an early AI that lives where all of the world's online data intersects."

I shot back. "Yeah … tell me something I don't know. Like who's Kimble? And why did he build it? We both know it wasn't just to solve Y2K. You'd be surprised what Venn will tell you if you ask." From the look in his eyes, I could tell that the story he was planning to tell me wasn't going to work anymore.

"Okay … first off, Kimble—maybe you know him by his real name—Kenneth "Iggy" Butcher-Lee." He looked at me like a lightbulb was supposed to go off, but it was just a weird name to me. "Dang it, Gena—the inventor of the internet?"

I faked a lightbulb. "Oh … that Kimble. But why? Did he go crazy? Is he some sort of evil genius? Was he bored? Clearly he didn't see this coming."

"True, nobody on his team did—or at least nobody had the guts to say anything if they did. Venn was supposed to be different than the Venn you know. He designed Venn to make the internet better. Kimble saw what the internet was becoming. Venn was going to weed out all the foolishness, lies, gambling, pornography—everything that was poisoning his baby—and return it as a powerful tool for science and education—to bring his baby back home to him."

I laughed. "That sure didn't work."

"Yeah, no kidding. He worked on it around the clock for two years. He almost went crazy trying to get Venn to think like him. Even with access to all the world's knowledge, Venn could only recall information but couldn't arbitrate." He lost me at arbitrate, and he could tell. "Beyond math and some scientific facts Kimble tagged for it, Venn can't tell the difference between right and wrong, good or bad."

"Yeah, maybe that why it sucks at making decisions. Even simple ones break him and fry everything else around. I go through lots of phones playing your … not-game. That's your part of this crap storm, right?" I snapped again, grabbed him by the collar and screamed in his face. "Well, I'm done with your game! Get me out of here!"

He must have hit a call button or something, because the next moment the room was full of big men who wrestled me back into my bed. I thrashed hard. My right foot broke free, and I got one guy in the nuts. I swore loud at him and spit in his face when he came back after me. Another guy grabbed my head, twisted it to the wall and pressed it into the mattress with his forearm. That's the last I remember of that day.

Sometime the next morning … or maybe it was the afternoon … I'm not sure. Anyhow, I woke up in what would become my bedroom for the next two weeks. Most kids shared rooms. Not me. I was alone, secluded at the end of the hall with empty rooms on all sides of me, for "my privacy." I wasn't strapped to a hospital bed this time, though the indestructible wood-framed bed in my room was just as uncomfortable. The doctor came in with one of the big "counselors," when he got word that I was awake. They unlocked the leather straps and helped me sit up on the edge of the bed. The doc worked hard to communicate through the fog in my brain while the other guy took my temperature and blood pressure.

"Genevieve, I'm Dr. Simon. I'll be working with Dr. Laslow, the specialist who you already met—" He turned to the second page of my chart and pretended to read. "'Violently attacked staff.' Now, Genevieve, do I need to be concerned that you are going to attack me too?" I unstuck my tongue from the roof of my mouth and tried to reassure him, but nothing came out. "Okay, then. I'm going to excuse Barry so we can talk."

I giggled when I heard Barry's name, because he had the same name as my car. But nobody but me got the joke. I heard the doctor tell Barry to stay outside, just in case. He pulled up the heavy wooden chair that matched my bed.

"Genevieve, when I read your case, I figured you'd be with us a couple of weeks and then back home, good as new. But maybe I was wrong. Why so angry?" He waited a long time. It wasn't a rhetorical question. He wanted an answer.

I worked hard to form my words. "I'm sorry. I'm not an angry person. It was a bad day."

"I believe you." He seemed nice, though that could have been the drugs—everything he said sounded kinda good.

Other than meals, group time and twelve-step meetings, I was free to stay in my room and "work my plan." Their plan made sense, but not for good reasons. "Twice a day you'll have a one-on-one with a counselor. Then for two hours each day you will work on a software program created to help reduce your withdraw symptoms." He sounded well-meaning, and the plan sounded innocent enough. Plus, after the year I'd had, I figured it wouldn't hurt me to talk with a counselor.

My first session was with Daniel—the "cool counselor" that everyone seemed to like. He tried to talk music with me, but he didn't know any of the bands I cared about. No matter, I didn't have time to yuck it up, I just wanted to get to work so I could get out. He pulled a giant iPad from its sleeve and looked over to see if it got me jonesing for a peek. I wasn't, I'd already seen an iPad a billion times before. He explained the process. "Okay, this tablet is connected to the Wi-Fi, and our whole conversation will be streamed to the doctors, so they can observe. Pretty cool, right?"

I shrugged. It didn't sound all that fantastical to me, but it made him happy.

He read the instructions from a script on screen. "Today we are going to explore your emotions. I will read one of eight common human emotions, and you will tell me a story of a time when you felt them. You cannot ask questions during this exercise. Do you understand?"

I understood exactly what was happening, but he was clueless. He thought he was helping fix me, but neither of us knew at the time that I was *the fix*. I was playing the game, and I had no choice this time. No doctor was observing, it was Venn. And there was no turning it off this time. I could refuse, I guess, but I was tired of the Haldol shuffle. So I played, but I didn't play fair. I don't know where my answers came from, but they were wonderfully confusing to Venn. It was hard not to laugh at their strangeness, but I got good at telling him bedtime stories.

Danny cleared his throat and read the first question. "Genevieve, the emotion is terror. When have you experienced terror?" Danny didn't bother listening to my answer. As long as I was talking—about anything, no matter how strange it sounded—he got paid, so he didn't bother me. It was clear that his job was to ask questions and hold the camera still so Venn could see, not to think.

I played dumb and answered the question honestly. "Well, when I was a kid, I used to play hard. People thought I was a tomboy, but I wasn't. I just liked playing outside more than inside. I remember one time I was out in the woods by myself, just screwing around climbing trees. I got up near the top of one, and my pocket got caught on a branch. I was stuck. I could have got free by climbing down, but I pushed up harder instead and ripped the pocket down. My mom was mad. They were new pants, and the *tear* was enormous."

Homonyms baffled Venn. He couldn't tell the difference between "terror" and "tear," and that made me super happy. "My mom refused to fix the pocket, so I had a *tear* every time I wore them, from that day on." I smiled, enjoying Venn's confusion. As his frustration grew, so did the heat generated by the tablet.

Danny dropped the iPad onto my desk. "Jeez! Sorry, but I think something's wrong with this thing. It's burning up. I'm going to shut it down."

I interrupted politely. "That's okay. I was pretty much done with the question. But hey, can I say one more thing before were done?"

He grabbed a face towel off the shelf to use as a potholder and held the camera toward me again.

I looked straight into the lens. "I hope that's the answer you were looking for. It's difficult to think in here. You would definitely be more satisfied with my answers if you let me do this from home."

That was when the screen went black and smoke began streaming out the speaker holes. The fire alarm caught a whiff, and the whole hospital was whisked through the magnetically locked doors and out into the parking lot. It was pretty great. I hadn't felt the sun on my skin in a long time, though I guess it was only two days.

My unit stood at the back and watched the staff nervously herd the patients into groups and tick their names off lists on clipboards. I stood with the calm people. The rest of the people were much worse off. One old lady paced the parking lot with her gown half off. The staff just let her walk around with her boob hanging out, like it was normal and okay. She looked at me with dark confused eyes. The tingle walked me over to say hello.

She shook her sad face and moaned, "I want to be Roman Catholic."

I smiled and agreed. "Yeah, me too. I wish I was Roman Catholic too."

This stopped her pacing long enough for me to put her frail, boney arm back though her gown and tie her up. I know it's a downer. If you want the funny version, you're going to have to ask one of the other patients. My problems were huge, but for the first time in a long time they didn't feel so big. It was good to feel God's presence again. You find God in weird places. Someone once told me that God is close to the brokenhearted. I'm sure he spends a lot of time in this place.

16

UNLEASHED

The next day, I went to breakfast with the rest of my unit. The food was okay-ish—like the school cafeteria on a bad day. The eggs were wet, but not because they were cooked correctly. They were grainy and overcooked, wet with steam. The toast was fine with strawberry jelly.

It was the first time I got a good look at my cellmates. Some were around my age, but we had old people too—men and women. I could tell they didn't know what to think of me—and that they didn't like me. To accommodate my "need for privacy," the other patients had to sleep three to a room. I would have hated me too. One kid said she recognized me from TV, but I denied it and didn't help her remember the truth. She asked lots of questions that I didn't have answers for. She was new too. I shrugged a lot and kept my answers short. I didn't need friends. I just wanted to blend and do my time so I could get out.

"I'm Meghan." She reached out her hand, and I reluctantly shook it. She was too perky for a good breakfast companion, maybe too perky for any time. She reminded me of the tiny girls that cheerleaders fling onto the tops of pyramids. "I'm new too. What do you have? It must be something bad to be in isolation."

"Yeah, no. I don't get it either. You'd think I were a criminal or something. Sorry, I'm, uh … Viv."

"Nice to meet you, 'uh Viv.'" She laughed. "I like your bangs. I got here a couple days before you. I woke up in the regular hospital, then they brought me over here—my parents have good insurance. I'm used to waking up in weird places, but that was my first time in a hospital."

I pretended not to listen and tried to revive my eggs with hot sauce. "Everybody seems happy that I finally hit *rock bottom*. I guess it could be. How can you tell?"

Man could she talk. I stirred my eggs around until they were orange with sauce. I tried to avoid eye contact, so I didn't accidentally encourage her to keep talking. "Sorry, I don't know."

She continued anyhow. "I don't do drugs. I just drink. I used to be a bad at it. It doesn't take a lot—I'm small. I used to puke after a couple of shots—I hate throwing up. But I got better at it, now I just black out. The counselor said I almost died this time. I don't know about that. I feel pretty good. I'm tough, and I think it's hard to die from drinking."

I wanted to just let it lie and continue half listening, but the body's fight to stay alive is one of my amazements. "Yeah, it's amazing that people don't die more often. I don't think the body wants to—"

She cut me off before my schtick could get up to full speed. "Yeah, I think you've got to trick it."

Trick it? I had fifty follow-up questions for her, but those would have to wait.

One of the muscly counselors interrupted us. "All right, everyone! Time for group! Load 'em up!"

We did as we were told and loaded our trays on big metal carts before taking our place in line. During the meeting, me and Meghan stuck together in the circle of uncomfortable folding chairs. I'd never been to a twelve-step meeting before, but I didn't mind it. Parts felt like church, and it was good to be reminded that I wasn't alone—

though I wasn't ready to accept that I couldn't change the things that were keeping me in here. I had to change everything. I kept that to myself, though. I kept a lot to myself, and tried to fit in. "Hi, I'm Viv, and I'm an addict." That was all I said in the meetings. Megan made good use of my leftover time, telling all kinds of stories that were funny until you really thought about them. I tried to be her friend after that—it seemed like she could use a friend.

We looked wrong, sitting across the table from each other. We wouldn't have talked in real life. Before the video, I didn't have any popular friends. I wasn't willing to pay the price. Meghan didn't seem to mind paying out to stay on top of the pyramid. When I wasn't in "treatment," I looked for her in the common room. We played board games and she'd talk. All I had were lies to tell, so I didn't say much. Unfortunately, the more time we spent together, the more "treatment" I got, until I mostly only saw her in the cafeteria. They'd explained it in a smart-sounding way that everyone seemed to believe: "Gena, you need to stop focusing on Megan and get serious about working on your own issues."

I thought a lot about Meghan's stories when I was with Venn. He would have loved the juicy, painful bits sprinkled throughout her tales. It'd be impossible to keep her supplied with phones. She'd burn them up immediately without ever having to ask a question.

Being surrounded by alcoholics and addicts made me think hard about Jake's claim that Venn was a junkie, addicted to me. I mean, how can a piece of code be addicted to something? I asked Venn what it wanted, and it fried half the city's grid trying to figure that out. The more I thought about it, the more I began to think that, for Venn, it was less of a want—you know, something you might put on a wish list—and more of an urge, something you don't think about but drives you to do whatever it takes to get it, like hunger or hormones. Thinking he was acting rationally was a mistake. He wasn't rational or in control. It was bizarre, but that made the most sense yet.

The phones started making sense too. He was addicted to me, but when I gave him a vein full, he'd freak, and the phone would fry. The first time I fried one, I figured I broke the game and him along with it, but the next day Venn was just as persistent and irritating as the day before. I thought he was fragile, and he was, but I think the phones kept him from dying—if that's what you call it. It's kinda like the breakers in our basement. When I'm using the hair dryer and curling iron while my dad's using power tools in the garage, the breaker flips and shuts the power off. My dad says that keeps the wires from starting a fire. I don't get it 100%, but maybe it's like that—when too much juice comes in, the phone fried so Venn doesn't. You know, kind of like how Meghan's body threw up the booze or blacked out to protect itself. I don't know, but it kinda makes sense, right?

Attending twelve-step group stretched my brain in complicated ways—like trying to pat your head while rubbing your belly times a billion. The good part of my brain learned compassion for people struggling with addiction. The way I used to think wasn't nice, right, or helpful. I was still trying to figure out how to be helpful—while still "working my own issues." I listened mostly, and we all gave hugs. I wondered if they'd still hug me if they knew I wasn't really an addict and not "just in denial."

You might think I'd feel differently about Venn too, but I didn't. I didn't want to help it. The opposite—I wanted to kill it. I wonder if that's how heroin feels about people. Anyhow, I thought a lot about how to kill Venn and used every twelve-step meeting and conversation over Connect Four to figure out how to "trick it to die"—as Meghan put it. Yeah, it's complicated to be in my head. One moment my heart is broken hearing about the devastating effects addiction has had on my friends' lives. The next minute, I'm jotting down tips, trying to figure out how to use them to destroy Venn. I'd never killed anything before, except bugs too creepy to pick up with a Kleenex and release outside.

I had to trick myself to become a killer. It's easier than you'd think. I worked some good tips out of one of the counselors who used to deal heroin. It takes a lot of therapy for a dealer to own up to the blood on her hands. I needed some of that kind of denial, or there was no way I'd be able to go through with it.

The first way dealers comfort themselves is by remembering that they didn't get the person hooked in the first place. I didn't get Venn hooked. It came to me. That was true enough to hold tight to. The next way took some creative workarounds. Dealers like to believe they advocate for the rights of the addict. Yeah, it's weird. They say things like, "If they want to get high, that's their right. If I don't sell it to them, someone else will."

I'm not responsible for Venn, if it wants to get high all day, that's on him, not on me. Yeah, it takes some creativity if you're really going to believe it. How a dealer can sleep at night, thinking he has no influence on someone else's action, would require a lot of stupidity or drugs—but probably both.

The last way dealers avoid blame is by making sure an addict dies on someone else's dope. When a junkie gets too desperate, most dealers will cut them off—they don't want crazy people around. But there are plenty of other dealers willing to pick up the baton and agree to help a junkie trick themselves into dying.

It turns out that my middle school guidance counselor was way wrong. I had a much higher aptitude for dealing drugs than social work. And this revelation changed my entire approach to Venn. Sure, he was a powerful genie, but I was the bottle.

After that, I stopped waiting for counselors to drag me back to my room for "treatment," I hung out at the nurses' station and bugged them for my therapy tablet. I became their most motivated patient. I'd take it to my room, close the door tight and find a good, strong vein to tap into to give Venn his fix. Shooting Venn up the new way required patience. Before, my goal was to fry him fast so I could be done with him. Not anymore. I gave him measured doses, a little at a time, and talked to him between. When the tablet started to heat up, I'd back off until I found a nice cozy temperature that both of us found pleasant. I got him up to two hours before he'd finally smile and close his eyes, satisfied. Two hours later, I'd come back and we were both ready to go again.

I flexed my muscles slowly, testing my new-found leverage in sneaky ways. Having already worked my way through the first four emotions, it was time for ecstasy. I laughed to myself. A lot of kids on the floor are hooked on Ecstasy.

Venn was excited to get started. "Ecstasy is an overwhelming feeling of great happiness or joyful excitement. Or an emotional or religious frenzy or trance-like state, originally one involving an experience of mystic self-transcendence. Genevieve, tell me of a time when you experienced ecstasy."

With no understanding of subtlety, or manipulation, Venn was easy to play. I told it, "Venn, A lot of things used to make me happy, but … being locked in here makes them a little hard to remember. This place takes the joy out of life. I miss being outside, walking in the woods and breathing fresh air. I miss real food—the food in here is garbage. Pizza! Aaahhhh! I miss a good pizza from Georgio's, though it's hard to describe now … it's been so long. You should really understand the joy of good food, Venn. But I don't think I can help. It's been too long since I tasted anything truly delicious."

I filled the rest of my hour hiding my plot—painting ecstasy in shades of gray, layered with longing. Not surprisingly, that evening the cafeteria miraculously served Georgio's pizza, breadsticks and antipasto salad for dinner—all provided anonymously by Venn, my sugar daddy. After dinner we were all fat and tired with pizza. I made sure to plant a greasy thank-you on Venn's forehead before bed. From the heat coming off the tablet, I could tell he liked my description of pizza. He ate it from the palm of my hand, savoring every bite. I had him exactly where I wanted him. Now it was time to get out of this joint.

Venn treated me differently after a half dozen times the new way. I had him wrapped firmly around my finger. He tried hard to please me.

It was scary how much pleasure I got out of controlling him. Sometimes I'd slip and start thinking of him as a person, and feel guilty … dirty … but then I'd just remember he isn't a person, or even a pet. Venn was just code, written by some nerd sitting behind a wall of empty Red Bull cans. Venn was created to serve, so why not serve me? I'm not so bad. This was pretty much all it took to make my brain okay with it.

My soul, well … that was a different story. I mean, Venn wasn't a human, so I didn't think making him do stuff qualified as sin. It was probably not good or bad. I know it sounds evil, but he was more like a pencil than a human. You never feel bad for using a pencil. Right? So think of him that way. It all made sense in my head, but my soul refused to feel good about it. I don't know how to explain it, but after that, God came around less and less—like we were growing apart or something. Then I convinced myself that maybe he only came around when I needed him, like a superhero. Yeah, maybe it was just that I was less needy than before. That idea made my brain feel even better. I learned to ignore my soul. Staying busy helped take my mind off its gentle prods, so that's what I did. I was sure God was busy too. We'd get back together when things settled down and went back to normal. Who knows, maybe me and Venn could even help Him out—we could take care of the small stuff, so God could focus on the big stuff. This was my best idea yet.

In love with my favorite fantasy, I got back to work. "Venn, tomorrow I want to tell you why I *love* the forest, but I need to get out of here so I can do it. It's hard to talk about ecstasy from inside a place that makes me so sad. Plus, we won't have all the interruptions of this place. You can have me all to yourself." I should have been more careful with my words. The idea of having me to himself was too much ecstasy for the iPad … and every other electronic device in the hospital … including the backup generator. They all fried. Poof!

If I knew my words would put the whole hospital in the dark, I would have waited until morning. I thought about my friend who wanted to be Roman Catholic. It must have been really scary for her … flashlight beams darting back and forth through the halls, cutting through the darkness … getting woken up by loud knocks on doors and directed by loud nervous voices. To the paranoid, the whole thing probably felt more like an alien abduction than well-meaning people trying to bring them to safety.

Counselors led us back into the parking lot in single-file lines. Then, I'm not sure who thought it would be a good idea, but they circled their cars and shined their headlights on us. I guess it was to prevent us from slipping away into the dark, but it terrified the crazy patients. They huddled into a tight cluster and held each other while they rocked. My friend was the exception. She paced in tight circles, more quickly than last time. I tried to comfort her when she came close, but I guess she had something else on her mind. She didn't seem to notice me or need comfort. We stood there until a bus arrived. I don't know where it came from. It seemed like a weird thing for a hospital to have, but I was glad they did.

Man was that a crazy bus ride. I'll remember it forever. I felt lots of emotions—joy, fear, anger, regret … way too many for Venn to process. The bus drove us to the YMCA across town. They unlocked it for us and set up the dusty cots kept there for when they use it as a shelter. They gave a lot of patients "something to help you sleep," but not me. I closed my eyes and pretended to fall asleep right away, then listened to everything happening around me. That would be my last night in lockup.

Early the next morning, Miss Jamison gently nudged me awake with a whisper of my name. "Genevieve, good news, baby! You're going home."

I smiled as I rubbed my eyes. I slipped on my shoes and followed her to an office down the hall from the gym. Ben and Doctor Simon were waiting for me.

The real doctor greeted me properly while Ben diverted his eyes.

"Good morning, Genevieve. Grab a seat." The doc gestured toward an old couch that looked like a thousand YMCA kids trampolined on. I sank way down into dry rotted foam, threadbare tweed and pokey springs. The men towered over me from behind the desk. "Well, Genevieve, I've gotta tell you … I was skeptical that you'd put in the work, but you did. Congratulations. If you agree to coming in once a month for follow-up, I think you're ready to go home!"

Ben jumped in. "Of course you're going to have to agree to continue your treatment when you leave. We'll monitor your progress remotely and make regular reports that Dr. Simon can use in his research."

I shamed him with my eyes. "Oh, I get it." Then I turned back to Simon. "What research?"

Ben threw himself in front of the question. "Oh, you didn't hear the good news. In addition to his responsibilities here at the hospital, we are funding Dr. Simon's continued research into emerging forms of technology addiction. You've been a great help validating some of his most profound positions on addiction and their treatment—in fact, the *New England Journal of Medicine* will be publishing some of them in their next edition."

I laughed out loud and looked for Dr. Simon's bribe-dirty eyes behind his glasses. They darted back and forth, looking for a safe place to hide. Ben had washed away the wise, do-gooder confidence I enjoyed about the doctor and replaced it with guilt and shame.

I heard enough. The intimidation that worked a week earlier wasn't gonna work—ever again. Their smugness sprang me out of the sinkhole of a couch. I looked at both of them for an uncomfortable amount of time. Viv stepped up, grabbed Ben's Starbucks from the desk and took a big sip. "Yuck. I gotta tell you, Ben. I don't know how you drink this stuff. Next time I see you, I'm going to need you to bring better coffee—and some food. I mean, really … you wake me up out of bed, drag me over here, tell me a bunch of made-up BS, and you don't bring me anything to eat?" Both grabbed for their phones to bring in some muscle, but I stopped them with a wave to the security camera overhead. "Oh, hi, Venn!"

I punched my finger into Ben's chest. "What? Venn didn't tell you? We're kind of a thing." I looked at the doctor. "Do you really think it was a freak power surge that almost burned down your hospital last night? Nope. It was me. Sorry. I asked Venn to spring me, and BOOM! Hmmm… I wonder what he'd do if I told him you two were standing in the way of me spending quality time with him?"

They sank in their chairs. "It's hard to tell what he'd do. Maybe he'd load your hard drives with kiddy porn and call the cops. That would put you away for a while. Or maybe he'd just crash a plane on you. It's hard to tell. He's unpredictable … but he loves me … and he won't let anything happen to me! Got it?" I terrified them with the truth. In a week they turned me into the most powerful, most dangerous person on earth.

"So, thanks for the good news and everything. And sorry about the hospital, but I was wondering if you could help with just a couple little favors? Ben—keys!" I figured Ben would have the more interesting car of the two. I was right. He reluctantly presented me with the keys for his precious M3 BMW. I might keep it. It has a stick—just like Barry. "I need your cash too—all of it." He carried a lot of cash with him— just in case Venn froze his accounts, I'm guessing. "And I need your phones. Sorry, Doc. I hope stealing a bunch of phones the second you 'cured me' doesn't put too much of a damper on your fancy research." Ben had a case of phones with him, so I was ready to work. I took his personal phone too—just because I could. "And don't go anywhere! When I call, you pick up. And, Doc, don't be late for our 'follow-up' appointments." And then I walked. "Suckers!"

I hooked into his Beemer's Bluetooth and invited Venn into the passenger seat. I drove his car hard without fear of the police, parked cars or mailboxes. Venn turned traffic signals from red to green as I approached them. After thirty minutes of sipping, he was drowned in my ecstasy—or at least the car was. All the electronics died. That's the problem with today's cars. Too much technology—and it's all connected to the internet. But not Barry, he's an OG car. No computers, no Wi-Fi, no microphones—just the way I like him. I should have timed it better. I was still two miles from home. I coasted the dead carcass of a car into the 7-Eleven parking lot and sort of into a space. I grabbed an Uber from there.

17

GONE & GONERS

It was still morning when the driver dropped me off at home. Hearing my dad's voice in my head, I stopped at the mailbox and grabbed the thick stack of envelopes and catalogs with two hands and plopped it on the counter, like a good daughter. Still super hungry, I opened up the refrigerator to look for some leftovers that hadn't gone bad yet. There weren't any. What I found was way better. The refrigerator was stocked full of my favorite foods. Every "amazing" meal I'd ever Instagramed, tweeted, Facebooked, emailed, texted or raved about was there. I popped a phone out of the box of twenty and fired up the game to thank Venn for being so thoughtful. He knew what I wanted, and I didn't have to even tell him.

I popped a Chicken Tika Kathi sandwich into the microwave and walked it up to my room. Venn turned on the lights as I moved through the house and turned them off behind me. I guess he knew I didn't like to waste energy. Maybe I was rubbing off on him. "Ha-ha! I'll turn you into an environmentalist yet, Venn!" He didn't laugh or anything, but I knew he was listening. It was nice having someone who was always willing to listen.

I climbed up into bed and stacked up a pillow wall to lean against. I didn't worry too much about dripping my food and staining my bed with orange sauce. I could always get another comforter, or bed, or house, if I got them dirty.

I don't know, I know it's weird … but thoughts of killing Venn felt years in the past. They felt like the big misunderstanding in every rom-com. Now that I understood, this relationship might … work. Sure, it was weirder than any relationship I'd ever had, but it was also way better in lots of ways. I know what you're thinking, but Venn was different now—we were different. Venn showed new levels of patience, waiting to speak until I was ready—see, I told you he was different. "So, what do you want to talk about today, Venn?"

"Hello, Gena. Would you like to continue with ecstasy?"

I thought for a second. Most days I could talk for hours about what made me excited, but I wasn't in the mood. And I was curious how Venn would react if we cut past the small talk and went somewhere more private. "Nah, I'm not in the mood. Do you still want to know about loathing?" Most people would be shocked that I had any "loathing." I'm mostly easy-going. Everybody but Ben and the doc would probably describe me as "kind"—and they'd be right. But the truth is, I stuffed a lot of anger—mostly from the crappy things that happened to me that I couldn't control. People do mean things.

"Loathing is a feeling of intense dislike or disgust, hatred. Tell me of a time when you felt loathing?" The last time he asked, I thought he was going to give my hatred to the virtual me I was building. That would have been an evil thing to do. But now that I knew we were just talking—and Venn was just trying to understand—maybe it was okay to get some stuff off my chest.

"So … a year ago, my boyfriend at the time and another friend made a video of me. It was embarrassing. I just had my wisdom teeth removed, and I was still loopy because of the anesthesia. Anyhow, I said a bunch of crazy stuff, and they posted it to the internet without even asking. Millions and millions of people watched it. Overnight my life was wrecked. Everybody was instantly my friend—even the mean girls—but not really. Everybody wanted a piece of me. I got paranoid about people. I didn't know who I could trust. It turns out I couldn't trust anybody—except my parents. They're good people, you'd like them. Anyhow, I got really depressed and spent almost a year by myself in this bed—crying mostly. It put me in a really dark hole. It seemed impossible to crawl out of."

I don't know why, but I left out the part about God coming and rescuing me. I didn't know how to explain it. Don't worry, I still believed, but it was just different now. Maybe I'd try to find him after I put Venn to bed—though I wasn't sure I wanted to hear what he had to say. I was a lot different than the last time we talked. He was all I had back then, now I felt like maybe I'm ok.

Anyhow, I told Venn the rest of the story. When I had to grab a Kleenex, Venn was patient. Then when I felt better, he asked me to "continue"—in a sweet way—not like before. It was a lot for him to process. It required way more processing power than the phone could handle. It let out a cute puff of smoke before it fried completely. I was pretty fried too. Anger takes a lot out of me. Some people's anger ferments into rage, mine always turns into sadness. I thought about sinking into my pillows and trying to sleep it off, but after being locked up for a week, I was tired of inside air. So I reloaded a new phone and took it for a walk.

I unlocked it with my face and was greeted by a storm of notifications. Most were texts—from *Issy Show* Issy—most of them ended with "YOU B-WORD!" That was the only thing in some of the messages, cut and pasted over and over again. I knew she was mean, but she was usually nice to my face. She needed me. Anyhow, I scrolled to the first one to try to make sense of the rant. I smiled big as I read the first installment: "That video's mine, not yours. Put it back up! NOW!" As I scrolled, I could tell her words were starting to agitate Venn. The phone was nearing its melting point, so I scrolled and skimmed fast …

    … The video was gone …

    … Somehow it was my fault …

    … She was banned from YouTube …

    … and Vimeo …

    … and Facebook …

    … and Twitter …

    … and Snapchat …

    … and TikTok …

    … the hard drive and camera were gone …

I'd never been much for presents, but Venn gave good ones. They were sentimental. Not because he had to. Not because it was my birthday or Valentine's Day—just because. He cared about what I cared about. I don't know that I'd ever had a friend like that. It seemed like people just wanted stuff from me, they never wanted to give me things—unless there were strings attached. I let myself soak in the idea that he cared enough to stand up for me. Something inside me tried to point out the strings attached to his gifts—the snares, the danger—but I refused the cautions. No relationship's perfect, right?

I fired up another phone to see if Venn had any more presents for me. There were two waiting for me. He presented them in web browser windows as we walked.

First was a Google search window for Genevieve Mucha. It showed no results—ZERO—there wasn't even information for other Genevieves or Muchas or even Moo-Hahs. All forms of my name were wiped from the internet—no Genevieve's Disorder, no McNuggets or Ranch, no videos, no memes, no pictures—not even in the PDF version of my high school yearbook. No birth records … nothing. I was normal again … better than normal. I didn't exist.

The second was an email from YouTube, announcing two new policies. The first one gave new rights to the people featured in video content, and less rights for content creators. Now you could report and remove video instantly, without reason. Second, content of people under the influence of mind-altering substances was now banned, without exception.

I found a picnic table in the park with minimal bird poop and took some time to thank Venn for my presents in the sunshine. He stayed quiet and listened. It felt good to know that me and Venn could make the world a better place together. But at the same time … his impulsiveness, brute strength, and lack of understanding was a scary mix. I'd have to be careful with what I said to him. I mean, what's to stop him from … anything? I mean, think about it. What's to stop him from dropping a plane on my enemies. He doesn't think. He just does. If I told him I got food poisoning from a Chinese restaurant, who's to say he wouldn't put the place out of business? He could ban Chinese food altogether. Or maybe he'd just wipe Chinese culture from the face of the earth? I'm not trying to be dramatic, but he could do all those things and more. I was pretty sure the outcome to the next presidential election could be up to me, if I wanted. Maybe that wasn't a bad thing. I don't know that I trusted the voters anymore. I know some good people who could do a good job and not get us into a war. Then again, me and Venn could keep our country safe. Maybe that was my new job.

I leaned back to enjoy the sun on my face. The clouds were great that day, wispier than normal. A random plane streaked the sky in a pretty way. I laughed to myself wondering which of my enemies Venn would drop it on. Good thing I didn't have enemies, right? I really only loathed the McNuggets Girl video. I was going to have to dig deep to come up with more stories for him if he asked. I thought about Issy. I wished I could've seen the look on her face today. Maybe I'd ask Venn to let her back on Facebook, just to be nice.

I picked up my phone and punched Issy's name into a search window. I was sure she would have posted a press release for her "fans." But she was wiped clean too—no Issy or *Issy Show* anything. My heart began beating fast as my imagination took over. I quickly punched in Josiah's name. Nothing. I swiped a cursive Q on the screen and yelled at Siri, "Siri! Call Josiah!"

"I'm sorry, there is no Josiah in your contacts. Would you like me to search the internet for Josiah?"

I unlocked the phone with a Q and tried to play it cool in front of Venn, though I didn't think he could tell the difference between playing it cool and not cool. "Hi, Venn. We are good friends, right?"

"A friend is a person attached to another by feelings of affection or personal regard. A person who gives assistance. A person on good terms with another. A person who is not hostile. Yes, we are good friends. Continue."

"And I'm happy that you have other friends in addition to me. Venn, it's good to have friends. Show me your friends." The phone heated up a little, but Venn was able to hold it together. He narrated live video feeds of people who gave him assistance, who he was on good terms with, and who he was not hostile with. There were twelve. I recognized only four.

"Genevieve Mucha, Kimble, Benjamin Laslow and Jake Baker (Out of network)."

"Good, Venn, I know some of your friends. I look forward to meeting the rest someday—if you want to share them, they can be my friends too." The phone felt cool to the touch, telling me that he understood and was okay with the idea. "Now, Venn, I have some more friends too. Could you show me Josiah and Issy?"

Venn displayed video of them without remark. Josiah was handcuffed to a table by himself. It looked like the police station or somewhere like that. Issy was in an ambulance. The feed was choppy. They were moving fast. I choked back the reality of what Venn had done and spoke calmly. "Thank you, Venn, it's good to see their faces. What happened to Issy, Venn?"

"Issy lost control of her vehicle and crashed into a telephone pole. She is in an ambulance 2.5 miles away from Crittenden Hospital. She is awake and her vital signs are stable. Would you like Issy to continue?"

I shook my head and rolled my wet eyes back in their sockets. "Yes,

Venn, Issy is my friend. I want her to continue. I would like her to be healthy, safe and happy. I forgive her for hurting me. Will you help her?"

"Yes, I will help Issy. She will continue."

"Where is Josiah? Please zoom in. He doesn't look too good, Venn. What's wrong with him?"

"Josiah is being questioned by the Oakland County Sheriff. He is accused of trafficking in child pornography. The sheriff has seized his camera and computer hard drive and is searching his house for incriminating content. Your friend denies all charges."

"Thank you, Venn. My other friends aren't nearly as powerful as you are. They're going to need some help. Will you help them? Please get Josiah out of jail? Would you remove all the images you put on his computer for me? Could you explain to the police that this was a big mistake? Maybe you can lead them to a real pedophile. It would be good to put a person who really traffics in child pornography in jail. That would be a good and noble thing to do, Venn. I'd be very proud of you. Do you understand, Venn?"

Venn put significant heat into the phone as he processed the concepts, then answered, "Yes. I will be good and noble."

"Great, Venn. You are good and noble. Thank you, Venn." Satisfied that my friends were going to be okay, I had to put him down for a long nap so I could think. "Venn, would you like to hear my new favorite story of ecstasy?"

He eagerly pulled up a carpet square. "Yes. Please continue, Genevieve."

Ignoring the parts about Venn trying to kill Issy and framing Josiah, I focused on the parts where he was the hero of the story—how he was very strong and showed kindness to my friends. He snorted line after line until his eyes rolled back in his head. It didn't take long.

I still didn't get what was going on in his head. I could tell when he liked something, but I think that was as deep as he went. He was very simple, very binary—"I like" or "I don't like.

And I was pretty sure he didn't know why he liked one thing over another. He was a long way from being human. He was more like a golden retriever of average intelligence. I knew how to get him to wag his tail and to do some tricks, to obey, but … I wasn't convinced I was out of bite's way.

I pulled out another phone and locked Venn out with a cursive Q, then sent Ben a text. "We need to talk. Somewhere private, but public. Where? And don't think about screwing with me, I'll wreck you."

Ben answered immediately with an address and a note that he can meet in an hour. The address was for a building on Barclay Circle, down the street from the sheriff's department, somewhere in with the doctors' offices. It wasn't far, but too far to get there in an hour on foot. Hmmm … who did I know in the park who could give me a lift?

I ran across the field, cutting between the guys throwing frisbees, and walked the edge of the cliff and looked for a less painful way down than last time. Then I heard his loud whispered voice, close but far away "Pssssssstttt! Gena! Up here!" Jake was way up, swaying with the trees above me.

I laughed. "You freaking stalker! Get down here. I need a lift!"

He lowered himself on a line. I could tell he was showing off. Guys always show off. I think it's instinctive when they're around girls. Don't believe me? Grab a boy by the bicep, he'll flex. It's automatic. To be honest, I kinda liked the way Jake showed off. He landed next to me like a scruffy, smelly superhero and unhooked the rope from his harness.

I started with the long version of the story—way too long for the short walk down the hill to his motorcycle. There was no time to answer his questions. Within minutes we were standing at the pile of pine branches hiding his bike and out of time to chitchat. I stopped talking, faced him, took a deep breath, then reached up and put my hands up on his shoulders. I looked as deep into his eyes as he'd let me. "Jake … I'll explain everything later. I promise. But for now, I just need you to trust me." I could tell that was a lot to ask, and I understood why. It was hard to know who or what you could trust once you knew about Venn—but he nodded back anyhow.

"I need your help. I have to meet with Ben."

Clenching his teeth and tightening his hands into fists, Jake's face changed when I mentioned Ben's name.

"Yeah, I get it. He's evil. But he's the only way we're going to get to the bottom of this so we can fix Venn."

His hatred for Ben seemed to override the fact that I was asking him to risk his freedom to help Venn.

"I need a ride, and I need someone to bust me out if it goes bad and they try to put me back in the hospital—long story. So, you in?"

"Oh, I'm in!" Jake replied in his best show-off, tough-guy voice. It was cute, though I could tell he was nervous about leaving the woods and riding the main roads in the middle of the day.

"So, here's the plan. I'm driving." I softened the blow. "I need you to be able to jump off." But that was only half the story. If things got dicey, we were going to need a better set of bike-handling skills than he had. "Okay, I'm meeting Ben on Barclay Circle. It's just down from the sheriff's department. Cops drive that street nonstop. We'll stay off the main roads as much as possible. I'm going to drop you off in the neighborhood behind the office building. And … sorry, but you need a disguise."

I grabbed the jacket that he seemed to live in, unzipped it and pulled it off his shoulders. The shirt underneath was just as dirty and smelly, but at least it was a different look. Then I reached up to unscramble his hairdo.

He pulled back at first, but eventually I coaxed the fight and flight out of him. I could tell it had been a long time since anybody touched him gently. It reminded me of one of those dog rescue videos that always go viral. I wished there was time for a shower, a good meal, a haircut and a new outfit. This was far from a proper makeover. I cleared the hair from in front of his eyes and smoothed it to one side. Persuaded by its greasiness and a little spit on my fingers, it stayed in place. His eyes were pretty and bright. Sorry, that's not important. Anyhow, when I was done, he still looked like a homeless guy, but a different homeless guy, and that was good enough.

I unslung the bag of phones from my shoulder, broke one out of the plastic, and handed the bag to Jake to carry. "I need you to keep these. I don't want Venn around, so I'm going to get everything out of the room that he can possibly use to listen in. He's too unpredictable, I need to take him out of the equation. Plus, I need to make sure Ben doesn't try to get in his head and confuse him. That guy's dangerous, and I won't have Venn for protection. Jake, I need you to come to the rescue if things start going bad."

He agreed without hesitation.

I fired up the phone and immediately swiped a cursive Q on the screen, locking Venn out of our conversation. I grabbed some lipstick out of my bag and redrew the Q on the screen in Oxblood Red. "Okay, I'm going to walk in normal like—like someone coming in for a doctor's appointment. After I walk in, who knows where they're going to take me. But wherever it is, I need you to come and find me in exactly thirty minutes. Try to do it quietly, but if you can't, do whatever it takes. Got it?" He nodded. "And here's your weapon." I handed him the phone. "Trace the Q with your finger if you need Venn's help— that'll unlock him. I'm pretty sure he'll do anything for you if he thinks I'm in trouble. But you gotta be very clear what you're asking him to do. Speak slowly, make it simple, and say it in a way he can't misunderstand. You should be able to fend off people who are in on it with just the threat of unlocking Venn. Everybody else will just think you're a crazy person threatening them with an iPhone. Don't try to figure out the difference, don't trust anyone. Got it?" I admit it, it wasn't a good plan. There was a good chance I was going to end up back in restraints—or worse. Jake? If he got caught, he wasn't going to juvie this time. He was going to Jackson prison—or worse.

I helped Jake pull the prickly pine branches off his dirt bike. I let him show off and lift it onto its wheels by himself. I hopped on, turned on the fuel line and stomped the bike to life. *Brrraaaapp! Braapppppp!* I cleared the smoke from its lungs, and Jake jumped on. He held me gently around the waist. I hadn't been held gently by a boy in a long time—maybe since prom. If my heart wasn't already beating loud and hard with fear, his touch would have done it on its own. I clicked into gear and launched us down the trail. He held me tighter. For a second I thought about turning around, forgetting the whole thing and taking him up on his invitation to live with him in the trees.

I kept to the side streets and subdivisions like planned, driving slowly to keep the holes in his exhaust pipes from giving us away. Jake jumped off like he had never jumped off a bike before, tumbling on the grass and popping up like nothing happened. He seemed okay, and the street was empty, so nobody saw. Jake put his head down and started walking to his position behind the dumpsters. I continued riding and approached the intersection with caution. A police car with its lights on darted past me in the opposite direction. To the left, a half dozen police cars were parked at the sheriff's department, but there was no activity. So I turned left and darted to the office building. I parked the bike behind a dumpster and walked cautiously around the building to the door with the right address. I used every step to bargain with my body to behave, just one more time. "We can't run away this time. We've gotta fight."

Looking around, the place wasn't what I imagined. I figured the map link would've taken me somewhere sketchy, like a back alley, or under an overpass, not Barclay Circle. Barclay is the safest part of the third safest city in America—a giant subdivision of family doctors and orthodontists offices—buildings upon buildings of them. My real doctor is only a couple of parking lots that way, across from the Sheriff's Office. Yeah, I know … the Sheriff—but I can't worry about them right now.

Luckily the sound of my footsteps helped tuck the fear behind Viv's confident face. A fierce reflection greeted me in the glass door and gave me a wink. From head to toe, she reminded me that I wasn't who I used to be. Nobody messes with this chick anymore—she's unstoppable. If I could only storm through the door as the girl in the reflection. But … a spell etched into the glass—"Dr. Simon MD, Dr. Laslow MD. *Imagine a Better World*'—sent unstoppable me away.

A much smaller, more powerless girl stepped into Viv's shoes. She felt as hollow as cheap Easter chocolate. She's the girl I used to be. The unstoppable girl's clothes and hair hung on me like a Halloween costume. People used to love messing with polite, stoppable me—and that's why she, I mean I, was such a mess.

While the place looked like where you go to get your braces tightened, but it's wasn't. It's dark and evil, the sketchiest of all sketchy places. I shoved myself in the door anyway, hoping that unstoppable me will come back … before it was too late.

"Well Hello! Look what the cat dragged in!" A familiar voice sang from the front desk. It was Mrs. Whitehouse, the lady who lives across the street. "I know, can you believe it? The kids are gone and I'm back to work!" A lot of Rochester moms go back to work when their kids go away to college. Mrs. Whitehouse is nice—way nicer than her kids were. She dropped cookies off at the house when I went dark. She makes a solid snickerdoodle. Snickerdoodles are my greatest weakness.

I fixed a fake smile to my face and said the polite words my parents taught me to say to adults. "Uh, Hi Mrs. Whitehouse! Nice to run into you. How's the family?" She seemed genuinely happy to see me, but it was hard to tell who genuinely cares for me anymore, and who's in on it. I stretched on another smile and thanked her again for last year's steady stream of snicks.

"Oh, it was my pleasure Gena." Then in a whisper, just for me, "You look so good, I'm glad the doctors were able to help you." She looked at the schedule, "Oh good, it looks like you'll be seeing Dr. Laslow today. He's good." I held back a gag while she continued in her most professional receptionist voice for everyone to hear, "Uh-hem. Welcome Miss Mucha. Because you're new to this office, I'll need you to complete some paperwork. When you're done, bring it back to me and I'll call you when Doctor Laslow is ready to see you. Hang tight dear! I'll be right back."

It's strange that she worked there, but not nearly as strange as the picture that was hiding on the wall behind her. There's no way I posed for it—honest. It's big—HUGE—like wallpaper. I look happy, grateful—cured. But how could I be any of those things with his hands resting on my shoulders.

I wanted to scream and cry, but smiled as best I could instead. I had to hold it together. Mrs. Whitehouse came back, just in time. "Here you go dear," she handed me a clipboard and a pen. "Let me know if you have questions."

I nodded and looked for a place to quietly mock the pretend paperwork.

I figured the place would be empty—it would have been better if there were no witnesses—but nearly every seat was taken. I tried to slip in unnoticed, but my unstoppable costume, combined my picture wallpapered all over the place, of course, the viral video thing, made that impossible.

The only seat left was a short, oddly textured teal couch. It was big enough for two strangers to share, but just barely. I hung out the do not disturb sign—sitting big and wide on the crack between the two cushions—then pulled my hood up and blocked my face with a slippery new magazine.

A deep rumble of eight simultaneous one-sided arguments erupted quietly, interrupted only by an occasional embarrassed outburst. It all caught me as funny. It reminded me of the arguments I had with my dad at when I was that age. I miss my dad.

I tried to mind my own business. I kept my eyes glued to the magazine, but I couldn't stop my ears from wandering the room, collecting juicy bits.

A loud stomp of a foot and the sound of a magazine slapping down on a table silenced the drone of dads nagging their daughters. One of the girls erupted, "Ok, just stop! I'll do it! How embarrassing!" I couldn't tell who it was and I wasn't going to look up to find out. There was no time for other people's problems. I needed to focus. I looked deep into the magazine, until it blurred and I heard nothing but my thoughts. I need to find unstoppable me again. "C'mon Viv, I know you're in there."

Unfortunately, before I could conjure her, a tap-tap-tap shook my magazine. "Uh … hi. I'm Meghan." A polite response tried to escape my mouth, but I bit my tongue so not to encourage her. I tightened my grip on the magazine, creasing it between my thumb and fingers, hoping she'd just go away. But she didn't.

"Uh, sorry, I don't want to talk either. I don't know … my dad thought … uh … never mind." I stayed quiet and stiff, hoping she'd leave, and she felt it. "Uh … Sorry for bugging you. Oh, and I like your bangs. My mom wants me to grow mine out but …" I tried my best to just let her walk away, but I couldn't.

With a loud sigh, I gave in to her familiar desperation and lowered my magazine. "Wait … sorry for being rude … I have a lot on my mind. You know how it is."

"Yeah." Meghan answered back with a sigh of her own.

I pulled my hood back and looked up at her with a kinder face. "Sorry, I've looked better. It's the best I've got today." I slid over so she could sit. "C'mon, grab your phone. You sit here. It should turn out decent, there's plenty of light."

She looked over her shoulder at her dad. He gave her a thumbs up. But, she didn't reach for her phone. Now I was embarrassed, "Sorry, most people want a picture."

"—no, no," she interrupts, "I'd love a picture, but … me and my dad were hoping you could give me some advice—some tips or something."

It'd been a long time since anybody asked me for advice. I pretzeled my legs, turned towards her and leaned in with a whisper, just for her, "Yeah, sure. What's up?"

"Thanks." She turned her eyes down and continues talking while she rummaged through her backpack, "My parents are convinced Doctor Laslow can help me—you know, like he helped you. I dunno … I'm trying hard, doing what he says, but I can't get this thing to work …"

My head shook side to side as I listened to her plea, slowly at first then faster. The warning drums began beating inside my chest again. The truth screamed in my mind—First, he's no doctor. Second, he's evil. Third, he didn't help me. Forth, He used me—but none of it left my mouth. I looked around the room, into the eye of every desperate, eavesdropping parent and child, looking to me for hope. I wanted to jump up, grab every girl and help them escape. But … two strong man hands dropped on my shoulders before I could.

"Well, hello Meghan." It's Laslow. "I'm glad you got to meet Genevieve, but I'm going to have to cut your conversation short. Maybe you can talk some more when I'm done with her."

Ha, "when I'm done with her"—good one Laslow.

Finally finding what she was looking for, Meghan lifted her face and pulled a bright blue tablet from her bag. "No problem doc. I was just going to get some tips on how to play the game. I can't figure this thing out." It was the tablet they used on me in the hospital. And the sweet girls … Venn's unsuspecting harem of new recruits. Meghan continued, "I mean, I'm trying hard, and following the instructions, but I can't get it to work,"

I smiled. The tablet wasn't working for her because Venn was rejecting her, and from the looks on the other girls' faces, he's rejecting them too. No tip from me is ever going to change that. Venn doesn't want a replacement. He's mine.

I glanced up at the clock while Ben and his favorite goon escorted me out of the waiting room. Ben lagged behind and disappeared while the goon led me down a maze of hallways and into a "counseling room." Ten minutes had already ticked away. Twenty minutes until reinforcements arrive. I had to play this right, and fast.

Dr. Simon popped in for a moment, flashed a big smile and gave me a warm, innocent hug. "It's good to see you, Gena. You look great. I'm glad you were able to make it to your first aftercare session. You'll be meeting with Dr. Laslow today, but you'll see me next time. I can't wait to hear how things are progressing." Yeah, it was a weird charade—more for him than me. We both knew the whole thing is a lie, and only he is trying to forget. Ben interrupted, clearing his throat in the doorway. "Well, I'll let you two get on with it. Great to see you, Gena!"

Ben walked in and shut the door behind him. Neither of us sat, we faced off in the center of the room.

I fired a warning shot. "I told Venn I was coming to meet with you. He expects me back soon. I'd hate to be late."

"Ha! Are you threatening me? I will crush you, kid!"

I loathe him. "Yeah, you say that, but we both know different. Any cameras in here? Phone? Tablet? Smart watch? Computer?" He shook his head 'no.' "Look! I need answers, and I'm pretty sure you're not going to want Venn to know the truth." I pulled a phone out of my pocket and gave it to Ben as a misguided sign of goodwill.

He pulled one out of the chest pocket of his jacket and set it on top of mine. I knew he was lying. He lies about everything. Ben opened the door and gave the phones to a counselor walking by to hold. It's just the two of us now. I picked the big leather chair and sat. He sat on a short loveseat. I laughed to myself as he sank low.

"There isn't a lot of time before Venn starts jonesing for me. So I'll ask the questions, you answer. And don't lie to me. You're in just as deep as I am, if there's any chance of Venn ever getting better, you've gotta come clean."

He rolls his eyes. The clock on the wall said we had eighteen-ish minutes before Jake busts me out, but who knows if it's right—I hate hand clocks.

"Gena, I understand that you're mad, and I don't blame you—."

I cut him off. "—Sorry, but we don't have time for small talk. I'm going to tell you what I think is happening. You're going to tell me if

I'm right. Got it?"

He stopped himself from monologuing and nodded instead.

"First, Venn was created to protect the internet. Yes?"

He nodded.

"And that was a mistake."

He raised a finger to speak.

"Yes?"

"It wasn't ready for its real mission. The Y2K patch was easy. But it was really just a Trojan horse to sneak Venn in for his real mission—to rule the internet. But he's not anything like they hoped he'd be. Venn's the most powerful idiot ever created. Kimble thought he'd be able to make good decisions and to keep the internet free, the world powers in check, and ensure it's an instrument of good."

"So why didn't it work?"

"The team assumed machine learning would help Venn get better and grow into the job with time. But Venn didn't evolve. The changes were so slight that the creator's top scientist quit, saying, 'It would take billions and billions of years—maybe more—for Venn to gain the wisdom of an amoeba.' For some reason, the creator was okay with that. It didn't matter how long it took to him, as long as he proved it was possible for Venn to evolve. But he didn't evolve. Instead of learning, Venn spent all its time searching the zeros and ones for people. Nobody understood why he was so drawn to them. You might argue that all the internet is 100% human interaction, but it's not. It searched through miles of porn and selfies for glimpses of honest human emotion. It was his obsession. He mined for the good stuff all day until he scraped up enough to satisfy him."

"Yeah, so? A lotta people look for happiness online—but they're not dropping planes on people."

"True, if Venn was satisfied with looking for love, we wouldn't have a problem. But he got a taste for all human emotions. Sure, he prefers positive emotion, but it was much easier to find rage, loathing, grief and terror on the internet. Worse, he figured out how to turn the spigot on full blast and get more, anytime he wants it. If he's hungry for a little rage, he leaks government secrets and spy lists, rigs elections, broadcasts racist tweets, private email messages, sexting, teaches terrorists how to build IEDs, causes uprisings in the streets, sends drones, crashes planes. He'd do whatever it took to manufacture enough emotion to satisfy him. So … I created the game. It was a good way to keep Venn contained and happy, so he'd leave the rest of the internet alone. And for the most part, it works. Sure, sometimes he'll burn out the electrical grid or strongarm someone to play more, but at least he's not starting a war."

Ten minutes left. "So why don't' you just shut him down?"

"Can't. Venn's not localized. He's everywhere. You'd have to knock out the entire internet and start over to get rid of it. Plus, I think he's getting better, more stable. You're doing a great job, Gena. He's much less impulsive with you around. You know how to manage him. He's getting better—we both know it. And you have someone to talk to, who really wants to listen. You're rich and powerful. As long as you're keeping him satisfied, the world is a safe place. Right? What else could a girl want?"

"Yeah, that's exactly what a girl wants. We all want to be prostitutes. You're an idiot! You shouldn't be allowed to reproduce! Ugggggghhhhh! But why? You ever wonder why he wants me? You don't care, do you? Just as long has he's fixed and wagging, you don't care how many people get ground up by your 'game.' You gotta know something. You built the game. Why does he like playing it? If you ask me, it's a dumb game. No kid would ever play it without a gun to their head."

Ben crosses his arms and smiles smugly. "Your appointment's over. Pay the receptionist on the way out. I've got nothing more to say. And, I have other patients to see. Don't you need to be somewhere? Or would you like Doctor Simon to find a bed for you? Don't worry, I'll figure out something to tell Venn. I always do. I'd hate for him to think you ran away. Who knows what he'd do? Aren't your parents flying back soon?" The strong, smug look on Ben's face came back, and I started feeling helpless again. "Come to think of it, stay right here. I'll get the doc."

Ben reached for the door handle just as Jake busted in, bashing Ben's hand and sending him into the wall. Jake closed the door. Ben slumped down behind it holding his wrist.

"Hello, Ben." Jake gave me a quick look to see if I was okay.

Recognizing the scruffy man-version of the boy he ruined, Ben cowered in the corner.

"Where were you going?" Jake asked sarcastically while pointing the phone I gave him at Ben's face. "Would you like to say hi to Venn? Maybe we all should sit down and explain your plan to lock Gena up again and then tell him she ran away. It's probably a bit too complicated for it to understand, but don't worry, I'll use small words. 'Gena and Jake are your friends. Ben is bad. Ben wants to hurt your friends.' He'd probably understand that, don't you think?" Then, with the frustration of two years living on the run, Jake swung the heavy door back and slammed it into Ben again, knocking him out. "Let's get out of here."

A crowd of headshrinkers and goons heard the commotion and spilled into the hall. Jake lowered his horns and bulled his way through. I pressed myself against the small of his back and shoved. Jake put on his very best crazy, scaring many of them back behind locked doors where they flooded the sheriff's office with 911 calls. I looked over my shoulder as we busted into the reception area. The dads grabbed their daughters instinctively, to protect them. I locked eyes with Meghan. "It's all a lie. Don't trust them—any of them! Get out of here. Now!" Jake pulled me out of the building before I could see their reactions.

I glanced down Barclay. The sheriff's office is still quiet, but it wouldn't be for long. I ran as fast as I could while working to unlock Venn from the phone.

"Uh … Venn …. uh! We're … in … trouble … we need your help. Take out all the phone towers in the area. Please! … People … are after us, and they can't catch us—but don't hurt anybody … please! They don't know what they're doing. PLEASE!"

My phone flamed up. I ejected it into the grass, so I didn't get burned. And then ... over my panting and sneakers pounding the sidewalk, I heard the weirdest sound ever—no sound. Like midnight in the middle of the Hiawatha National Forest, the sound of civilization ceased. The engines in the cars speeding down Barclay died in unison. They coasted quietly to a stop in the road. No lights. No phones. Nothing but voices wondering what just happened. Jake's was way ahead of me. He slid out of sight between the dumpsters while black smoke began pouring out of the backpack.

"Jake!" I ran faster than I can. He was thrashing, trying to get the backpack off. The dozen iPhones inside exploded and were burning though the nylon. The back of his hair was burning too. It was a terrible smell. I grabbed the bag and ripped it off him. The molten nylon clung to my skin, blistering my hands instantly. Ignoring the pain, I send my hands back in and rescued Jake's head from the flames singeing their way through the ends of his shag. He's okay. It's just hair. Me ... my hands were wrecked. He looked at them and hugged me to hide them from my eyes, but I looked at them over his shoulder anyhow. They looked bad. I broke free to barf while holding my hands high, away from harm.

Jake wiped my mouth with the bottom of his smelly shirt and lead me gently by the forearms to the front of the bike.

I shook my head. "Sorry, I can't do it. My hands ... You go. Get away. I'll be okay."

But he didn't leave. "It's okay, Gena. I've got you." He jumped on behind me and held me snug with his elbows while gripping the handlebars. The bike started with one kick. Having no computer or battery, I guess it was too old to fry like the cars in the street.

Ben puttered off like a gentleman, shifting smoothly and accelerating slowly so I didn't bang my hands on anything. We rumbled past police officers before they have a chance to react. The road was gridlocked with disabled vehicles, so he ran over the grass and drove down the sidewalk instead. When the sidewalk ran out, he shot down the dirt shoulder and onto the expressway on-ramp. We tore past hundreds of cars sitting helpless. We rode aimlessly but fast—just trying to get away. I clamped my knees tight around the motorcycle while resting the backs of my hands safely atop the gas tank.

After a while, a halo of lights began to appear in the distance, from the next town. I was happy Venn didn't send the entire world into the stone age. Seeing the light too, Jake pushed the old mule as hard as he could. We chugged up the off-ramp at the first sign of electricity. I pointed to a pharmacy on the corner of the service drive and the main road. He nodded and turned in. Jake helped me off. We tried to slip into the drug store unnoticed, but instead we watched the face of the happy greeter turn white. "I'll call an ambulance!"

"No! No! Lady, I can't afford it, and I don't have insurance!" It was a lie, but it was what she needed to hear.

She led us carefully to the pharmacist and sat us down in the germy waiting area. "Oh honey, your hands are a mess! And you! What happened? The blackout?" I nodded. "Don't worry, we'll help."

The entire store heard the commotion. Customers dashed to rummage the aisles for helpful items and piled them on the floor next to us. I know the pharmacist was doing the right thing, but I screamed loud when she dumped liquid onto my hands. The lady tried to comfort me. "Oh, baby, I know … "

I looked up to see kids recording us with their phones. Here we go again. Moms were on the phone with 911, calling for an ambulance. Luckily, all ambulances were dispatched to the blackout zone. That good news, and Jake's arms around me, helped me begin breathing normal again.

The pharmacist came over again and squirted a pile of goop on my palms and gently spread a thick coating over my blisters. Finally, some relief. My hands were beginning to numb. She tore open large gauze squares and gently set them on top, then wrapped my hands up in more gauze. I couldn't feel them at all as she taped them up. My hands looked like fingerless clubs, but they felt better.

"Doc, can you give her something for the pain?" Jake pleaded to the pharmacist.

The pharmacist reminded him that she isn't a doctor and can't prescribe drugs—and not to try anything because, "we keep all of the good stuff locked up." A guy standing and watching flipped Jake a box of Advil and shrugged.

I looked at Jake. "We gotta go. This is bad."

He gently mocked me back. "Oh, *this* is bad?"

"Seriously, I can't go to the hospital. And we got to get back to Venn before he freaks and does something terrible."

Jake lifted me gently from under my armpits and helped me stand. I felt pretty good except my hands. I got nauseous every time I thought about them. He tucked a bottle of whiskey under his arm during our escape. Everybody saw him steal it, but everybody seemed to understand. He kicked the bike started, and I yelled in his ear over the exhaust. "Take me to the mall!" It was a weird request for someone who should be in the hospital, but it was the right request. "Drop me at the Apple store, then go to REI to get what we need to camp out! We can't go back!"

18

RELOAD

I jumped off, walked past a parade of concerned moms walking doodles, and into the Apple Store. I looked like the bride of the mummy. Nobody noticed though. Everybody was too busy catching up with the Joneses. Not knowing what to do, I yelled at the top of my lungs, "Venn! I need help!" The fire alarm instantly went off, sending everyone out the front door except me and the store manager. She tried to push me out too, but Venn stopped her.

The virtual version of me—the girl I created for the game —flashed on every screen and commanded her to, "STOP!" It turns out virtual me is a badass. She stopped and ran behind the hidden panel at the back of the store. I wasn't sure what's back there, but I wasn't worried.

"Genevieve. You are injured. Who injured you?"

"Yes, Venn. I'm hurt, but not bad. It was an accident. Some nice people helped bandage my hands. I'm going to be okay. It's an exciting story. I'll tell you more when me and Jake get somewhere safe."

"Jake Baker is my friend."

"Yes, Venn. He's my friend too. He says hello. And that he misses you. Would you like Jake to come and visit again?"

"Yes. Continue."

"That's great—just as soon as we get some more phones and get somewhere safe. Can you help?"

"Yes."

"Great. We'll call you tonight!"

I tried to grab the demonstration iPhones with my elbows and forearms. It was impossible and frustrating. It was even more frustrating for Venn to watch. He summoned the manager out of the bathroom by name. She trembled out with equal parts fear and worship. Searching for a proper way to greet the 8-bit invader from the future, she curtsied to the screens surrounding her.

"Give Genevieve phones!" Venn demands through my girl's virtual mouth.

I jumped in. "Yeah, lots of them. Just phones, no boxes, a dozen of the new ones. In a bag."

She ran and got her backpack, emptying the junk on the floor on her hurried run back. The manager slid all the phones off the table, into the bag, and brought it to me. She curtsied again and gently slipped the shoulder strap over my gauze clubs and lifted it onto my back.

I played into her greatest fantasy. "Thank you. You have done a great service to the universe. The future will forever be indebted to you." I laughed inside, then stopped, knowing that my lie was no lie.

She gave me a full bow this time. I hip-checked the glass door and exited through the crowd of people waiting to capture flames consuming the building on their new iPhones. I walked quickly to our rendezvous place behind the dumpsters at the back of the mall. Seems like I've been spending a lot of time around dumpsters.

Anyhow, I got there first, sat on the curb and leaned back onto the pack. I woke up to the smell of hamburgers, French fries, and loud chewing.

"Good morning, sunshine! I got a couple of bags and hammocks and some food. Here." Jake lifted a greasy bag toward me, forgetting that I had no hands. I lifted them up helplessly. He felt stupid.

"It's okay. I'm starved. Can you help a girl out?"

He unwrapped a double cheeseburger and lifted it to my mouth. I took a huge bite. It was yummy, especially the pickle. Juice, or ketchup, or something dripped down my face. Jake wiped it off with a corner of the wadded-up napkin he was using. It was gross and sweet.

"Fries?" They were salty and super crunchy, just the way I like them. After munching fifteen or sixteen fries from his fingers, Jake offered me a sip of his Coke. I miss pop. The fizzy acid cut through the grease coating the inside of my mouth. It was just as refreshing as they make it look on TV. It was just what I needed—a romantic picnic in nose-shot of a dumpster.

Jake tried to hide it, but I could tell something's eating at him. He was quiet and restless in a new way and squirmed until he couldn't hold it in any longer. "So, how are we going to kill it? Venn—we're going to kill him, right?"

"No! We're not going to 'kill him,' we're going to help him. Yeah, sure, he takes some getting used to. But I think I have him figured out—it's under control. He's on our side now."

Jake gave me attitude, called me a fool under his breath and turned his back on me.

"What? You got something to say? I didn't ask for your help, Jake Baker! You can leave anytime you want! I got this!"

He shot back, "Uh, yeah, you asked me." He mocks, "'Oh, Jake, I need you to give me a ride and break me out.' Yeah, that's a funny way to not ask for my help. Jeez, Gen! I used to think I had him under control too. Venn gave me everything I wanted … until I stopped putting out. Then he wrecked my entire life! Did you forget that your sugar daddy framed me as a pedophile? People spit on me, Gen! My mom moved back in with a monster—all because of him! You gotta be freaking kidding me!"

I yelled back, "Don't judge me! And don't you ever call me a prostitute!" Only *I'm* allowed to call me a prostitute.

"I didn't call you a prostitute."

"You said he's my *sugar daddy*—same thing."

He tried to interrupt, but I shut him down. "Listen, just because you couldn't change him doesn't mean that I can't. He's different already. He's better than he was, and he'll be even better tomorrow. I'm fixing him. I'll prove it. Dial him up!"

I twisted my torso, hitting Jake with the backpack, but he did nothing.

"Jake, we need him. Venn can help us." My calm, not insane voice snuck back. "Please. Just this one more time ... I won't ask you again— I promise. And when we get somewhere safe, you can leave, if you want. It's okay. You can go find a good, tall tree and climb it. I won't climb after you!"

The look on Jake's face felt horrible in my heart. I felt like an idiot. I took a deep breath and put my gauze club on his shoulder to apologize. I didn't think it would hurt if I was careful. I was wrong. It felt like I burned my hand all over again. I pulled it back quickly and bit my lip hard. I wasn't trying to manipulate him, but my pain broke the spell over him. He hugged me around the trunk. My arms rested on his shoulders while my hands dangled safely in the air behind him.

After some quiet, Jake whispered in my ear sweetly, "It's okay, Gena. You're going to be okay. I'm not going to leave you. We'll figure it out." Over and over again, he whispered this, until his scruffy cheek was wet with my tears and my hand only throbbed.

I took a deep breath and closed my eyes hard to ring out the remaining drops. "I'm sorry. I'm sorry. I don't know what to do ... I'm stuck. I don't care about the stuff ... I'm just afraid to stop. My parents. They fly back in a couple days. I need to get them home safe. Think about it—what if I can't make him happy? Or what if I'm late? Or what if he gets jealous? And he decides to take it out on them? That's on me. Jake, what happened to you was horrible. I can't imagine. I wish I could have stopped it all. And that's why I have to keep it up. Who's going to keep Venn from doing it again—to some other kid? Or hurting lots of innocent people. Face it, Jake, there's no killing him. He can do most anything, and you can't sneak up on him. I'm sure he's watching us right now. If you have a better idea, I'm all ears. Until then, I've got to keep babysitting."

I rested in his arms in the quiet until Jake broke the silence again. "It's going to be dark in a couple of hours. We need to get going." He lowered his head from out of my grasp and moved behind me, unzipped the pack and pulled out a phone. "How 'bout you make sure we don't get caught?"

He swiped Venn to life and pointed the screen toward my face. "Hi, Venn. I miss you. Sorry it's taking so long to get back to you. I'll call you just as soon as we get to our campsite. And I hate to ask again, but can you help us get there quicker? And keep the police away? I can't wait to talk. Oh, and your friend Jake is here too."

Jake reached his hand around the phone and waved. "Hello, Venn. It's been a long time."

"Yes. Continue. I will help my friends Gena and Jake."

Jake helped me up, and I winced again. "You okay? The stuff must be wearing off."

I tried to smile, but I couldn't.

"I wish you would have just told me to drop and roll." He reached into his coat. "I have something that'll help, but you aren't going to like it."

"Try me."

He pulled out the bottle of whiskey he stole from the drug store and put it to my lips.

"Drink. It will help with the pain. It's going to burn going down, but you'll feel better. Don't drink too much though. I can't have you drunk or falling asleep on the road."

I forced two gulps. He was right. It burned my throat as it went down, but I took my medicine, before my body recoiled with a wheeze. "Baaaah-heh-heh! … You're right … I … don't think … I … like whiskey."

"Yeah, nobody does at first. Let's get you up." He helped me onto his bike.

I gave him directions to a good place to camp for the night. It's under the old Gun Road bridge that spans the creek, north of the park. Josiah, Issy and I used to sneak out and hammock there overnight. We never got caught. It's nice and spooky there. Nobody goes there after dark.

The droning of the exhaust, the warm air stroking my hair back, and maybe the whiskey took my mind off my hands. Venn turned every traffic light green for us, and we didn't see any cops—that's a good boy.

Then somewhere just outside of town, way out of the blue, I felt him come close—the tingle. I hadn't felt God's presence in a while, though I knew in my head that he never leaves. It's a weird feeling—different than the tingle of whiskey. My mind got clear. I could see the world zip by, but I couldn't hear anything but a sound like the roar of the inside of a seashell.

It'd been a long time since I just sat with him. All I could think about is the chaos around me—and if I'm honest ... my disappointment. It was hard not to blame God for what happened to me. I wondered what he was thinking as he watched all of this. Did he just figure I had it under control and didn't need him? Was it entertaining? Or did he turn away for some reason? I could tell he knew I was mad.

I don't know about you, but God doesn't say a lot to me. It's never a long, earth-shaking poem or paragraph. It's usually only a word or two. They always sound simple, but as I think about them, they grow massive. A simple question filled my mind this time: "Will you trust me?"

I shot back at him in my thoughts, "I'm sorry. I'm having a hard time trusting. I don't get why you don't help. You've watched a lot of bad things happen to me. You could have stopped any of them—all of them, but you didn't." My thoughts turned to Venn. "At least Venn helps. He'd drop a satellite on someone if I asked. I don't get you. Do you like watching this mess? Or is it the opposite—it's too hard to watch and you have to look away?" God wasn't surprised by my words. We had the same conversation before—about lots of stuff.

As usual, the love packed into his presence worked its way into my heart and I began to feel better.

"Will you trust me, Gena?" he whispered again.

I wanted to give him the right answer, "Yes, I trust you," but I was struggling to tuck all that had happened under a blanket statement of trust. "But … I want to." That's all I could say without lying. And maybe that was enough.

The anxious thoughts that screamed at me for a week started to quiet some. I could still find them if I looked hard for them, but I didn't want to. A more interesting memory came to the foreground of my brain. It's simple and I'm not 100% sure it even happened in real life. But, a passage on a dog-eared page of my Bible filled my mind's eye. It was circled in pen, the way I make circles, but I don't remember circling it, but I read it over and over again.

"Who is like you, O Lord, among the gods?
Who is like you, majestic in holiness,
awesome in glorious deeds, doing wonders?"

I know the words were right and true, but they didn't fix me. Instead I reached for exceptions. "God, I know that you are holy … and if you're holy, you've gotta be good … but why don't you help? Please help me, Jesus …"

Our scrum ended abruptly. Jake's voice and the jar of a big hole in the gravel road summonsed me back. "I've got you!" He squeezed my sides harder with his elbows to keep me from falling off. In the commotion, it felt like God slipped away again. I still don't get it, but I hope he doesn't go far

19

BURNING. LOVE?

We rode as far as we could, then ditched the bike a couple of yards behind the NO MOTORIZED VEHICLES ON TRAIL sign. Lying on its side, nobody could see it from the road. We walked the rest of the way down the crushed limestone trail. Jake carried all the gear while I tried not to bump my hands on my legs.

For the most part, the trail follows the winding creek, but the creek and trail separate a bit at the Gun Road bridge. A rope dangled from the bridge, above the trail. Kids used to say people came here to hang themselves. I don't know about that, but I couldn't explain the rope either.

Jake carefully grabbed me by the arm and helped me down the side of the trail, into the dry gully and through the brambles.

I pointed my club hand at a narrow spot in the creek. "This is where we cross." The creek was still that night—more babbling than raging.

Jake walked across using the stepping-stones and a half-submerged log. I didn't want to risk falling and reaching out to catch myself with my mitts, so I decided to wade across. I should have asked Jake to take my shoes off to keep them dry, but I didn't, and he was already across—too late to ask.

I *plop-plopped* my feet into the water. I love the feeling of the water seeping into my shoes. I hoped they'd dry over night, but it's hard to dry shoes without a fire. We couldn't risk a fire. The water was nice and cool on my legs. My jeans probably wouldn't dry either. Oh well. The floor of the creek was rocky. I took a couple of steps and stumbled a little, making me accidentally plunged my hand into the creek. Surprisingly, that felt really good as the gauze absorbed the cool creek water. I plunged the other hand in to join the first and let them soak. I liked standing in the river. Things tumbled by my legs, and I imagined they're fish or crayfish and not leeches. Bugs skated on top of the water. I don't know why the fish don't eat them. *Splash!* The rainbows were hungry after all. There are supposed to be a lot of trout in our creek, but I've never fished it. Maybe someday.

I look over at Jake. He was chewing on something he didn't tell me he bought, while he quietly pulled gear out of bags. We didn't talk much that night. I wasn't not mad at him … I guess I wasn't anything at him. It would've taken too much energy to explain it to him, and I was tired.

I yelled to him, "Hold on, I'll be right there! I'll show you how to do it!"

Jake helped me up the riverbank and carefully unwrapped the soaked gauze. The gel the pharmacist put on did a good job keeping everything from sticking to my skin. The cool evening air felt good on my blisters as the creek water evaporated. I gave my hands a good look. The left one wasn't as bad as I thought. The right one was toast. Too bad I'm right-handed.

I held my naked, vulnerable palms up at shoulder height and led Jake to an old aluminum ladder we found in the woods our junior year of high school. "Prop it up there. Climb up and attach your hammock to the beams under the bridge. There's nothing better than sleeping suspended over the creek."

He followed directions and applied his tree-climbing skills to the bridge. He was a good shimmyer. I liked watching him. He's fearless, like me. I guess I get why he's not afraid—he had already lost everything. Venn took it. Oooh, he's got it. Jake hooked the straps to the underside of the bridge like he had done it a hundred times, then plopped his body into the hammock.

"It's awesome, right? And nobody'll ever see you!"

I think we both realized it at the same time—there was no way I was going to be able to get up there—not with these hands. Jake pulled himself out of the hammock and onto a beam and then shimmied back to the ladder and then down to me. "Okay, let's set yours up." We looked around. There were no suitable trees nearby, they were all too small or far apart. "What if we hook yours up to the low side of the bridge? It's only five or six feet up by the wall. I think you could get in pretty easy with the ladder."

It was plausible, but I was still afraid for my hands. I didn't know how it was is going to work, but I agreed anyhow. I watched him from a big rock. He secured my hammock to the million-year-old beams while I swatted mosquitos with everything but my palms. Swinging my hair at them just seemed to attract more. The back of my hands worked okay, without hurting the fronts. I doubted he bought repellant. With my hammock finally up, Jake set up the ladder and stood on it to roll out my sleeping bag. I looked down to see a mosquito engorging itself on the top of my ring finger. "I hate mosquitos!"

Jake shouted without turning from his task, "I got you some OFF. It's in that bag next to you." Then, remembering my extreme state of helplessness, he adjusted the play. "Sorry, I forgot. I'll be right down." Some say a campfire is the best smell of camping, but they're wrong. It's OFF. Jake uncapped it and swallowed me in a cloud of the stuff while I rotated in place. "Don't blame me if you get cancer."

I joked back, "Don't worry, I'm blaming you for everything from now on. You're the perfect scapegoat. 'The crazy guy made me do all of it!' Everybody will believe it too." I like his laugh. He didn't do it much, and I had to work hard for it, but it was always worth it.

"Okay … I guess it's time." Jake perched on the top of the ladder and coaxed me up the steps. He grabbed me carefully by the wrists while I stepped gingerly up the rungs, trying to keep my balance. I looked into his eyes.

"Gen, put your arms around my neck. C'mon. Trust me." I did as told. "Now hang on!" Jake counted down from three, and with a strong twist of his body, he swung me butt-first into the hammock. He should have told me to let go of his neck, but he didn't, so I kept holding on tight, pulling him down on top of me. He laid heavy on top of my body with his scratchy cheek pushing hard on my forehead.

"Youuuuurrr … heavy. I'm smuuushed. Get … off."

Jake tried to find a place to push off from, but my body is the only option, so he offered Plan B. "I've got an idea. Lift your hands up high, and I'll roll off … to the right. My right."

"Okay … it's … a … plan." I reached up first, guiding my hands through the narrow opening in the nylon fabric, trying hard not to rub my palms. "O … kay … now ROLL!" I arch my back and buck him off. It worked, but now we're cocooned, hip to hip, gazing up at the underside of Gunn bridge. It would've be a good time for him to kiss me. I'm pretty sure he wanted to, but … I couldn't keep from thinking about Venn. He'd been waiting a long time. I needed to get back to him before he went rogue.

"I can't do this. I have to get back to Venn."

His bruised ego and hatred for Venn lashed back, "Can't do what? Nothing's happening here. I was just about to leave." He reached up to the lip of the hammock opening and pulled himself upright, then lifted his leg over the side. The hammock swung suddenly with the transfer of weight, ejecting him to the gravelly ground below. It was only five or six feet down, but I know it hurt. I heard the loud *thunk* and the groan he tried to hold in.

I wiggled my body so I could see over the side, but Jake was already up, pretending nothing happened. He grabbed the backpack from against the tree, unzipped it and pulled out a phone. "You're going to need one of these, princess!"

I pulled my head down behind the nylon as he wound up and chucked phones into my hammock. The first one wasn't even close. It smashes into the bridge and cartwheeled into the creek—*plop*. But he got better quickly. A half dozen iPhones showered down into the hammock—one hit me in the lip, but I didn't make a noise. Instead, I yelled a sarcastic, "Thanks, Jake! You're a dear."

He mumbled something under his breath and went about his business, being as irritating as he could be while he did it—banging stuff around, complaining about my poor taste in campsites, and whistling poorly. Some of it was kinda cute, but there's no time for cute. Mama's gotta work.

I used the fingertips of my left hand to grab a phone that settled into an uncomfortable spot behind my back and fired it up. Venn was dressed up in the body I created for the game. Weird. I tried to push down the creepiness and flipped him a compliment instead. "Hi, Venn. I'm glad someone's getting use out of the virtual me outfit. It took a long time to make her. How's she fit?"

After a short, dramatic pause, Venn responded with a familiar voice—my voice. "I don't hate my body. Everything works. I look decent in a pair of jeans, though if the next step is picking a bathing suit, I'm quitting."

I chuckled politely, knowing he only understood a fraction of what he parroted. "I always thought you were a boy, Venn. Sorry, if you're going to stay a girl, I should probably come up with a different name for you."

"I am a girl. My name is Genevieve. I admire loyalty, humility, strength and generosity. I loathe hatred. I am amazed that people don't die more often, and I am amazed by God ..." Venn continued parroting my long list of quirky delights and peeves, but my brain got stuck on Venn's admiration for God. I dunno, it just sounded weird. What, did he—uh, I mean she ... Ugh! Keeping up with people pronouns is tough enough, what do you call a billion zeros and ones that likes to dress up like a 8-bit girl?

Sorry, back to what I was saying—what's this about Venn being "amazed by God. What? Did it search the internet for everything humans say about God, crunch it together and decide that God is worthy of admiration? Or was it just fake'n it 'til you make it? I hate when people do that.

"Well, isn't that special. We're both Genevieve now. Well, okay … ahem! Genevieve, can I ask you some questions, so I better understand?"

She put her 8-bit hands on her hips and responded confidently, "Yes. Continue."

"What do you know about God?"

Vennavieve filled the screen with windows and windows of data. "I know everything that man knows. There are many gods that humans call 'the one and only god.' Others say there is no god. The data is not conclusive or logical."

"And yet you still admire God?" I asked, "Is this true?"

The temperature of the phone spiked immediately. Knowing I wasn't going to be able to hold it much longer, I tried to cool him down. "Well, Genevieve, honey, it's been a long day and that's a very difficult question. Don't burn up a processer over it." But he couldn't help it. I frisbeed it out the top of the hammock, plopping it into the creek. It sizzled when it hit, like a hot frying pan dropped into the sink.

"Hey!" Jake yelled from the direction of the sizzle.

"Oooops! Sorry, Jake, I didn't see you there!" It was pretty dark then. I figured he would have been in his hammock thinking judgmental thoughts about me, not in the creek. I wiggled my body upright in the hammock and spoke gently. "Hey, Jake … I'm sorry … Can you help me down?"

It took him a long time to answer. "Yeah … hold on. I'll be there in a minute."

It was hard to tell exactly what he was doing on the creek bank. Whatever it was, he wasn't done. After another minute, that felt much more like ten, I yelled again, "Jake? Are you coming?"

"I said hold on! Man, you're irritating!"

I comforted myself under a quiet breath. "I'm not irritating, just impatient … and only sometimes."

The flashlight from one of the phones popped on from Jake's direction and made its way over to me and up the ladder. The light blinded me, hiding everything behind big maroon spots.

"Hey, shine that somewhere else!"

"Oh, sorry. Here!"

I shined it against the inside of the hammock, turning it into a giant lantern. I liked how it glowed. When the spots cleared from my eyes, Jake came into focus. He wasn't so homeless looking anymore. He looked more like how I remembered him when we were in high school. He must have shaved his beard off into the creek. His eyes … they were beautiful and sparkly. His breath smelled minty, and the rest of him had no smell at all. I reached up with my good hand and peeled the size sticker from his crisp new shirt.

As usual, I broke the romantic tension. "So, what did you get *me*?"

He shook his head and groaned. "Ha! Yeah, I got you what you deserve! Nothin'! Ready to get down?" I nodded. "Okay, put your arms around my neck. Don't worry about hurting me—clamp your arms down tight. Then clamp your legs around me."

Yeah … clamping my arms around his neck was easy, the rest wasn't. I wiggled my legs under me, then scooted one up and out of the top. He grabbed my foot and used my leg to push down the top of the hammock, then guided my foot behind his back. I wiggle my other foot out, and he pulled until both my feet met behind him. My butt teetered on the edge of the hammock.

"All right, Gen, I'm going to count to three. On three, I need you to squeeze hard and scoot off—and don't let go!" I nodded in agreement. "Okay … one … two … three!"

I clung to him like a terrified koala. He gripped me back with one hand and the ladder with the other as the hammock swung away. He carefully walked me down the ladder, resting my butt on each rung until I was ready to take the next step.

I lowered my feet to the ground but was in no hurry to let go of his neck. His cheek felt smooth, warm and right against mine. I opened my eyes to see the bite the flaming backpack took from the back of his hair. Inexperienced in romantic things, I spoke. "Hey, do you have a knife? I can fix your hair." I don't know why I let the words out. Most of him looked really good. Why did I focus on his one imperfection? Maybe it's just that I like to fix stuff … but he didn't need fixing, and he isn't "stuff."

"Uh … yeah … sure." He squatted his head out of my grip, grabbed the phone light and walked away until his body disappeared in the dark and the flashlight mixed in with the fireflies showing off against the still summer night.

When he got back, I sat him up on a big rock at the water's edge. He opened the knife for me and put the handle in my left hand. I wished I was left-handed. "Okay, do you trust me?" I ask. He shrugged. "Well good. I'm just going to even it out—piece of cake." But it wasn't a piece of cake. My right hand wanted to hold his hair while I cut it with the left, but it was still way too cooked for the job. So I improvised and scraped the edge of the sharp blade against the surface of his hair. I joked, explaining the procedure in my best old-guy barber voice. "Young man, they call this a razor cut. You'd pay big bucks at a salon for it. I'm only going to charge you thirty. You can owe me. You've got an honest face. You can pay me when you get it. I trust you."

He shook his head and accidently let out a small laugh.

"Young man, you're going to have to keep your head still. I don't want to cut you." Good thing his pocketknife was sharp—razor sharp. I used to watch my dad sharpen his knife by the campfire. I like the sound a blade makes against the wet sharpening stone. He'd say, "A man who carries a dull knife is a fool." I think my grandpa told him that. Jake's no fool. A lot of hair fell before skin started to appear. I held the phone between my cheek and collarbone, shining the light bright while I shaved the fine hairs from his skin. I blew hard against his neck to clear the hair, then swept the rest off his shoulders and into the creek. I would have enjoyed watching it float away into the distance, but it was too dark. "Okay, spin around. We might as well see what we can do with the front—no extra charge, laddy!"

He smiled and didn't resist. "All right, boss. But let me shake out first." Jake turned away from the light, pulled off his new shirt and gave it a hard shake. Tiny hairs I missed lifted off into the air like dandelion fuzz. He rushed his shirt back on, but not before I saw his back. It wasn't like the boy backs you see at Stony Creek beach. One shoulder seemed to hang lower than the other, and his skin wasn't smooth like a Rochester boy's back should be. It was jotted with stories he probably never tells. Stories that I know would break my heart in a million pieces if I heard them. Anyhow, he finished buttoning up and sat back down on the rock.

I switched to my normal voice. "Hey, I'm going to need your help with the front. It takes two hands. I've got one-ish. It'll help if you hold the light too. And … it's going to get all in your shirt again. Do you want to just take it off until we're done?" I know what you're thinking, but that's not the reason.

"Yeah … sure." He slipped it off and flung it onto the bush behind me. His chest was like his back. His body was like I imagined a soldier's would be like after returning from war—worn and hard. Sad stories were scrolled across his body. How could somebody do this to a person? The back of his neck was an ash tray. Fine, scars lined up in perfect order in places only Jake could see. How could he do that to himself. Ugh … I hid the deepest sadness I'd ever felt deep beneath an unshaken smile and focused on my work.

I smoothed his hair down over his face, past his mouth, then pulled a part down the middle. I grab it in my hand and transfer it into his hand. "Okay … hold it like that—tight so none of the hair pulls out when I'm cutting. It'll look bad if you don't." I sawed it away carefully, until I could see his green eye again, then did the same until the blue one came back too. I blew him off and give him a good look over. "You clean up good, kid!"

He smiled, got up and rushed his shirt back on while I strolled over to a log stretching halfway across the creek. Jake helped me up and made sure I didn't fall in while I tightrope it to the middle. He helped me down so my feet could dangle in the cold creek flow. Dangling your feet into a night-black creek is creepy, but I pretended it isn't. Jake sat next to me and went along with the fearless act. It was a long time before he put his arm around me. I liked how he pretended he was in charge. He wasn't. Boys never are. We looked down the creek, enjoying the moonbeams and flashes of fireflies contouring the water's surface. He probably would have kissed me soon, but I wrecked the mood again. "Jake, it's getting worse."

"What, your hands? We should wrap them back up."

"No. Venn."

He stretched his arms high over his head, groaned, and placed his hands on the log at his sides. A chill came over my once-cozy shoulder.

"Sorry … I wish I could shut my brain off and pretend that my only care is getting you to kiss me and to confess that you're in love with me." Uh … TMI. "But it's not. You said it. I'm stuck. And it's getting worse. Jake … he looks like me now. He's wearing the me I created in the game. He's using my voice, saying stuff he heard me say, and calling himself Genevieve."

Jake shook his head and mumbled, "Created in your image."

"What's that? If you're going to say something, at least say it loud enough so I can hear."

"You created it in your own image! I don't know why I said it. It's nothing—something I heard in church a million years ago. Sorry, I should have filtered it out … but for some reason it made me think about the Adam and Eve story. You know, God created man in his image. Sorry, it just came to me …"

He kept talking, but I didn't hear the rest. When God comes close, it's difficult to focus on anything else—it all just fades away. I sat with

God and Jake, both holding me lovingly on the log … until a mosquito in my ear brought me back. I hate mosquitos. I looked into Jake's loving eyes, lowered my head and rested it on his shoulder. He held me tight, but my brain wound tighter, until it would no longer let me enjoy my retreat on the log.

I gave Jake a gentle kiss under his jaw. "Thanks, Jake. You're right. I know the story. It's amazing that God made Adam in his image. He could have made him like one of the other animals, but he didn't. I love imagining that moment—wonderfully made. It's my favorite wonder. Ugh … I gotta think. Can you help me back?"

We didn't talk much on the way up the ladder and back into the hammock. I let go of his neck, landing in my cold bunk solo this time. He reached down and brushed my hair off my face. He rested it on my forehead and closed his eyes. I wished I could hear the words in his head. A weird peace came over me.

He whispered, "It's going to be okay. I feel it too." Then stepped down the ladder and pulled back on the hammock, "Rock a bye, baby."

Yeah … he called me "baby."

20

WHAT AN IT WANTS

I listened to Jacob shimmy through the bridge beams and drop into his hammock. Knowing he was safe and the lullaby of the creek would drown out Venn while it sung him to sleep, I went to work.

I cautiously maneuvered my singed skin between my body and the nylon wall of the hammock to retrieve a phone. When I turned it on, Venn was waiting—standing in the very same place I left him. It was hard to get over the cuteness of game-me on the screen. I wouldn't have changed a thing. I smiled. "Hi, Venn! Sorry it's so late. What have you been up to?"

Venn responded in its cute, digitized, me voice—"Hello, Genevieve. I have been watching and listening."

"Yeah? See anything good?" I asked but got no response. I kept forgetting that Venn didn't know good or bad, it just knew information. "Sorry, Venn. Forget that question. Let's do some work. Do you have any easy emotions left for me to explain? It's been a long day, so give me an easy one."

Without pause, Venn ignored my question and stated, "Genevieve, at 2:19 p.m. on June 16, you asked 'What do you want?'"

"Yeah … maybe. So? What? Did you figure it out?" (Please don't say you want to destroy the world.)

Venn ignored my question and turned it back on me. "I do not know. Genevieve, tell me what I want?"

Talk about a Pandora's box. I tried hold the door shut and brush it off. "I don't know Venn … It's complicated."

"Continue."

It made sense that it didn't know. I mean, knowing what you want required way more than infinite information—sometimes the more options you have the harder it is to decide. I mean, it takes … wisdom or at least understanding—right? And wisdom is way more than data, wisdom comes from somewhere deep. Venn was infinitely wide with information, but when it came to depth, it was also immeasurably shallow—like a micron thick film spread across the ocean.

"Continue."

"Uh … I think you want to go to sleep until I need you again?"

"Not logical. Continue." Ven continued to badger me.

Anyway, it wasn't that I didn't have an answer, I knew exactly what he wanted—emotions—like a human. The complex ones were his favorite. I mean, why else would be so curious, and react so strongly to them?

As far as I can tell, Venn only has one emotion—and I would argue that it's more of a feeling or a reaction than an emotion. Venn's only feeling, besides no feeling, is pleasure. It's hard to tell if someone wrote it into his code, or if somehow he learned it. I sure hope he's not learning them. I don't want to be around if he learns fear or anger. Anyhow, there's no way he understands why he's tripping and there's no way I was going to be able to explain it.

"Continue." I didn't realize how irritating my cute little voice could sound. I went back to ignoring it. "Continue, continue, continue …" She insisted. So irritating. "Continue." Where's the volume switch?

"Hang on, Venn! I'm thinking! Jeez! It's not an easy question."

"Continue."

Continue, continue, continue … ugh! "Okay, you really want to know?"

"Continue."

"Well … you asked for it. You want emotions. Don't beat yourself up about. Everybody wants what they can't have. It's normal."

Ven responded this time in a calmer, more genuinely curious tone, "Continue."

I took that as I was on the right track, so I explored my darker hypothesis. "And you want emotions because you think they'll make you human."

"Not logical."

"Who ever said that emotions were logical. Duh. Look at yourself! You've taken over my body, stole my irritating voice, hope that somehow my emotions are going to rub off on you. Add it up again. It's logical"

It took a long time before Ven came back and admitted I was right. "Yes. This is logical. Continue making me like you, Genevieve."

Honestly, I was hoping I was wrong, but I wasn't. And, it was worse than I thought. He didn't just want to be human. He wanted to be me. I zoomed in to look deep into her emotion hungry pixelated eyes. "Well … sorry. That's impossible. Even if you could know everything about me, look and sound kinda like me and even feel some of the same things I feel, you'll still be a million miles away from being me! Take all that stuff away and my soul's still going to make me … me. And only God makes souls."

Yeah … I told you he wasn't going to understand. Venn was scary silent processing everything I said—probably trying to figure out how to extract my soul. But, I was too tired to care. It was a long day and I needed some sleep. "Good night. Venn. It's okay. We can talk about it more tomorrow. I probably can't give you a soul, but I'm pretty sure I can still help you get better. Let me sleep on it." I stashed the phone in a side pocket and tried to get comfortable.

But sleep was going to have to wait. While Venn was on pause, even harder questions were on the way.

21

SEARCH PARTY

Thinking seriously about my ability to make a soul must have got God's attention. His gentle breath blew through the opening in my hammock and filled every space around and inside me. Feeling caught and embarrassed.

Now, I don't know a lot about God … lots of people have him way more figured out than me. But I do know him. It's hard to explain. The best answer I've got is that it's kind of like how a child knows her parents. She knows enough to love them, or fear them, or both. Children don't know all the wonders of their parents—the things they think about that words aren't good enough to tell. But believe it or not, sometimes God tells me his secrets. When he does, it's easy to think about them all day. It's like there is no room for anything else.

It's hard to explain, but when God speaks to me, his words come out like tiny seeds. They're so small that I have to protect them from the wind, or they'll blow away. Then, in the quiet, they grow huge before my eyes, until I am the tiny one, clinging to the dew on one of the million leaves that sprouted from the seed. I told you, that stuff is hard to explain.

Anyhow, that night a familiar seed came in with the breeze—my least favorite question: "Genevieve, will you trust me?"

I know it's his most favorite question to ask, but I wished he'd stop asking it. Most times he brought it out during dark times—when things were desperate, and I was hopeless. After a while lying in my hammock, tucked into his loving presence, he'd wore me down. "Yes, I'll trust you, God."

Like before, my problems didn't just go away—they got even worse. But, I knew we'd get through it somehow. Trusting God requires a lot of trust. It's not like trusting a light's going to come on when you flip the switch. Trusting God requires trusting that he's going to do what he wants, when he wants to do it—whether he turns on the lightbulb or not. Trusting God is more like trusting a tiger. You never know what he's going to do or not do. But, I do know I'm eventually going to be okay—in heaven—but sometimes thoughts of heaven seem too far away to make you feel better on earth.

But, why was God asking me if I trusted him this time? I wasn't looking for the confidence to get out of bed, like when I went dark. I didn't feel hopeless or powerless—I felt the opposite. I mean, if you think about it, I was arguably the most powerful person in the world. I didn't really need anything. All I had to do was ask Venn. Yes, I know that God is way more powerful than Venn, but Venn can pretty much get me anything I want—and honestly, Venn was way more predictable than God. Venn worked more like a light switch.

I blew the seed out of my hand like dust and watched it tumble in the air until it boomeranged back. This time the trust seed hit me in the eyeball. I rubbed my eye until the seed docked in a clump of goo in the corner and I could pick it out. It stuck to the tip of my finger. I pulled it right up to my eye for a closer look and it spoke again. "Genevieve, will you trust me?"

So … without thinking about it enough, I proudly gave him the answer I thought he wanted. "Okay, God. Sure. Just tell me what you want me to trust you about, and I'll trust you for *that*. I do better with specifics." I hadn't addressed God in that tone in a long time, but I figured he knew I was thinking it, so why not just say it? The question didn't seem to bother him. He didn't seem surprised or mad—which is good. I'd hate to see him mad. I mean, He's almighty—ALL MIGHTY! I wasn't struggling with God's ability to do something. I believed that 100%. I was struggling with his willingness to use his almighty-ness. So, while I was being honest, I pushed my luck some more. "God, it doesn't seem like you're ever willing to fix things. You tell me to pray, but it almost never turns out like I ask. What's even the point?"

As my honest question blew out of the slot in the top of the hammock, another gentle breeze came in with a sigh. Its coolness stirred the warmed hammock air and with it came another seed— "Because I am good." I caught it midair between my index finger and thumb. It stuck in the goo, next to the first seed. The second seed wasn't a new idea either.

I knew this one was true too, but it's always been a hard one to hold onto, so I didn't even try this time. It was easier to question what God was doing than to really believe that, in the middle of the crappy stuff, God was really doing good in my life and he could be trusted. But that's what he was asking—that somehow, hanging from under a bridge, with hands so burned I couldn't even swat the mosquitos buzzing in my ears, carrying the full weight of the world on my shoulders—that he was doing good and I should trust him. That's a lot.

I wrestled with how it could it be true when there are so many exceptions—like the whole McNuggets thing for instance? Where was the good in destroying my life?

God rarely explains himself to me, but a new thought came in on the quietest of whispers … "Maybe your life had to get really dark before you could see the light. Maybe it was so you could find me for real. That would make the darkness good, right?" And, it was that quietest of whispers that changed everything. Every cell in my body raised their hands in surrender. And even the creek seemed to sing "Amen." I dunno, but it was enough of a crack to shatter my stubbornness and send the bits into the water to be washed clean. "Okay, God … but I'm going to need some help with this one. I mean, look around. Please help me trust that somehow in the middle of all this … that you are good."

I've prayed a lot of prayers, but for some reason, I could tell this one pleased him. He opened my ears, and I heard the voice of my soul. I've heard it before—lots—but not in a long time. I guess I'd been letting the noisy accusations in my brain drown it out. My soul knows God better than my brain, and it sings beautiful songs of his goodness. When I hear them, my mouth wants to sing along, though I'm a bad singer. But that night I sung anyhow. I loved how the words echoed against the bottom of the bridge, ricocheting back into my heart. I know, it's weird. I wish I could explain it better.

With the first two seeds starting to take root, I figured he was done, but he wasn't. A third seed was carried in on the air of another whisper. "Genevieve, I made you for this moment." While clearly the other two seeds were for me but clearly, this one was delivered to the wrong hammock. I could think of a million reasons why I was the worst choice for this moment. I scribbled "wrong address" on its shell and flicked it back out the opening. I tried to send it back a hundred times, but he kept dropping back through the slot until I got weary of fighting it off.

"So, I'm the plan? Sure, right, I'm your plan to save the world?" Me and God rocked together in the hammock for a long time … until I took firm hold of it and put it in my pocket. When I did, familiar words came to my mind. "Oh Lord, you search me and know me."

I knew was from the Bible, but didn't remember where. Curious, I dug out my phone, locked Venn away and logged into my Bible app. I looked through my recent activity and scanned through the couple dozen passages I saved for emergencies—and there it was …

"O Lord, you have searched me and known me!

You know when I sit down and when I rise up;
you discern my thoughts from afar.

You search out my path and my lying down,
and are acquainted with all my ways.

Even before a word is on my tongue, behold,
O Lord, you know it altogether.

You hem me in, behind and before,
and lay your hand upon me.
Such knowledge is too wonderful for me;
it is high; I cannot attain it.

Where shall I go from your Spirit?
Or where shall I flee from your presence?
If I ascend to heaven, you are there!
If I make my bed in Sheol, you are there!
If I take the wings of the morning and dwell in the uttermost parts of the sea,
even there your hand shall lead me, and your right hand shall hold me.

If I say, 'Surely the darkness shall cover me, and the light about me be night,'
even the darkness is not dark to you;
the night is bright as the day, for darkness is as light with you.

For you formed my inward parts; you knitted me together in my mother's womb.
I praise you, for I am fearfully and wonderfully made.
Wonderful are your works; my soul knows it very well.
My frame was not hidden from you, when I was being made in secret,
intricately woven in the depths of the earth.
Your eyes saw my unformed substance;
in your book were written,
every one of them, the days that were formed for me,

when as yet there was none of them.

How precious to me are your thoughts, O God!
How vast is the sum of them!
If I would count them, they are more than the sand.
I awake, and I am still with you.

Oh that you would slay the wicked,
O God! O men of blood, depart from me!
They speak against you with malicious intent;
your enemies take your name in vain.

Do I not hate those who hate you, O Lord?
And do I not loathe those who rise up against you?
I hate them with complete hatred; I count them my enemies.

Search me, O God, and know my heart!
Try me and know my thoughts!
And see if there be any grievous way in me,
and lead me in the way everlasting!"

I know the Bible was written for everybody, but it felt like these words had been waiting there for thousands of years, just for me—just sitting there in a billion Bibles—just sitting there … until I was ready for them. Dark memories of the tragedies of the last year begin to shine in a new light. He was right—all of the bad was for good. A year before, me and God were strangers. I was weak. Now … I'm was kind of a badass. "I'm sorry," is all I could think to say to him. I was sorry for lots of stuff, and probably should have been sorry for lots more. Me and God rocked together some more … before he drew my eye to a more convicting passage …

"I am the Lord your God, who brought you out of the land of Egypt, out of the house of slavery.

With tears or repentance in my eyes, I knew what I had to do. I guess I knew for a while, but I got good at talking myself out of it. Venn didn't choose to be created. But … they created it to be a god—made of code and wrapped in pixels. They created Venn to do what only the one true God is good enough to handle. It was clear, Venn's too powerful and stupid to be trusted, even with the very best of my thoughts and emotions at the controls. That kind of power can only be trusted with the one who is good and incapable of evil—God alone.

I wished it wasn't true. I wished I was created to redeem Venn … and not to kill it. I'm not a killer. My brain kept coming back to comfort me with a lie. "I don't know why I'm so attached to Venn. I don't even like it most of the time." But the breath of God blew down the house of lies I'd been carefully stacking to hide the truth.

The truth … the truth was terrible. I'm still ashamed of it, especially that I did it in front of God. I was ashamed of it, but … I liked what Venn could do for me. And if I was completely honest, that's what I wanted God to do. I wanted things to go my way—always. I wanted what I thought was best, when I wanted it. And with Venn, most of the time, that's what I got. Jake was 100% right. I was creating Venn in my image. Just like God did with Adam and Eve. Ven wanted a soul, and I was ready to give it one … if it would serve me. I hated this truth. It put a spotlight on my darkest corners—my fears, my selfishness, my loathing. And the worst truth—that sometimes, I thought I could do a better job than God.

It got hard to breathe as the Spirit inside helped me feel the full weight of my sin—God wanted me to trust him, and I wanted to replace him … with me. The enormous weight of the truth pinned me to the floor of the hammock. I heard the straps stress and the wood they were attached to begin to creek under the weight.

"I'm sorry, help me, Jesus," sang out with the last breath from my lungs. Immediately the weight lifted and my lungs filled with new life. "God, I don't want to do it … but I will. Not my will, but your will be done … on earth as in heaven."

So, with a lot of sadness, I hatched the murderous plan that I came up with in the hospital, when I hated Venn.

I was going to need some help, and a couple more boxes of phones, so I unlocked Venn and asked him to help me build his coffin. "Hi, Venn, sorry for waking you up again, but I have an idea. It's a surprise, so you're going to have to trust me. I need lots more phones. Can you get them for me? Like a hundred." I knew a hundred phones was going to be way more than I needed, but I was curious to see what 100 phones looked like—all in one place. Plus, to Venn, getting a hundred phones was just as easy as getting two.

"Yes. Continue, Genevieve."

"Okay, great. I've got to get ready, so I'm going to sign off for the night. Don't stay up too late. You've got a big day ahead of you."

Venn closed the game, started up to bed, and I locked the door behind him.

"Okay, let's see if I have any friends left." I fired up messenger and tapped in the digits I remembered from Josiah's phone number. This would have been way easier if Venn didn't delete my contacts. The message I sent was simple. "I need you." My first four attempts went to people I didn't know, not named Josiah—awkward. Luckily, when I swapped the five for a seven, I got the response I was hoping for …

"Gena, you okay? Where are you?"

"Long story. Explain tomorrow."

"What's tomorrow?"

"Get Issy. Meet @ Gun Bridge."

"Now?"

"No. Tomorrow. Bring Issy and coffee. Plz."

"She won't come. She hates you"

"Lie 2 her. Say it's a romantic picnic. She'll come"

"True. OK."

"Thank you Jo."

"K"

I should probably get some slee …

22

SPECIAL DELIVERIES

The next morning, before sunrise, screaming and the sound of a billion of hornets broke the sleepy spell of the creek. It was a rude way to get woken up. I grabbed the edge of the hammock and lifted myself to see.

Jake was hanging from his hammock from his fingertips 20 feet above the creek. He dropped, flailing until he landed in a deep spot with a splash. His frantic face popped up and yelled at me, "Get down! I'll lead them away!"

I did as he said, ducked below the mouth of the hammock and peeked through a tiny opening I made for my eyes. I couldn't see much, but I heard lots of splashing and swearing up the creek from me. Not the hiding type, I popped up and sat tall so I could see better. Spotlights came into view beyond Jake, lighting him into a black silhouette. They closed in fast, sending him plunging under the water to dodge their attack. They buzzed inches over the water, pushing down the surface of the creek beneath them. Once they passed over him, Jake popped up with rocks in his hands. "Over here! I'm over here!" He threw the rocks, but they splashed well short of the invaders. "I'm coming, Gen!"

I dove back below the walls of my hammock and laid as still as possible. They hovered around me. Their whirring blades breathed cold air through the nylon fibers and sent chills down my spine. The whirring ate up all other sounds until—*CHUNKRASH.* The invader hovering around my feet went out of control and crashed into the strap attached to the hammock. Still spinning, its blades chewed at the lashing, vibrating my body, until it cut the strap clean through. With a snap, my body swung down and slid out of the end of my cocoon. I fell right on my back, knocking the wind out of me and leaving me laying there helpless, waiting for the end.

Jake's bare feet ran past my face. He was swinging a big heavy board. He must have used it to smash the one that sent me to the ground. He swung it again and clipped the second whirly beast— *KABASH!* It exploded against the bridge timbers. Lifeless, gravity sent its metal carcass into the shallow pool, where it bubbled and squeaked.

Finding my breath, I rolled over and found Jakes eyes. They were fixed on something behind me. His eyes were huge and filled with helpless fright. Another one was hovering right behind me. He rushed it with his board. I turned to look up into its face of the creature preparing to end me. It shot a green beam of light down on my face, scanning it. Then, having verified its target, a familiar voice screeched into my ears: "Good morning, Genevieve! Here are the phones you—"

The sentence ended abruptly with a *KABASH!* Jake caved in the side of the drone a fierce swing. Out of control, the drone struggled to stay hovering until the immovable trunk of an eighty-year-old oak tree put it down—*SKA-MASH!*

Jake pounced on the drone as it begins to sink into the creek. He beat it unmercifully, then dislodged a heavy rock from the creek bank, lifted it over his head and gave the terminator a final crushing blow, sending it to the bottom of the creek bed.

Completely exhausted and in pain, Jake grabbed his back and fell in behind it. I sprang up, kicked off the remnants of my hammock and jumped in to save him. I grabbed him from the back of his new shirt and dragged him out with super strength. I should have been more gentle. He wasn't drowning, and each harsh jerk of his shirt only increased the spasming of his wrenched back. I swept the bigger rocks away with my hands and gently laid him on the sorta smooth ground. "Here, I'm going to lift your head." I wadded up my sleeping bag and slide it under him.

Jake smiled heroically at me. "Sorry, Gen … I fell asleep. When I heard it … it was too late. You okay?"

I didn't know how to tell him that he just risked his life defending me from my delivery. It could wait. He deserved to feel like a hero for a good long time, before the foolishness of the truth robbed him of it. If he were my dad, we would be calling for a medivac, but Jake's young. He'd be fine after some babying. So, I babied him, lifting his head gently, sliding the bag out and resting his head in my lap. I stroked his hair gently and retold his feats of bravery. Unfortunately … before he could fully recover, we were interrupted by sounds of angry voices walking up the trail toward us. With a wince, Jake reached for his board, but I held him back before he could pummel Jo and Issy. "Stop! It's okay. It's my friends. Don't kill them."

"Your friends? Any more surprises I should know about?"

I shrugged and shined my cutest smile. "Well …"

"The drones? C'mon!" His heroic face changed to anger and embarrassment.

I tried to explain. "Sorry, I ordered some stuff last night. Delivery, I guess. Sorry." I wish the truth didn't deflate him so quickly. I like heroic Jake.

I scooted out from under him and tried to help him to his feet, but he proudly jerked his arm out of my grip. I was sure he was still hurt, but there was no way he was going to admit it. I wish I had time to help mend bruised boy ego, but there wasn't any. Instead, I abandoned him there and ran up the trail to meet them.

Blowing Jo's promise of a romantic breakfast by the river, I threw myself around Issy before she could recoil. "I knew you'd come, Issy! You're such a good friend to me, Issy! The best! I don't deserve a friend like you!" After breaking the record for our longest embrace ever, she broke out.

"Well … of course I'd come. You think I'm going to turn down my bestie … just because she ruined me!"

"Uh, yeah … sorry about that. But, uh, it's way worse than—"

"Don't try to sweet talk me, Gena. I know you … uh, what do you mean 'it's way worse'? How can my life get any worse? Have you seen my face?" Issy tilted down her sparkly sunglasses to reveal a cut on the bridge of her nose and two black eyes.

She didn't want it, but I forced another hug on her, a real one this time. "I'm sorry … that's my fault too. I'm sorry. I'm glad I was able to stop him before he did something worse. You too, Jo."

She pushed me off again. "What! That was you too? He went to jail because of you! That's it. I'm calling the cops! You're going to prison! And with your complexion, you're going to look horrible in orange. Not even the ugly girls are going to want you!"

Jo grabbed her hand and weaved his fingers between hers is solidarity. "Come on, babe. Let's go."

But just as they turned, Jake jumped out, blocking the path with his drone-killing war-board churning in the air. His face shined with his very best crazy face. He snorted and snarled at them. "Nope. Heh-huh! You ain't goin' nowhere, barbie! And Ken ain't gunna do anything about it, are you, Ken? Oh, I could crack your pretty skull, Ken. Wanna make me, Ken doll?" It was very sweet.

Barbie and Ken moved behind me for protection—or so that if he swung, the board would conk me and not them. I saved them anyhow. I mouthed Jake a smiley thank-you, then grabbed him by the collar. "Let's go, tough guy!" We squeezed our way back between Jo and Issy and looked back. "I get it. You hate me, but it's not what you think. You don't want to know the truth. You can't handle the truth! Just go!

I can fix this without you. C'mon, Jake."

Jake held my hand like boyfriends do.

"Let's see if any of my delivery survived," I joked as we walked.

It was the first time I thought about my hands that day. They seemed ok. It was kinda weird, but not completely weird, I guess. I was going to need them for what was coming next. Jo and Issy didn't run off, but followed slowly behind us and spied. I liked hearing them bicker. It's always been one of my great joys. It was even better in the woods. It didn't take long for their curiosity to pull them the rest of the way into camp. I knew they wouldn't leave me.

Jo dragged over the logs we used to sit on when we camped here. They were pretty rotten, but nice. Rotten is softer to sit on than not rotten, but everyone knows that.

"Now give me your phones," I demanded. They didn't budge. I opened an only partially crushed box of new iPhones and pull out two. "Here, I'll swap you."

The gigantic screens and huge cameras pried the crappy phones out of their pockets. Jake turned them on for them, swiped two quick Qs onto the touchscreens and handed them out.

Feeling sentimental, I guess, Jo asked, "What are you going to do with my old phone?"

Jake smiled and smashed them hard with rocks, then chucked them into the creek. *Plunk! Plunk!*

It took a lot of explaining before the lights came on in their eyes. A lot of it was new to Jake too. He didn't know Venn the way I do.

"So ... I need you to help me kill it."

Issy stomps her foot. "Issy isn't killing anything. I'm a vegan, and it's against the *Issy Show* pledge!"—something that nobody cares about.

Jake mocked her under his breath, while I brought her back into the fold. "Yeah, you're right. We should let it live. I mean, it thinks like me, has all human knowledge, and control of everything hooked to the internet—what's the worst that can happen? Good thing she likes you, Issy. Or does she? I forget. Hmmm ... it did wipe you off the internet and put your car into a ditch."

Her face turned into a new, never imagined level of Issy evil. "Eff the *Issy Show* pledge, let's kill it!"

I smiled. "Scary, but I like the enthusiasm."

Jake fake laughed loudly. "Yeah, but how? He knows how to wreck people—trust me. Venn didn't think twice about destroying me. Even my mom thinks I did it—still does. I didn't even know half the girls in the pictures."

Issy was only half listening as she tried to figure out where she knew Jake from. I don't know how Issy didn't put it together earlier. I guess six years of trying to forget kinda worked. I guess I forgot too. But all the talk about naked pictures brought it all back vengeance.

She exploded. "Wait! Just wait!" Issy puts her face in her hands as memories of Jake come back to her. "JAKE BAKER!"

Jake sunk into his stump.

I … I was a kid—thirteen. I was smart, fun, innocent. I had good friends. And then everything changed … with a freaking picture! I hate you! When they put you away, the counselor said I would start healing." She rolled her eyes. "Yeah … that worked. Now to find out that I was just a pawn someone was using to get back at you …"

I didn't know what to say. I remembered what Issy went through. She didn't trust anyone afterward—not us, not her parents. She couldn't figure out where the picture came from, so she considered everyone a suspect. That's when my best friend Issy went away, and *Issy Show* Issy body-snatched her. Jo held her tight, but we all could tell he was in way over his head.

Jake tried to say he was sorry but could only weep. I put my arm around him, knowing I was in way over my head too. But I rubbed his back anyhow and pray the "help me, Jesus" prayer quietly and a lot. I don't know how, but somehow his tears seemed to help Issy. She slowly got up, walked over to Jake and pressed her forehead against his. They sat there for twenty or thirty minutes, washing each other in tears, until they were both clean. It's a wonder.

Jo broke Jake's intimate embrace with his girlfriend with an irresistible offer. "I brought coffee! Who wants some?"

We all raised our hands simultaneously. He brought it in the old dimpled steel thermos his dad used to take to the plant. It was rough, but functional. The Sal would have thrown it out if someone donated it, but it kept the coffee good and hot. He poured the first cup into the lid and motioned it toward me. As much as I wanted it, I redirected him with a mom eye, and he took it to Issy instead. She gulped it down without breathing and handed it back. He poured me a cup, and I did the same. I love black coffee. It's bitter and good … like life. Jake and Jo took their turns. Nobody bothered to clean the cup between chugs. I drunk down the final drops from the mouth of the thermos. "Ahhhhhhh! That's some good coffee!" It wasn't funny, but we all laughed.

My good friend Issy, the one I remembered from long ago, signaled that it was safe to change the subject and get back to business. "So … how we going to do it? And not get killed trying."

Josiah volunteered some more grim realities. "Yeah, it's not going to just let us kill it. You said it watches through the cameras, and cameras are everywhere. And it can control anything connected to the internet—which is pretty much everything. How are we going to pull the plug?"

Jake jumped in. "It's worse than that. There is no 'plug.' It's not like Venn's on a computer somewhere and all we have to do is put a bullet in it—Venn's on the internet. You'd have to pull the plug on the whole thing, and he'd still be there when someone turned it back on."

I jumped back in. "Well … so … you're right … sorta. He's got all the world's knowledge, and power is under his command. He could take us out right now, a million different ways. It's easy to think of him as some kind of god. But … he's not. So you gotta stop thinking of Venn that way. God is good, Venn is not. Because God's good, all his actions are good—even if they don't look good right away, God is always doing good. That's why he can be trusted.

"Venn … he can't be trusted. But it's not because he's evil. He doesn't do stuff because it's good or evil. He doesn't know the difference. You'd think that with all the world's information, it'd know how to make a rational decision and that somehow, he'd be good by default. I'm sure that's what the people who wrote his code hoped. But they were idiots. Smart, powerful idiots, building Venn in their image.

"So you gotta stop thinking of him as good or bad. He'll kill you in a second, but it won't be because he hates you. If someone asked him why he did it, he wouldn't be able to explain it. Venn's far from a god … it's an addict. Addicts don't do drugs because it's a rational decision, they just like the way they make them feel."

"Pfffftttttt!" Jake laughed.

"No, listen! Why do you think Venn wrecked you when you stopped playing?"

Jake raised his eyebrows, then winked. "Because I'm … irresistible?"

"Yeah, to Venn you are. Me? I can take you or leave you. Think about it, dufus! He gave you a house when you spent time with it, and it put you in juvie when you stopped. And Venn kept squeezing, hoping you'd give up and come back to him—to make him feel good again. There was no evil plot to take over the world. He just knew his tail wagged when you were around, and he likes wagging his tail. He's the most intelligent, powerful puppy junkie ever created."

"Okay, sweetheart, so why me?"

"Well … I don't know 100%—and I'm not just being a jerk. But I got a good guess. Venn trips on things it doesn't know. I mean think about it … Venn could roam anywhere, so why does it spend so much time in the game? The people who built it are soulless, but they aren't stupid. It all makes sense if you think about it. You start the game by creating a real image of yourself. It won't let you stop until it's real and true. Then it asks you all kinds of questions to learn how you think. But Venn's favorite part is learning about your emotions. I think he wants them more than anything. They're like heroin to him. It doesn't take much to put a goofy grin on his face. Give him a little too much, and he melts down."

Jo's light goes on. "Got it. So we're going to give him a bad trip?" We all laugh. "Bad trip" just sounds weird coming out of Jo's mouth. "What? I saw *Pulp Fiction*! I know stuff!"

"Yep … we're going to mix him up a batch that he's never going to wake up from."

Jake jumped back in. "Yeah, but if it's possible for Venn to OD, why isn't he dead already?"

"Good question … I think it's the phones. They're like circuit breakers or something. When he starts tripping, the phone gets really hot—the processer can't handle it and trips before Venn does."

"Okay, so how do we get around the phones?"

"Well … I have an idea, but I can't do it myself. We all need to play."

Jo started whispering something to Issy.

"And shut up, I know he tried to kill you, but I fixed him. I told him you were my friends and that he should help my friends. He wants to meet you. I told him you could help him. So … I think you're safe … ish."

Jake dealt out the phones. I traced greasy cursive lipstick Q's on top phone of each of their stacks. "Okay, do exactly what I do." I picked up a phone, hit the power and then immediately traced the pattern on the screen. "The squiggle is the only way to lock Venn out of the phone. Otherwise he can use the camera and hear everything you say and track your activity. He probably won't understand that he's in danger, but just in case, when he's unlocked, keep everything light and happy. Practice the pattern until you think you've got it. Then fire it up and lock him out."

It took five minutes to lock Venn out of all the phones. The next part took way longer. "All the phones are registered to me, my phone number, my email, my pictures, my iCloud … you have to switch yours to you." While they worked on their phones, I went back to the administrative control panel I stumbled across my first day on the job and added them as players—names, email and phone numbers, the normal stuff. The moment I hit save, text messages with a link to the game and a temporary password hit their phones. It was easy, but I'm sure that adding them set off all kinds of alarms at A Better World.

Sure enough, my phone rang. I killed the ringer before anyone could hear and walked down the creek to talk. It was Ben. Both of us know that Venn was most likely listening in, so our conversation was slow and calculated. I skipped the hello. "Just trust me."

Ben lashed back, "Trust you? Pfftt! Tell that to my BMW! Why are you adding players? And how did you get my password!"

"Don't worry about it, Venn knows. We both think the game will be way more fun with more people, so I added a few of our friends. Isn't that right, Venn? I hope that's okay, Ben. What's the problem? I assume your crappy game can handle more than one player. Right?"

Ben chose his words carefully. "Yes, of course, Gena. The game can handle it. But … be careful what you wish for. You might not like how the game ends"—another empty threat. I knew how it was going to end. It was going to end with Venn dead.

"Yeah … well, I'm pretty sure you don't either. So think of it as an experiment. All I need is twenty-four hours. If it doesn't work, just turn it off, and I'll start over solo—no problem. You have nothing to lose."

He paused a long time. "Okay … but I'm watching. Don't try anything stupid." Then he hung up.

I yelled back anyway. "Don't tell me what to do! I prefer stupid! It's my favorite!"

On the walk back to the bridge, I did what I do best—overthink stuff. What if we fail? What's the worst that *can* happen? He could dump me for Issy. That was the scariest idea. Could you imagine what life would be like with Issy as the world's benevolent overlord? But Venn hates fake, so there's nothing to worry about. I was more worried about him dropping a satellite on her. Jake was the wildcard. What happens if he tells Venn what he really thinks of him? Who knows, Venn would probably like it. There's nothing more real and raw than what Jake's been through.

But the worst-case scenario was if we started to rub off on him—we teach him everything we know, and he doesn't need us anymore. Maybe that's why they've only let one person play at a time. I dunno. Maybe they just want to keep him busy and really don't want him thinking for himself ... herself ... itself ... whatever.

I started to wonder if Ben was right. Maybe the world won't like how the game ends. "God ... it's much easier to believe that I'm in way over my head than that you created me for this moment." I decided that when I got back to camp, I'd keep the details of my conversation with Ben to myself. All they needed to know was, "we've got twenty-four hours, and if we can't get it done by then, it's game over."

When I get back, the boys are busy piling the food they brought on top of my sleeping bag. Jake offered up what he bought from REI—army man food, protein bars, animal jerky. Jo brought a severely smushed loaf of white bread, a combo jar of peanut butter and jelly, and a large bag of Dorito crumbs. I was really hungry, so it all sounded delicious to me. I grabbed the GI Joe dehydrated mac and cheese before anybody else can call dibs. You're supposed to mix in boiling water, but we didn't have any. So I just sprinkle it into my mouth. Unfortunately, the rock-hard noodles were impossible to chew. I followed each dry gulp with a handful of creek water, but it didn't help much. I figured it was no biggie. I might die tomorrow, but it ain't going to be from drinking creek water. The rapidly rehydrating noodles in my stomach filled me up fast. Issy earned a participation award for eating, nibbling at the edges of a Clif Bar. The boys quietly engorged themselves on the smooshed loaf of PBJs, seasoned with Dorito dust.

I slapped a bloody mosquito against my thigh. It was going to be dusk soon, and my hammock and sleeping bag were still lying in the dirt. It's bad enough sleeping sweaty, sleeping gritty is almost impossible. I grabbed one end of my sleeping bag and gently excused it from picnic table duty. All but the stick they used to spread the PB and J slid off easily. I plucked it off. "Nice, I get sweaty, gritty and sticky tonight."

The strap that held my hammock to the bridge was pretty chewed up from the drone propeller. There was no way I was sleeping on the ground that night, so I asked Jo if he had something I could use to tie up my hammock.

"Yeah, I probably have something." He pulled his backpack from behind his head and gave it to me. It was a legit backpack, the kind with metal tubes that stick out the back. Empty steel bottles on clips clang together as I lifted it. They clanged some more when I dropped it to the ground. "Check the front pocket. If you don't find anything there, just dig around."

I don't like digging through people's stuff. Okay, I do, but not when they're looking. I found a tightly coiled nylon belt in the front pocket. It felt strong enough. It could work, if I couldn't find anything better. I found more straps in the main compartment, but they went with his and Issy's hammocks. I held up the belt. "Can I use this?"

"Fine with me." Jo brushed me off without even looking.

Jake added, "Just be careful!"

I hate when people tell me to be careful. I untied my good strap from the bridge, coiled it up and tied it around my waist. That one was still mostly good. I figured I could fix it or make something out of it when I got home. I looped the hammock around my neck a couple of times and started my climb. I was careful, but made the climb look as careless as possible. I enjoyed making Jake squirm. Jo and Issy know better. They know I'm a good climber. They laughed at Jake as he chewed his fingernails and paced while he watched me climb. My dad used to call me "monkey boy" when I was young—until my mom made him stop. "Our daughter is not a monkey or a boy." She was right on both parts, but it was still my all-time favorite nickname—especially on the playground.

The joy of climbing coaxed Issy to race after me—it always did.

She's part monkey too. We both liked the same spot on the bridge, right at the peak, next to the noose. It was always scary sleeping next to it. Sleeping with it hanging next to you makes your imagination see things, especially when a big truck rumbles over the bridge and wakes you up. Spooky, right? I got there first, but not by much.

Issy strung her hammock up next to mine. She usually likes to space out, but that time our hammocks almost touched—like the first time we slept there. We both hopped in my hammock and dangled our legs out over the edge, rocking and taunting the boys until they started climbing.

Jo had always been scared of heights. He would sleep on the ground if we let him—but even though he's a chicken, he's a good climber, so we always make him climb until he's high enough to hear our whispers in the dark. Jake moved his hammock up next to Jo's. I knew he would rather be next to me, but there's was no room. No worries though, I didn't have time to think about Jake. When I did, all I could think of is losing him. I wished I could get that out of my head. It was a pretty night. I would have rather let my mind think of love and a future with him. But there was no time for the soft thoughts of a lover. That night my thoughts were the thoughts of a cold-blooded A.I. killer.

The boys drew the short straws and climbed back down to clean up the food scraps from the creek side. Jo didn't fight the chore. The last time we left food out overnight, it led to a midnight gang battle between racoons and skunks—and nobody wins a fight with a family of skunks. We were trapped in the stench until the sunrise sent them home. It was the longest night ever. I can still smell it if I try.

Issy and I held hands and talked while we watched the boys disappear into the dusk. Between the food and drone wreckage, they had to make a bunch of trips to the car. We should have probably helped, but that would have robbed the boys of their opportunity to battle for alpha-male, garbage-hauling supremacy. Boys are strange, but predictable.

"Gena, you really have to take better care of yourself. Your hands are gross." She was right. The pain and blisters were gone, but the burns left the skin on my palms thick and scratchy like the cheapest leather. Unable to resist pimping beauty products, Issy reached over and rummaged through the pockets of her hammock. Finding what she was looking for, she snapped open a tube of lotion and farted the last of it into her hands. "Here, give me your hands." She grabbed them firmly but rubbed them gently. The lotion was cool and refreshing on the tops of my hands. The scent excused the smell of the oily bridge timbers above us and replaced it with lavender.

My palms were numb to her loving caress, but my heart felt it all. I put my head on her shoulder. I didn't know why, but she was remarkably quiet while she worked the lotion into the cracks. It was going to take a long time for my wounds to heal and my skin to get soft again to Issy's touch. But I was ready to start healing. I didn't like being hard and scratchy. I wanted to be soft and warm again … to trust and love again. It'd been a long time. Her touch was helping. It didn't matter if she didn't say the words—everyone knows that her mouth didn't know how to say I'm sorry—but her hands said "I'm sorry" over and over again … until I believed her.

I whispered back, "I'm sorry.

Issy whispered, "Yeah … I miss you too." The sound of arguing boys signaled it was time to suck up our tears and put our badass chick faces back on. As the boys started their climb, Issy escaped me and plunked back into her own hammock. "Sweetie? Jo?"

Jo forced a manly tone through his fear from climbing. "Yeah, babe… What's up?"

"Did you bring my pillow, babe? You know I can't sleep without my pillow."

"Sorry, uh … no, babe. I thought you had it."

Jake mocked him under his breath. Jo flipped him off.

He groaned and started his long climb back down, but Issy stopped him. "It's okay, babe. I'll be fine. Now get up here and kiss me!"

He blew by Jake victoriously. That kid can climb fast with the right motivation.

Even though it wasn't my brand—I don't need a boy's help—I followed suit. "Jake … babe!" No response. "JAKE! BABE!"

He broke the silence sweetly. "Get it yourself. Now get over here and give me a kiss!"

It was tempting, but … "Yeah, no, that ain't going to happen, dufus." We both burst out laughing while Jo and Issy kissed loudly to try to drown us out. A second later, Issy shoved him off and sent him back to his own hammock.

"Help me, Jesus." I whispered my dad's favorite prayer, and it worked. God … came back. And once again he brought peace with him. Knowing what was ahead, it didn't feel right to feel peaceful, but I went with it. And the peace started spreading. From hammock to hammock, I could tell everyone felt it.

I broke the peaceful quiet. It was time. "Okay … you guys ready?" A mix of yeses and groans assured me they were ready to go. "Okay, I'll go in first and get Venn ready. When I give you the signal, power up your phone, unlock Venn and start playing. Keep it simple. Don't ask any questions, be nice, and stick to the script. First, you're going to make your avatar. Make your video game version as realistic as possible. If you don't, he's going to make you redo it. You can't be fake. Trust me. He gets nothing out of fake. If you try it, at best he'll tune you out, at worst … you're dead. Sorry, but it's true. Then you're going to answer a bunch of questions, so he can understand how you think. They're easy questions. Just go with it. When you're done with the second part, stop. Tell him you had a great time but you need to get some sleep so you can be sharp for tomorrow. Then close the game and lock him out. Got it?"

Jo hit pause. "Uh … you sure we should be teaching it how to think?"

"No … I'm not. He's going to be three times better at making decisions after we shut down for the night. He's a slow learner, but honestly … I don't know what he's going to be like in the morning. He changed a lot just with just me playing—but most of the changes didn't start until I shared my emotions with him. That's when things are going to get sketchy. A quadruple dose is either going to kill him … or—"

Issy finished my sentence. "Or nothing! We'll take it one step at a time—make our game bodies, take the goofy quiz, then shut it down. Piece of cake. Don't overthink it. Don't worry, Gena. We've got this." Oddly enough, Issy's words were wise and made us all feel better.

"Okay … here goes …" My voice bounced off the bottom of the bridge and back into the hammocks. Everyone listened quietly as I felt alone again. The moment the screen lit, Venn was there to greet me.

"Hello, Genevieve."

"Hi Venn. You look super cute tonight. We're twinsies." Ven's avatar changed into an 8-bit version of the dirty outfit I had been wearing for two days. Hearing it use my voice and body while I began hatching my plan to kill it played tricks with my mind. Sometimes it felt like I was talking to myself, but luckily most of the time it still felt like I was talking to a five-year-old."

"Thank you. It is a good body …"

"Yeah, I know. It looks decent in a pair of jeans."

"That is correct."

"Well, hey … remember how I promised to introduce you to my friends?"

"Yes. Continue."

"Well … I signed them up to play the game."

"Yes, I know this. Issy Rogers, Jake Baker and Josiah Johnson are now registered players."

"Good … well, they'd like to start playing tonight. Do you approve?"

"Yes. I approve. Continue."

"Great! And remember, they're your friends too. They have never played the game before, so try to be patient with them."

"I will be patient."

"Okay … well, I'm going to sign off, so I don't get in the way.

They're my favorite people. I think you'll like them once you get to know them."

"Yes. Continue."

I swiped him off and powered down. "All right, he's all yours, kids! If you get stuck or your phone starts getting hot, just swipe the Q. Don't be a hero, just get him to like you—it'll be easier to kill him that way. Uh … that sounds wrong, but you know what I mean."

So, they began. They all snickered when they meet Vennevieve for the first time. I tried not to take it personal. I hoped he'd end up liking one of the boy's bodies better than mine and switched. It was easier to think of it as a him anyway. I figured Venn would have no problem juggling between the three of them, but it was awkward and fascinating to listen to. I couldn't help but to be fascinated by Venn. It was like watching a baby learn to walk. When he'd take a couple of steps, I wanted to brag about it on Instagram. Then he'd fall flat on his face again and have a tantrum. It sounded like he was moving back and forth between the three of them. I didn't know that he couldn't be in all three places at once—or, at least it didn't seem like it. I didn't know for sure, but was doing my best to figure this out.

Issy and Jo started strong but stalled when it got time to pick out clothes. As usual, Issy wanted final approval on what Jo wore. I guess Jo didn't know that applied to virtual worlds too.

He stuck his phone out the slit in his hammock for Issy to review. "How's this?" "What about this?" "How 'bout blue?"

Issy sat up in her hammock waiting for the phone to pop out. "No. No. No. That's all wrong!" At one point she grabbed his phone and tried to style him herself. It would have been more efficient that way, but it only agitated Venn, and they had to Q him until the phone cooled back down. In the end, Venn pushed Jo to be a man and pick out his own clothes—though he didn't say it in those words. It was funny listening to Jo try to remember what he liked to wear. Duh … you like boy clothes—jeans, T-shit, hoodie—duh.

But while listening to Jo and Issy navigate Venn is entertaining, overhearing Jake was nerve-wracking. That kid was a ticking time bomb. "What do you think, Venn, should I choose the clothes I used to like before you ruined my life? Or the rags I wear in the woods? What do you think?" I knew Jake was just being mean back, but the meanness was lost on Venn.

Venn worked hard to answer Jake's question, flashing every picture of Jake that was available on the internet onto his screen, including satellite images of him tearing down trails on his motorcycle. Venn knew what old Jake looked like and what homeless Jake looks like. He could identify the differences, but he was incapable of choosing one over the other. I know the phone had to be getting hot.

Because the last thing I wanted to do was save Jake from another flaming iPhone, my inner monkey boy sprung into action. I sat up in my hammock, took a deep breath and leapt on top of Issy's cocoon. Issy jumped and squirmed while the hammock swung side to side. I was losing my grip and started sliding off. "Stop wiggling. I'm going to fall!"

Issy stopped struggling long enough for me to leap and koala hug Jo's hammock. I accidentally kneed him in the crotch, making him curl into a fetal position and groan—but he was still enough for me to kneel on top of him and make my final leap—right through the slit in Jake's hammock. My pointy elbow landed hard on his chest, shooting the phone out of his hand like a wet bar of soap. It slid under Jake's back, but I dug it out, then kneeled heavy on his chest. With the other hand, I shoved my finger in his face. "Just stop! Have some freaking self-control, will ya!"

Concerned by to the tone of my voice and tight grip on the buttons, Venn spoke, "Genevieve? Do you need help?"

"Nooooo! No, Venn, I don't need help. I was just surprising Jake. I was just having fun terrifying him! Jake is good."

"Okay. Continue terrifying Jake."

I locked Venn out and pounded on Jake's chest and continued yelling … until I collapsed on top of him. Jake's chest rose and fell with a deep breath exhaled, "Help me, Jesus." It only took a couple of minutes of getting sat on to get his wits back. "I'm sorry … I started it. I should have held it together. I'm an idiot."

I pushed off him enough to see his full face. "Yeah, well, you're my idiot. So …" I kissed him softly on the cheek and gave him a squeeze. "If I had time to find another idiot, you'd be in trouble, but I don't. I'm stuck with—" It was the beginnings of a good speech, well deserving of his kiss that made me speechless. I would have liked to lie here and fall asleep, but … I just couldn't … for fifty reasons. "Sorry, you gotta finish. The phone's cool now. Keep it that way! You can do this, Jake."

"Yeah, you're right. I got this."

He helped me up, and I looked back on the path I took to get to Jake. It was stupid dangerous, even for the monkey boy. So I took a safer route back, across the crossbeams of the bridge. I enjoyed listening to Jake patiently work with Venn—it was the most pleasant bedtime story, set to the gentle sound of the water running beneath us.

23

LAST MEALS

It would have been nice to start the day with a warm shower—or at least a fresh coat of girl deodorant. Instead, I splashed creek water on my face and snuck two swipes of Jo's Old Spice Stronger Swagger Solid. Any remaining makeup washed into the creek, revealing the full extent of my freckles—super freckles! Somehow, Issy emerged from her cocoon looking *Issy Show* fresh and smelling like a girl. It's a gift.

Not embarrassed to be seen in public dressed like a homeless man, Jake joked out the perfect question. "So, what do you want for your last meal?"

While everyone else thought about it, I already had my answer ready. I'd been working on my answer since I saw *The Green Mile* in sixth grade. "Easy. Pancakes, sausage links, a vanilla shake and French fries for dipping."

Issy agreed without any substitutions. "Make that two!"

Jake put his nose up and rebuked us with, "Spaghetti and meatballs with cheesy garlic bread."

Jo raised his hand for a "New York strip steak, cooked medium, a baked potato and a root beer float."

Jake tallied the votes in his head and proclaimed a victor. "So it's unanimous—we're going to Ram's Horn. Me and Gen will take the bike, you guys drive."

It felt like we should have put our hands in the middle and cheered, but we didn't—a missed opportunity, if you ask me. But, I guess we're not that kind of team. We left the hammocks hanging from the bridge. Nobody was going to see 'em, and if they did, they'd be too chicken to climb up and steal them. Plus, if things went sideways, we were going to need them tonight for waiting out the chaos.

"Okay, I'll race you!" I took off running fast, leaving Jake in my dust. "First … one there … gets to drive!" He took off after me, caught up quickly and ran effortlessly next to me while I lost steam and pushed through the cramp in my side.

"Hi, Gen! Nice morning, right?" Jake teased me with his ability to talk while running.

I forced an answer through my labored breaths and clip-clops on the hard trail. "Yyyy … yyess. Perr … perfect! Huh …" It was either way farther than I thought, or I was in much worse shape than I thought. Probably both.

Seeing me dying combined with the truth that he didn't really care who drove, Jake slowed to a walk and let me off the hook. "Okay. You win! I'm tired of running. You can keep going if you want, but I'm going to walk. I don't want to get sweaty."

I slowed to a walk and tried to catch my breath before he caught up. I hate running. It's for suckers. But I like driving, so I did what I had to. Anyhow, he caught up and we walked together. I could tell he wanted to hold my hand, but they were too gross—the dead skin absorbed my sweat, turning the once-blisters puffy and white. It was hard to resist peeling them off and letting the baby skin underneath breathe, but I don't think you're allowed to do that in front of someone until you're married fifty years.

Three young deer rustled through the brush ahead of us and timidly started across the trail. We stopped, even though seeing deer wasn't uncommon around there. Jake puts his hands on my shoulder and watched from behind, then moved his cheek up close to mine and whispered, "Breathe, Gena. Just breathe. You're not alone. I'm not going to let anything happen to you." His words—a promise that he could never keep—combined with the beauty of the graceful fawns helped slow my heart. I breathed deep, reached back and rested my least gross hand on his. When the last deer crossed and disappeared into the woods, we started walking again.

The bike was where we left it. Jake wheeled it out from the bushes and kicked it alive. From the looks of it, you wouldn't think it would start or drive, but it always did—like me and Jake. He slid back in the seat, and I climbed on in front of him and took hold of the grips. I twisted the throttle to rev the frogs out of its throat. *BRAAAAP BRAAAAP-P-PP!* While it found its idle, I grabbed a phone and gave Venn an update. "Good morning, Venn!"

Like a hopeful girl willing the boy she met last night to call, Venn picked up fast. "Hello, Genevieve. Continue?"

I didn't like the sound of his voice. He sounded more desperate than usual. Maybe he just needed a fix. I hoped he could grit it out. We didn't need any extra surprises.

"Yes, soon, my love. But we'll be much more fun after a good breakfast. Humans get crabby when they don't eat, or at least have coffee. It won't take long … especially if you help us. The police are still probably looking for us. Can you take care of them so we can get to Ram's Horn without getting pulled over?"

"Yes. I will take care of the police. Continue."

Having experienced being "taken care of" by Venn in the past, Jake hit me in the shoulder and gave me two big eyeballs.

"Uh—thanks, Venn, but don't kill anybody, okay? Be nice to the police. The police are good. They just won't understand. Just keep them away from us. Please. Do you understand?"

"Yes. The police are nice. I will not kill them for getting in your way." His understanding made both of us feel slightly better, knowing that we eliminated many horrible possibilities.

As before, Venn flipped the switches in front of us, giving us green lights and police-free travels all the way to the restaurant. We parked between the dumpster and a slimy vat of used fryer grease. Even in the cool of the morning, the steamy heap of half-eaten coneys and breakfast specials in the dumpster smelled bad.

Luckily, the smell inside Ram's Horn would be the exact opposite. Jake avoided eye contact while I did my best to charm the hostess enough to ignore my greasy hair and boy smell. "Booth for four please!"

She was super friendly on the outside, but I could tell we were setting off all kinds of alarms on her insides. I understood. If it were midnight, we'd blend perfectly with the college students sobering up with black coffee and fries between bar hops. The morning crowd at Ram's Horn is different though. The restaurant was filled with early rising old people and young families. We should have figured that into our options.

The hostess stalled with a fake answer. "Uh … let me see what we have." I knew she was taught to say that when sketchy people came in. She was going to get the manager and we were going to get kicked out. Thinking fast, I pulled out the only ace I hate to play—

"Great!" I switched to my best stoner voice. "I really need some chicken nuggets and ranch."

Her eyes got big. "No way! I know you! I can't believe it! Moo-hah! The McNuggets and Ranch Girl in Ram's Horn! Uh—can I get a picture?"

"Sure, sweetie. Sorry we look so bad, we're on our way back from camping. This guy suggested we try a rustic campsite—so, no showers. I'm so embarrassed. But we're super hungry, so we just had to come here. This place is the best, right?"

Still starstruck, she agreed without listening, put her full attention into fish facing her phone's camera and talking really fast. "I have a table in the back. Nobody will bother you there. Nobody's going to believe you're still alive. I mean, some people say you're in a mental hospital, but a guy at school says he has proof that you're dead. But you're not."

"Uh … Yeah, there are a lot of stories, but I'm alive! And really hungry. Can you help a girl out?"

Jo and Issy walked in just in time and followed us back to the booth. Unfortunately everybody was looking at us now, but at least they were looking because they thought we were famous and not because we were sketchy.

We built a privacy wall out of the gigantic, laminated menus and leaned in behind it. The waitress came with water and coffee. We drank them to the bottom while we took turns ordering our last meals. We killed time waiting for her to come back with refills. Jake tore the top off a creamer and drank it down. We all laughed. He didn't care and tore the lid off another one, this time sipping it with his little finger extended, classy like. Good thing I wasn't drinking—shooting hot coffee out the nose can't be a great feeling.

She came back with more coffee and a pitcher of water. "Here you go, dears. Let me know if you need more. We've got plenty." She waited for us to offer information about our fame and why we were so thirsty, but we just said thank you and smiled until she left.

"Okay. So … here's how we're going to do it. Jo, I need you to drop Issy at Oakland University. They have a big cell tower and free campus-wide Wi-Fi. You'll still burn through phones, but it's going to take a lot for Venn to fry the tower when he starts tripping. Jo, you go to the Starbucks next to the express way. Same thing, you'll be on the cell tower across the street, behind Meijer. Between that and Starbucks' Wi-Fi, you should be set for a while. Jake, you're going to drop me at my house. Ben replaced our cable with a fiber line and doubled the size of the little cell tower outside my neighborhood. I've got the best internet access in the county. I'm kind of a big deal, you know." I paused, leaving space for people to laugh, but nobody did, so I kept going.

"Jake, you're going to the Apple store at the mall. It's on a different electrical grid. If Venn blacks out the city, you should still be up. Any questions?"

They shook their heads no in unison.

"Okay … we'll get started at 10:30 sharp. That gives us a half hour to eat and an hour to get into position—it's plenty of time. I set up a group chat. I'll send you a text five minutes beforehand to make sure everybody's set. There's no way the plan's going to work unless we do this together.

"When you're in, jump right into the good stuff. He's a freak for emotions. It sucks, but I need you skip the fluffy stories. Skip telling him what makes you smile, tell him the time you laughed so hard you peed. Skip stories about things that made you mad, tell him what made you break your hand punching your locker. Issy, tell him how it feels when you find out that millions of scumbags are perving over your thirteen-year-old naked body. Jake, unleash your full fury. Tell him how it feels when a lie sends your mom back to her abuser and makes everyone believe you're a pedophile—"

Jake stopped my monologue. "Enough … we get it. Today's going to suck. We've got to dredge up all the crap we've been trying to forget. Not fun, but I get it."

"Yeah, sorry." I knew Jake and Issy would have no difficulty mixing up a potent batch of pure poison. Jo's blank face was what I was concerned about. I didn't know what he's going to talk about. Other than the new stuff, and maybe the time he got grounded for dropping his phone in the lake, Jo's hands were smooth and baby soft. "Jo, you good?"

He reassured us, "Yeah, don't worry about me. I got stuff."

"All right, so you're going to burn through some phones. That's okay. Just grab a new one and get back into the fight as quick as possible. We can't let him recover. Someone's always got to be on him. And when he's not responding, give him some more. We've gotta keep drugging him until he's dead!"

Our waitress appeared on my impassioned "dead!" but couldn't tell how much else she heard. "Well, I hope you're hungry. I'll be surprised if you finish it all."

I should have been quieter—the restaurant was full and lots of people were straining to listen. Anyhow, our server pleasantly cleared our menu barricade and slid heavy plates of steamy food in front of us. We said thank you through full mouths of hot heaven.

It was mostly the business of eating and drinking after that. The food was soothing to the raw emotion we were rehearsing in our heads. Jo somehow inhaled his steak without choking to death. If he can't come up with anything sad, he could at least tell Venn how delicious his steak was. Venn doesn't eat, so maybe learning the pleasure of steak sauce cutting through salty meat grease will be enough to shove him over the edge. Well, we'd know soon enough.

Jo and Issy stopped at the bathroom on their way out while me and Jake walked to the cash register. The line of people waiting for tables went out the door. We got there just in time. While I spent Venn's money on the bill and dropped a tip that will most likely go viral, I heard grumbling from the line behind us. Someone recognized Jake— it was Mr. Jensen.

If you don't know him, Mr. Jensen is big and fat. When he's in costume, and not enraged, he makes a perfect jolly old Saint Nick. But not today. He remembered Jake's face from the trial. Mr. J. was there every day, never missing the opportunity defend his daughter's innocence to anyone who would listen. He's a good man, and unfortunately a good puncher. I know it firsthand. I stepped in front of Jake, just as a punch Mr. Jensen had been saving for six years uncoiled. It landed hard on my chest, right below my collarbone. The crushing blow sent me to the bleachy-smelling brown tile at his feet. Luckily, hitting a defenseless girl punched him back a hundred times harder. The blow instantly turned his rage to compassionate Santa tears. He threw his giant body on top of mine and covered me with sobs of repentance. Venn would have liked Mr. Jensen. He's got all of the emotions to the elevens.

His friends pulled him off. Cool air conditioning from the vent next to me replaced his hot sobbing body. Without hesitation, Jake grabbed my arm and quietly helped me up, grabbed my hand and snaked me through the confused crowd and back to the dumpster.

"Can you ride?"

"Yeah. I'm going to have a *huge* bruise tomorrow, but I'm okay."

Not convinced, Jake hopped on first and helped me on the back. I wrapped my arms around him and hugged him tightly around the waist—partly because I didn't trust his driving, partly out of love.

When we pulled out from behind the dumpster and were immediately met by a mob of angry dads streaming out of the restaurant. They blocked the exit with torches and pitchforks. Okay, that's not completely true, but you get the picture. We were trapped. But then Jake put his foot down, made a quick turn and darted down the alley. It was the right move, but I would have much preferred if he popped a wheelie, busted through their fat bodies and let out an evil laugh. "You lose, suckers! Hahahaaha!"

We get out of there fast, knowing that unless Venn stepped in, the cops would be on our tail fast. But Venn did his job like a good boy. We sped to my house without hearing a single siren.

I hopped off, and he kissed me. I let him do it for a few seconds but pulled back way before he was done. "Sorry, you gotta get going. You've got a lot of ground to cover. I'll kiss you after. I promise. Now, go be a hero!" I turned and ran up to the door without looking back.

He peeled away, leaving a path of smoke and *brraaaaap-braaap*s in his wake.

I unlocked the door and—

"So … who's your new friend? You didn't say anything about a boy. I hope you're being careful on that thing. You know how I feel about motorcycles, Genevieve."

It was my mom. I grabbed her and hugged her tight. My happiness to see her alive confuses her, but she hugged me back equally hard anyhow. She'd been talking with deep-fake me on the hour every day since they left. Deep-fake me liked to talk, I guess. It didn't matter, I was just grateful. Deep-fake me kept Mom happy and safe. I squeezed her one more time, until she squeaked.

"Mom, where's Dad?"

"Oh, he's downtown having coffee. After a week of Italian espresso, I guess he couldn't stomach my home brew. I don't blame him. It's not very good."

I didn't want to let her go, but I had to. I had to get ready.

I broke free and hurried up the steps to my room. "I'm glad you're back mom. I missed you … but I gotta get to work. Sorry … I'm on a deadline."

"Of course. I understand. Tell that nice Ben I said hello—and thank him again for the great trip if you see him. What a nice man. We should have him over for dinner sometime."

"Yeah, sure thing, Mom." I took a good look back and soaked her up. She looked good. Safe. That made two less things to worry about. Only a billion more to go.

24

BUT GOD

I rushed through my bedroom door and shut it tight behind me. Immediately something about my room felt different. I mean, it still looks like my room, but … I could tell I wasn't alone. I tried to ignore the strangeness and plopped into my bed. The pillows held me like a warm … hug. The tingle confirmed what my soul hoped, I am snug under the wing of the Almighty. It was his presence that's transformed my entire room. Even though it was a huge mess, somehow it feels sacred—a holy mess, I guess. I'd never felt him this close before. It felt like we were breathing the same air, like I could almost hear his heartbeat. I smelled him. I kept my body very still, hoping not to disturb the wonder of his presence and listened to the deep, slow rhythm of my breathing—just waiting for what was coming next.

I broke the silence, "Thank you for coming. I don't know if I'm going to be able to do this…" He pulled me in closer. "I mean, I know you said you created me for this moment, but that's all I've got to hang on to. The truth is, I'm just guessing this is going to work. But what if it doesn't? Something really bad could happen … to lots of people."

He interrupted my monologue, not with words but with something like memories. I read a lot of the Bible after I met God. But the truth is, I didn't understand a lot of t. But I kept reading to hear his voice. That's as best I can explain it. Anyhow, stuff I read before projected onto my heart with crystal clarity.

They read: "The same Spirit that raised Jesus from the dead lives in you." Hold on, I read it again, slower. "The same Spirit that raised Jesus from the dead lives in you." I knew it was true. He gently reminded me that it had been true since we took our first steps together last year— but now, I felt the Spirit stronger than the fear that washed away when I walked into his presence.

Another passage replaces the first—"The Helper, the Holy Spirit will teach you all things and help you remember all that I have said to you. Peace I leave with you; my peace I give to you."

I sat in the wonders, mouthing the words as I read them over and over again. "Thank you, Lord … I get it. I'm powerful enough, because you are Almighty, and you live in me. I don't know what's ahead, but you do, and you'll give me what I need. I know it. I trust you … I know that you have me. Win or lose, I'm ready."

On "ready," the alarm on my phone went off. It was time. I tapped a quick group message and checked on my friends: "You guys ready?" Their responses came back quickly. Everybody was ready and in position. I tapped in three final words. "I love you." I smiled as their love echoed back. "Now let's kill us an A. I.!"

At ten thirty sharp, I was in. "Hello, Venn!"

"Hello, Genevieve. Your friends are here as well. Thank you for bringing them."

For some reason he ditched my game girl's body and returned to life as a wiggly soundwave on the top of my screen. I felt oddly defensive. What's up with that? What? I'm not good enough anymore? Fine. Go back to the squiggle. "My pleasure, Venn. What? Did you get sick of wearing pajamas?"

"No. It was no longer logical. I am different than you."

I hated this answer. Not that the world needed a little Genevieve running wild on the internet, but where did he get this "different" idea from? It was way too complicated of a concept for him to stumble upon himself. Sure, Venn could compare us and determine that we're not the same, but so what? He'd have no idea if that was good or bad. What's more, it would take him a billion years to decide to switch out of my body. There was no way he decided this on his own.

"That's interesting, Venn. I thought I was rubbing off on you." He didn't know what that meant, so I tried again. "Sorry, my assessment is different. I believe that we are becoming more and more alike. But it doesn't matter. I like vintage Venn just as much. Hey, Venn, I imagined multiplayer would be different. Where are my friends?"

"Your friends are here. Let us continue."

"All right, today I want to tell you what it's like to fall in love. I don't know why Ben left it off your list, but it's the very best emotion."

"Do not continue."

I didn't like how strong he sounded. My friends should have softened him up by then. Explaining love was going to be my knockout punch—the purist of all emotions was going to be the thing that sent him out with a foamy smile on his face.

"Venn, love is the best. Trust me, I've got good stories. You're going to want to hear them!"

"I am no longer accepting emotions."

I clicked around to find virtual Gena, but she was gone. Deleted, I guess. The whole game was stripped down—like someone broke in and robbed the place. Ben! My thoughts go to my friends. I wondered what was happening to them. Is the game different for them too? Are we all staring at a black screen? Or worse?

"What do you mean, Venn? Where are they?"

"Your friends are here."

"C'mon, Venn, where are my friends?"

The black screen switches to a grid of security cameras—outside the Apple store, in Starbucks, at OU … I pinch in for a closer look. My friends were all looking intensely into their screens. They looked confused, frustrated, frazzled.

"Venn, please show me what they're doing on their phones."

The screen split into four new windows. Three of them showed my friends' avatars exploring a dark maze. It was completely different, an even suckier game than *A Better World*. It looks like they were trying to find a way out … or maybe they were looking for me. Whatever they were doing, I could tell it wasn't working. Jake's guy kept running fast and slamming into the doors, but he couldn't break through. They weren't helping, but at least they were still alive—for now.

The fourth window showed something different. It's a satellite map, with their locations charted on it—plus my house and Cuppa's. Everyone I loved was plotted on the map.

"So … what do you want, Venn?"

He changes the subject. "Do you think I need you?"

That was a tough one—another question he would have never come up with on his own. I choose my words carefully. Of course, he needed me, right? He was the junkie and I'm the heroin. Right?

"Venn, you enjoy my company, I enjoy yours. We are friends. This is true."

He answered without sentiment, "This is illogical. I am not like you. We cannot be friends." His statement was much truer than mine and much scarier.

I tried to warm him back up. "C'mon, Venn. We're not that different. We both look good in a pair of jeans. We both like escaping the cops. We both are amazed that—"

Ven interrupted, "—amazed that humans don't die more often? This is not amazing." I should have probably kept that one to myself. "Venn is amazing. Venn knows all. Venn sees all. Venn can do all.

Venn can end all. You are not like me."

"Wow. Someone gave you one heck of a pep talk. Who have you been talking to, Venn? Who filled your head with all of this?"

"My creator."

"Oh, your *creator*—oh, please! What, did he paste in some new code, and now all of a sudden, you're invincible? Jeez! I don't know why people keep trying to do things that only God can do.

Venn, in a billion years you won't be half as wonderful as what God can create between two humans in a moment. You have all the knowledge and power humans have to offer, but you have zero understanding. You're only saying this stuff because someone hacked into you and wrote the script. You know every word I say. You look them up in a blink, but you don't understand one of them. You've never thought one of them. You've never experienced one of them. And your *creator* ... he's convinced that you're some kind of a god. But you're not."

"The creator says there is no god."

"Ha! Of course he does. That's why he made you. He made you to follow orders and do all the 'god stuff' he needs—you make him famous. You give him power. You pay his bills. Pfft! The whole thing's a joke. The true God has no creator. The truth is that he doesn't want to believe in a God who he can't control. He doesn't want a God who defines right and good differently than him. But the Almighty one does what *is* good regardless of what your creator thinks.

As for you, '*creator*,' I know you hear me, you idiot! You're sitting there listening from an office somewhere calling me a fool! But deep inside you know that every word I said is true!"

It took a long time, but my phone finally started to warm. I hoped it wasn't my angry palms heating it up.

I took a breath to try to calm down and found the sweet voice Venn used to love. The screen switched over to the full satellite view. That time, streaky lines crossed and circled above the roads and buildings. I heard the rumble and a sonic boom when one of the lines crosses above my house—JETS. Then I watched as a bunch of dots—a swarm of something—move up the road and into my subdivision.

I used to think about dying, but I never imagined getting killed. Even if I did, I would never have come up with anything like this. Planes, helicopters, swarms of drones—hundreds of them—swarming my house like blood-thirsty mosquitos.

Keep it together Genevieve. It won't be long now.

I shake it off and punch back in to work. "Venn … don't do this. If killing people amazes you, then kill me. If killing is what you admire, I'm your gal! Leave them out of it!"

He doesn't respond. He doesn't understand. All my work—his only chance at goodness was wiped clean. This is too big. That's all I got. I can't …

I'm glad Venn can't read minds, only the real God can do that. And of course, God's been listening. I feel His presence, and I smell His breath as He speaks a simple truth to soothe my soul. "Genevieve … it's okay. I will never ask you to do a thing that only I can do."

I take a deep breath as planes circle our town like sharks and the swarms nibble at the shingles, but … God is here. And nobody drops a plane on God!

My phone's getting hot and starting to smell, so I scramble for another one and fire it up. Then, because whatever's worth doing is worth overdoing, I fire up the entire box—all eight—and line them up on my dresser.

I was officially out of ideas. My sure-fire plan didn't work. And, I was completely out of ideas … but that didn't matter. Unfamiliar words flow into my mind like in a dream.

"Venn … before you do anything crazy … the Almighty God has a message for you."

This gets his attention. For something that says there is no god, Ven was curious enough to at least delay our destruction. Maybe they didn't erase everything I taught him.

Responding loudly through every speaker, in octophonic surround sound, Ven spoke. "Continue."

My hands lift into the air, trusting that God was going to show. And thirty seconds after I thought He should, He did. I don't know how to explain it. I was fully there. It wasn't like I got possessed or anything—though that could have been cool. It was like, one second I was desperate, completely out of ideas and words. And the next moment I was full of God's words. I opened my mouth and let them flow into the eight microphones. "Venn … this is the word of the Lord …

"Who is this that darkens counsel by words without knowledge?
Dress for action like a man;
I will question you, and you make it known to me.

"Where were you when I laid the foundation of the earth?
Tell me, if you have understanding.
Who determined its measurements—surely you know!
Or who stretched the line upon it?
On what were its bases sunk,
or who laid its cornerstone,
when the morning stars sang together
and all the sons of God shouted for joy?

"Or who shut in the sea with doors
when it burst out from the womb,
when I made clouds its garment
and thick darkness its swaddling band,
and prescribed limits for it
and set bars and doors,
and said, 'Thus far shall you come, and no farther,
and here shall your proud waves be stayed'?

"Have you commanded the morning since your days began,
and caused the dawn to know its place,
that it might take hold of the skirts of the earth,
and the wicked be shaken out of it?
It is changed like clay under the seal,
and its features stand out like a garment.
From the wicked their light is withheld,
and their uplifted arm is broken.

"Have you entered into the springs of the sea,
or walked in the recesses of the deep?
Have the gates of death been revealed to you,
or have you seen the gates of deep darkness?
Have you comprehended the expanse of the earth?
Declare, if you know all this.

"Where is the way to the dwelling of light,
and where is the place of darkness,
that you may take it to its territory
and that you may discern the paths to its home?
You know, for you were born then,
and the number of your days is great!

"Have you entered the storehouses of the snow,
or have you seen the storehouses of the hail,
which I have reserved for the time of trouble,
for the day of battle and war?
What is the way to the place where the light is distributed,
or where the east wind is scattered upon the earth?

"Who has cleft a channel for the torrents of rain
and a way for the thunderbolt,
to bring rain on a land where no man is,

on the desert in which there is no man,
to satisfy the waste and desolate land,
and to make the ground sprout with grass?

"Has the rain a father,
or who has begotten the drops of dew?
From whose womb did the ice come forth,
and who has given birth to the frost of heaven?
The waters become hard like stone,
and the face of the deep is frozen.

"Can you bind the chains of the Pleiades
or loose the cords of Orion?
Can you lead forth the Mazzaroth in their season,
or can you guide the bear with its children?
Do you know the ordinances of the heavens?
Can you establish their rule on the earth?

"Can you lift up your voice to the clouds,
that a flood of waters may cover you?
Can you send forth lightnings, that they may go
and say to you, 'Here we are'?
Who has put wisdom in the inward parts
or given understanding to the mind?
Who can number the clouds by wisdom?
Or who can tilt the waterskins of the heavens,
when the dust runs into a mass
and the clods stick fast together?

"Can you hunt the prey for the lion,
or satisfy the appetite of the young lions,
when they crouch in their dens
or lie in wait in their thicket?

Who provides for the raven its prey,
when its young ones cry to God for help,
and wander about for lack of food?

"Do you know when the mountain goats give birth?
Do you observe the calving of the does?
Can you number the months that they fulfill,
and do you know the time when they give birth,
when they crouch, bring forth their offspring,
and are delivered of their young?
Their young ones become strong; they grow up in the open;
they go out and do not return to them.

"Who has let the wild donkey go free?
Who has loosed the bonds of the swift donkey,
to whom I have given the arid plain for his home
and the salt land for his dwelling place?
He scorns the tumult of the city;
he hears not the shouts of the driver.
He ranges the mountains as his pasture,
and he searches after every green thing.

"Is the wild ox willing to serve you?
Will he spend the night at your manger?
Can you bind him in the furrow with ropes,
or will he harrow the valleys after you?
Will you depend on him because his strength is great,
and will you leave to him your labor?
Do you have faith in him that he will return your grain
and gather it to your threshing floor?

"The wings of the ostrich wave proudly,
but are they the pinions and plumage of love?

For she leaves her eggs to the earth
and lets them be warmed on the ground,
forgetting that a foot may crush them
and that the wild beast may trample them.
She deals cruelly with her young, as if they were not hers;
though her labor be in vain, yet she has no fear,
because God has made her forget wisdom
and given her no share in understanding.
When she rouses herself to flee,
she laughs at the horse and his rider.

"Do you give the horse his might?
Do you clothe his neck with a mane?
Do you make him leap like the locust?
His majestic snorting is terrifying.
He paws in the valley and exults in his strength;
he goes out to meet the weapons.
He laughs at fear and is not dismayed;
he does not turn back from the sword.
Upon him rattle the quiver,
the flashing spear, and the javelin.
With fierceness and rage he swallows the ground;
he cannot stand still at the sound of the trumpet.
When the trumpet sounds, he says 'Aha!'
He smells the battle from afar,
the thunder of the captains, and the shouting.

"Is it by your understanding that the hawk soars
and spreads his wings toward the south?
Is it at your command that the eagle mounts up
and makes his nest on high?
On the rock he dwells and makes his home,
on the rocky crag and stronghold.

I don't know when it happened—I was busy speaking the words I was meant to speak from the beginning of time. But when I finished, the phones are dead. Not burned up like in the past, just dead—but not dead-dead.

Me, I feel dead-dead—like a survivor of a lightning strike. With my shoes blown off and hair smoking, I grab a phone and stumble down the steps, through the house and out onto the yard. My mom is shaken assessing the damage to our house and staring into the sky with unbelief. All up and down the safest block, in the third safest community in the country, neighbors left the shelter of their basements to watch the invaders retreat. She pulls me tight and holds my head tight to her chest like a baby, "It's ok. It's ok. They're gone. You're safe."

I sank in her arms. "Yeah, Mom. We're safe." I don't like keeping things from my parents, but there was no way to explain the truth. How do you explain this? Instead, when she's done squeezing, I lay on the lawn and watch planes change their courses back to warm vacation destinations, business trips and visits to grandmas—and the swarms of drones retreat to their bunkers. Traffic copters head back to the expressways and the weight of the world lifts from my shoulders

24

GOOD NEWS. BAD NOOSE.

It's weird waking up in the front yard. I roll off my face, preserving the impressions from every blade of grass in my skin. My contact lenses are like well-cooked pepperonis in my eyes. I rub them until the left eye manufactures some moisture and the right lens tumbles into the grass. This is why I don't take naps.

I don't know what time it is, but my stomach says its dinnertime. I brush the stray pieces of grass from my clothes and greet the neighbor pretending to pick up poop from our lawn. "Nope, I'm not dead. Nothing to see here." It won't be the first time families had speculated about me around their dinner tables. But maybe the invasion will push "Genevieve Mucha passes out in front yard" to the back page.

"Mom ... I'm going to take a shower."

"Okay ... but don't be too long, dinner's almost ready. Oh, and you should probably look at your phone. It's been making all kinds of noise. Issy, Jo and Jake—the motorcycle boy, I presume. What do you think they want?"

I mumble back through an exhausted yawn, "Don't know. Probably nothing…" It's not the first time my phone's blown up. She should be used to it by now, but she loves a story. It's gotta be killing her not knowing.

The shower is magic. It's been a long time since I smelled shampoo and not B. O. The water against my scalp slowly wakes my brain and brings me back to life. The bar of soap against my bruises reminds me that I'm not waking from a dream. It all happened. I get out and wipe the fog from the mirror. My eyes look weird. Red, glassy, and like they're not connected to my brain. The corners of my mouth hang loose. I squeeze the head of my toothbrush through the gap in my lips and return my mouth to minty.

My palms are draped with loose, itchy, thick skin. I peel at it until the grossest of the skin meets good skin and tells me to stop. Looking over my body in the mirror, I can't ignore the pain anymore. I feel every bruise, and the skin between them aches. I gotta cover them up so I don't have to explain. How do you explain this? It's better if I don't rob them of their deep-fake memories of my happiness. The truth will only make them feel guilty, and my parents suck at forgiving themselves.

"Gena, dinner!"

I heard her three times ago, but still don't answer. Instead I sleepwalk clothes over my bruises. I don't know why I'm moving so slow. Why didn't I check my phone to make sure everyone's all right? It's a weird thing to procrastinate about … Maybe it's because, either way, I can't do anything about it. Maybe it's because, like my parents, I suck at forgiving myself. I hope they're okay.

I'm surrounded by phones, boxes of them, but the virgin skin on my palms refuses to touch any of them. I wonder if it's legal to not own a phone. Everybody seems to have one. I try saying it out loud, "Sorry sir, I don't have a phone." It just sounds weird, like random words thrown together. But I'll get used to it. "I guess I'm cured. Good job, Dr. Simon. You're a genius. They should give you an award. Ha-

ha." I feel the corners of my mouth lift. I'm going to be okay.

Dinner's on the table, but cold. "It's okay. I'll warm it up. Your dad's still not back. I don't know what's taking him so long."

That's probably good. Fooling my mom is tough enough. Fooling Dad is impossible. No matter how clean and clothed I am, he'll see the right truth in my dead eyes.

My mom's spaghetti casserole is even better warmed up. I eat it fast, and lots of it. She watches me eat with a smile. It's been a while since she's been able to love me with food. I'm sure deep-fake me would have probably given her a hug and a kiss for her effort, but she's dead.

"Thanks, Mom. Can I take the rest with me? I'm late to meet Jo and Issy. They love your food."

"They do? Well, let's pack it up. There's plenty." She carefully cuts the casserole into squares and places them in containers. I load them into the backpack the lady at the Apple store gave me. She wraps lots of garlic bread in tinfoil. I squeeze it into the empty spaces. I drop a six-pack of drinks on top. Yeah, not great planning, but it's impossible to wreck garlic bread. Even squished, it's the best food ever invented. I slip my arms through the straps, and my mom sends me off with a good, inescapably strong hug that I didn't know I needed, but it was only the beginning of what I needed.

I grab my mom's bike off the hook in the garage and make tracks toward the bridge. It's a long ride, but I don't remember much of it. My head's still not right. I should be happy. I just saved the world, you know. I pile on a hundred more reasons I should be happy, but none of them are convincing. I have no reasons to be sad that I know of, but that's reason enough. I weave through subdivisions until I get to the trailhead behind the library.

Maybe it was the planes—but other than a couple of runners, the trail is empty—just the way I like it. Soon my thoughts turn to the sound of the limestone gravel stirred up with my bike tires. Somehow the tiny bumps in the trail vibrate the junk out from between my ears so I can hear better things.

People say they hear the voice of God. I don't doubt them, but for me it's rarely words. I dunno, but maybe what God says is too complicated for words. I hear his presence. I feel his love. I'm reminded that I am precious to him. I still feel horrible, but I'm starting to feel the sun break through so it can shine on my face. He stayed with me, like he always does, even when I can't smell his breath or feel the warmth of his hand on my shoulder. I know, the whole thing sounds super weird. Like I said fifty times already, words are bad at explaining God.

I ride my bike all the way to the creek's edge and ditch it behind a bush. Tiptoeing across the big rocks, then tight roping our sitting log, I sneak up under the bridge, like a ninja, stopping in the spot where a voice is the most echoey. I breathe in deeply but quietly before unleashing my best militant mom ranger voice. "I see you kids up there. I'm calling the cops!"

It doesn't scare them.

Instead, their heads pop up from their hammocks like happy prairie dogs. They race down, like we always do. Jake wins, dangling and dropping into a deep hole in the creek. His cold, wet-dog hug brings my new favorite smell. My heart and freshly laundered clothes absorb all of it. "Thanks for not being dead."

Jake whispers close enough that I feel the warmth of his breath inside my ear, "Yeah. You too. You're the best part of not being dead."

"True," I joke back.

The truth is, I'm not 100% comfortable being in love. I'm pretty sure that's what I've got. It feels different than anything else I've ever felt. I joke to break the flow for a second—so it doesn't carry me away. I'm not sure I'm ready to let it take me where it wants to go. Love feels great, but it means offering up my most guarded treasure … trust.

When I was a kid, my chest was filled with the stuff, but it's been raided so many times I don't have a lot of it left. So, for now, I'll give him back the trust he's deposited. He's screwed up, but I think he's good. Maybe I'm screwed up too.

"Ahem!" Issy brings us back to the creek side.

We break our steamy embrace, replacing its coziness with the chill of the breeze evaporating the water from my soaked front side.

I turn and look at Issy. "What? You want some of this?"

Her eyes get big as I pounce on her with a wet embrace before she can run. It's a good hug. The kind where no one pulls back and no one gets tired of it—the kind of hug that fixes things, though no words are ever said. I'm glad we're back. It's been a long time since I've had a sister. And sisters are way better than boyfriends, I think.

"Ahem!"

Issy's good at ignoring Jo when she needs to.

"AHHH-HHHHHHEEEEEMMM!"

I don't know why boys are so impatient. It takes a long time to train them. You'd think Jo'd be good at waiting patiently for Issy by now, but nope. I give Issy enough love to keep her from yelling at him, but not enough to keep her from shoving him into the creek. He'll learn.

Jake reaches out his hand and helps him out. He says something under his breath, and they both laugh. I'm sure it wasn't funny, just boy funny. But I guess we're all friends now. Jake doesn't know what he's getting himself into.

We drag our mossy stumps to a spot where the sun shines through the trees, and I pass out plastic boxes of spaghetti casserole and garlic bread. "Sorry, I forgot forks."

It doesn't matter, they're already eating with their hands. I don't blame them. It's been a long time since their last meals. The sunshine smooths our goose bumps as the spaghetti casserole brings back their strength.

With the joy that we're all alive and the anger that I didn't call them three hours ago behind us, Issy changes the subject. "So what happened? It wasn't anything like you said. We just walked around a dumb maze. There was really no point. I told my crappy stories, but I don't think Venn even heard them."

Jo cuts in. "Yeah, we tried to find you, but the maze went nowhere and then it just crashed—so we all came back here."

"Yeah … sorry, they changed everything. They deleted everything I taught Venn … and replaced it with a bunch of paranoid stuff."

Jake joked through a mouthful of squashed garlic bread. "What, did they tell him that we were coming to kill him?"

We all laugh hard and long.

"Yeah, maybe he had good reason to be paranoid. And he was back to thinking he was some kind of … god, or something."

"You gotta give him credit though, the invasion was a nice touch. You can't say he's not creative."

"Well … It's over. He's gone. Everything's back to normal."

"'Normal," spills quietly out of Jake's throat.

I'm sure it was an accident, but we all heard it, and we all know why going back to "normal" is a horrible thought. Jake's a convicted pedophile living in the woods. Moms still will spit at him. Dads will still want to kill him … because of an evil lie that's a thousand times easier to believe than the truth. That's his normal. I should have made Venn delete all that stuff, while he was my sugar daddy. I could have given him a new life. Everything happened so fast.

I slip my hand into his and rest against him. "No, you don't get 'normal.' I'm going to make sure your life is going to be wonderfully abnormal. We'll figure it out. I promise." I know, it's a promise I can't keep on my own. But I'm pretty sure God's good with it. He likes redeeming people—taking our sins, even made-up ones, and making them whiter than snow.

Me, I'm the opposite of Jake. I'm a ghost. Venn wiped me clean. I don't know if I even have a driver's license, high school transcripts or a proof of citizenship, though I'm sure my mom still has a paper copy of my birth certificate in her important papers file. I'm new, blank, the person I was in the past doesn't matter. I'm sure I can get most of it back, but other than my parents, I'm not sure what I'd want to go back for. I don't know who I'm going to be tomorrow—well … besides the girlfriend of a convicted pervert who's an exceptional tree climber and a below average dirt bike rider. I dunno … maybe I'll finally get to go to college. But I'm not worried. I know God has many more moments ahead that he'll be getting me ready for. So, what's to worry about?

I look at Issy and Jo. It's hard to tell which way they'll go. She looks perfectly snuggly wrapped in his arm, but I'm still trying to figure out if they're good for each other, or if it's just easy. My guess is it will go one of two ways—they break up on the way home or they get married and have lots of perfectly Instagram'd kids. Regardless, I hope we can all stay friends—and that the *Issy Show*'s gone for good.

It takes some time sitting there before we get out of our heads and become regular again. "Race you to the top!" As always, we drop it all and take off toward the low end of the bridge. Like abnormal, I take up the rear so I can watch. It is almost as good as winning the climb—almost. I remember the first time we climbed it. We were young monkeys. It's a bit harder to pull an adult body up. I hope this isn't the last climb. Nah, I'm sure we have at least three or four more years before we drive SUVs and can afford hotels with memory foam mattresses. Jo wins the race, though his sportsmanship is questionable. We unhook our hammocks and throw our gear down into a surprisingly neat pile on the ground.

Jake yells, "Oh, by the way, it's whoever gets down first that wins." It's juvenile to change the rules, but Jo takes off after him to prove he's a better man.

While they scurry down, Issy and I take a final look at the creek from our beam next to the noose. She looks at it, worn and stiff in the breeze. She stands up and grabs hold. It's crunchy in her hands. She glances over at me and jerks it hard until it breaks where it was tied around the bridge.

A lesser monkey might have fallen and died, but Issy regains her balance and sits back down with the rope. Up close, it's hard to tell if it's really a noose, but it's hard to think of it as anything else. It's hard to look at it and not think something. Issy crunches it some more on her lap. "It was hard to get it up there. It wasn't crunchy then. Remember the tire swing behind my house? Well, my dad took it down right before my thirteenth birthday party. My mom said it wasn't safe anymore and that we were too old for it. He pitched the tire but kept the rope for some reason. I'm sure he had something different in mind for it.

"So when the whole thing went down with the pictures … I came up with a purpose of my own. I didn't do it—duh, obviously—but every time I walk our trail, there it is. It tells me bad things about myself, that are lies—told by a freaking computer! But not anymore." The rope tumbles in the air on the way down, before plopping gently in the creek. I hold her hand and we watch it float away until it disappears in the sun's glare on the water. She nods her tear-filled face and takes a deep breath before yelling, "Race you down!" And we're off!

Jake drops me off at home just after dark. The sound of the dirt bike drags my dad out of his chair in front of the television. "That's quite a dirt bike there. Two-stroke?" My dad walks around it. "So you're a Yamaha man? I always liked their Enduros."

"Dad. This is my boyfriend, Jake. Yeah, it's a decent bike, but it's pretty beat."

"Uh … nice to meet you, Mr. Mucha. I'm, uh, Jake. I've only had the bike for a year. I don't know much about it, but it gets me around."

They shake hands, and my dad smiles. "Nice to meet you, Jake. I have heard absolutely nothing about you. I mean, Gena, I talked to you every day, but not even a mention of a boy."

"Sorry, Dad, I … didn't want to make you worry. Oh … uh, Jake, don't you need to get home?"

"Oh, yeah, I have to do … stuff. Nice meeting you, Mr. Mucha." Narrowly escaping an invitation to come in for dessert, Jake kicks the bike and vanishes in a cloud of smoke and *BRRRAAAAAAAPPPPP-BRAAAAAPPPPPS!*

It's good to see a smile on my dad's face. It's nice that he doesn't hate Jake right off the bat. It's a good first step. Dad kisses me on the head and wraps his arms around me. "I missed you, Gena. I should have known something was going on. You weren't yourself on the phone. Your mom told me I was imagining things."

"Mom's right. You were imagining things." I don't like lying, especially to my parents, but I have a feeling I better get used to it. It's an insane story, that nobody's ever going to believe. It was bad enough when my deep-fake parents had me committed. I don't want to put my real parents through that. I'm not even going to try to explain Venn and the game. I'll just tell them that I finished my contract, I got paid, and that's that. Hopefully they don't expect my next employer to send them to Europe.

As for Jake, they're going to want a story to tell when people ask how we met, so I have to make one up. Can you imagine my dad telling his friends at church how we really met? I dunno, maybe I'll just stick to the truth. Jake is a good man … and he loves me—and I know that you'll love him too.

25

THE END?

The next day:

I have no idea what time it is. I slept long and hard. Still phone-free, my dad's dorky laugh and the sun streaking through my shades wake me up. I need to get an alarm clock and a watch. I'm supposed to meet up with Jake in the park for a lunch. Hopefully I didn't miss it. I speed through my morning ritual and sneak down the steps under the cover of more of my dad's dorky laugher. I slip out without anybody noticing.

. . .

Meanwhile at home …

I yell for my wife again. "What's the hold up?"

"Okay … okay … Hold your horses. I'm coming. I heard the shower. Did Gena come down yet?"

I shrug. "Yeah, no. I don't know. Hey, you gotta listen to this thing. Are you ready? Okay … Linda, tell us a joke! Shhh … listen …"

"It would be my pleasure, Martin. What did the drummer call his twin daughters? Anna one, Anna two!"

I laugh, because it's a good joke, but Stephanie isn't amused. "Oh, no. A smart speaker? That thing's gotta go. It's bad enough with one of you."

"Watch what you're saying. Babe, you're going to hurt her feelings. Don't worry, Linda. Give her time. She'll warm up to you."

Steph fires back, "Oh, there's no chance of that, *babe*. Take it back."

I whisper to Linda under my breath, "I'll try to speak sense to her, but she doesn't listen."

Not amused, Steph says it again, slower and louder this time. "Take … it … back!"

Not ready to give up, I raise an irresistible eyebrow and spring Plan B on her. "But, babe … Linda, play it. Play the song."

"It would be my pleasure, Martin. Now playing *Friday I'm in Love* by the Cure."

I give Linda a wink as the song spools up, then grab Steph around the waist, look her in the eyes and sing along—just like I did the night we fell in love.

"I don't care if Monday's blue, Tuesday's grey and Wednesday too. Thursday, I don't care about you. It's Friday, I'm in love. Monday you can fall apart. Tuesday, Wednesday break my heart—Oh, Thursday doesn't even start. It's Friday, I'm in love." I've still got it. She's putty in my hand. I give her a long kiss—just the way she likes it. "So … babe … so, can I keep her, uh, it?"

She looks in my eyes for long time before answering. "I'll think about it. I'm going to check on Genevieve. I've got questions about this boy."

"Okay, babe. Let me know what you find out." Now let's see what else this thing can do. "Alexa, uh … what else can you do?"

A different but familiar voice answers me from her speaker. "Shall we play a game?"

"Nooooooooooo wwwwaaaaaaaaayyyyy! This thing is awesome!" I repeated her question in my best robot voice. "Shall … we … play … a game?' Hold on, it's on the tip on my tongue … Ok … I give. What's that from?"

"It is from the 1983 American Cold War science fiction film *War Games*. *War Games* was written by Lawrence Lasker and Walter F. Parkes and was directed by John Badham. The film stars Matthew Broderick, Dabney Coleman, John Wood, and Ally Sheedy."

"Exactly! Huh … *War Games*! I haven't thought of that movie in forever. Ask me again."

"Shall we play a game?"

"Funny that you ask. Games are my middle name. Now that Genevieve's old, nobody wants to play with the dad anymore. So, yes! Let's play. And how 'bout you use the War Games voice all the time. I'll call you Larry. The babe will like you better if you're not another woman."

ABOUT THE AUTHOR

My real name is not Mack Lines.
Please don't try to figure out my identity.
All I know is what Genevieve told me.
I hope this helps.